A SHADOW
ON THE SUN

A SHADOW
ON THE SUN

Francis Cottam

SIMON &
SCHUSTER

LONDON • SYDNEY • NEW YORK • TORONTO

First published in Great Britain by Simon & Schuster UK Ltd, 2005
A Viacom company

1 3 5 7 9 10 8 6 4 2

Simon & Schuster UK Ltd
Africa House
64–78 Kingsway
London WC2B 6AH

www.simonsays.co.uk

Simon & Schuster Australia
Sydney

A CIP catalogue record for this book is available from the British Library

ISBN 0 7432 6324 3 (hb)
ISBN 0 7432 6325 1 (tpb)

Typeset by SX Composing DTP, Rayleigh, Essex
Printed and bound in Great Britain by
Bath Press Ltd, Bath, Somerset

For Michael Hodge, for your generosity and belief

ACKNOWLEDGEMENTS

This is a work of fiction, but historical fiction only works if it carries the conviction of truth and two factual books were particularly helpful in enabling my attempts to achieve that here. These were Robert Dalleck's *John F Kennedy: An Unfinished Life* (Penguin Books); and *Rat Pack Confidential: Frank, Dean, Sammy, Peter, Joey and the Last Great Showbiz Party* by Shawn Levy (Fourth Estate).

NEVADA, 1960

On her seventeenth birthday they took her to see Sinatra at
the Sands. He sang a song for her. He sang, 'It was a very
good year'. And he dedicated the song 'to my beautiful
Polak niece', which sent a polite ripple of
uncomprehending laughter spreading through the crowded
tables. The dedication was inaccurate and insulting and
funny and sweet and typical, she thought, of his wilful
contradictions. The lyrics of the song told a story that was
melancholy and inappropriate, ardent as it was with longing
for lost youth. But it was a song she loved and of course he
sang it beautifully and she was very flattered.

'Did you prompt him?' she asked her mother at the
interval. Her mother shook her head.

'Bill?' she asked her godfather.

Bill smiled. 'No.'

Afterwards they went to see him in his dressing room and
the man she had called Uncle Frank since as long as she
could remember took a single bloom from a bouquet and
gave it to her and said, 'Happy birthday, kiddo', and she

twirled the flower in her fingers as the short walk to their waiting limousine leached life and moisture from its petals in the desert night.

And seated between Bill and her mother, aware of the heavy Martini smell on Bill's breath and the weight of him, and her mother's perfumed aura of Joy and French tobacco, she had to chide herself for thinking the thought that none of this was real.

Before air conditioning turned the interior of the car cooler, she was able to smell the residue of dry-cleaning fluid in Bill's tuxedo and the starch in the white shirt underneath. The lights of the strip went by through the limousine windows in flashing stutters of chattery neon. The smells inside the car grew fainter as its air grew cold.

And none of it was real.

There were no pedestrians on the street. There were no children in the city. There were no dogs or bicycles or paper boys or picket fences bordering suburban homes. Climate was something you controlled with the flick of a switch on an electronic console on your desk or dashboard or in your hotel room on a panel between twin beds. Las Vegas was not a place. It was a conceit. And she chided herself for conspiring with that conceit, for sharing it, on this day, on this specific night of celebration. But it was only one night, after all. And all American kids celebrated their birthdays as a celebration, really, for their folks. That was the American way, wasn't it? And she was still, technically, a kid, wasn't she? Even if she had been obliged to grow up more swiftly than she suspected most American children were obliged to do.

At a machine in a casino lobby she put the silver dollar Bill had given her for the purpose in the slot and pulled the handle, and watched the symbols giddy on the reels until they stopped and coins bucketed out of its metal belly in a heaving, glittery flood. Casino staff, dressed like minor functionaries from some Ruritanian principality, stooped and gathered the coins in plastic pails from the carpet and guided her to a teller behind brass bars in a glass cage who stacked the coins in cylinders and then carefully counted out five one-hundred dollar bills and placed them in a gold envelope for her.

'Quite a night,' Bill said, his face flushed with whiskey and collusion as he tipped the teller an indiscreet wink.

'Yes,' she said. She was flushed herself, thrilled by the criminality of it. She was gambling in Nevada four years below the age at which the law entitled her to. Under Bill's protection, in the kingdom of Las Vegas, she could do pretty much as she pleased. She put the envelope into her purse. And in the glass of the teller's booth she saw her mother's reflection as her mother stood, studying her.

Back at their hotel, after nightcaps, an hour later, she discovered what her mother had been thinking, then.

'You've grown so beautiful,' her mother said. And her mother's smile seemed almost doubtful with the conflict of pride and nervousness in her face, her eyes. 'So beautiful, 'Tasha.'

Her mother almost never used anymore the tender contraction Natasha remembered from childhood. Now, hearing it brought the sharp sting of tears. She was a child no longer; today she had taken another symbolic step towards responsibility, towards the nowhere to hide accountability of adulthood. She had embarked upon her eighteenth year.

'I've had a lovely time,' she said. She looked at her mother's face, at the fierce loveliness under the subtle lines time was imposing across her mother's forehead and at the sides of her mouth. She knew that her mother had her hair expensively coloured once a month. She knew that under the salon dye, Julia Smollen's hair had turned, with time and whatever torment she concealed, entirely grey.

'I hope so,' her mother said. 'I hope you have.'

She suspected the grey hair would look magnificent, framing the bones of her mother's face, a pale contrast to her brilliant green eyes. But she knew it didn't do to age conspicuously. Not in her mother's profession, it didn't. Not in her mother's world.

She lay in bed for a long time without sleep. She fancied she could hear Bill snoring boozily across the hall, but knew this was nothing more than spite or imagination. Bill and her mother did not share a bed. And anyway, Bill didn't really sleep. He would be at the casino, settling the bill for that neat jackpot trick with the one-armed bandit. Or he would be in Sinatra's suite, the tobacco-coloured air lush with stories about Liston and Brando and West Coast and

East Coast wise guys and Kentucky bloodstock and some hot new European broad off the boat from Naples or the plane from Rome and maybe the young senator from Massachusetts bidding for the presidency. But more likely he would be alone in a bar, playing out his own suicide song.

That was what Sinatra called them, didn't he? Suicide songs? 'Set 'em up, Joe, it's getting on time to go . . .'

Natasha Smollen stirred between immaculate cotton sheets. She could smell something spicy and sharp, the scent of the potpourri in the bathroom mingling with beeswax from her polished wooden bedhead. Her sense of smell was impossibly acute— 'A gift from your father,' her mother had more than once wrily observed. She could smell the desert too, arid and deathly beyond this extravagant refuge of refrigerated air.

He had said something to her, had Sinatra, as he presented her with the little bloom from the bouquet on his dressing-room table next to the champagne ice-bucket and the fan-spread of cigarettes in their filigreed silver box.

'Make your mother proud, sweetheart,' he said. And he winked and then gave her that look she had seen on his face when he wanted you to know that he was being sincere. Being sincere, or in close-up, his mind on an Academy Award nomination, in one of his more serious movies. It was his *Man with the Golden Arm* expression, she thought, grinning in her bed in the darkness. It was his *From Here to Eternity* face.

Unable to hold Sinatra's pale blue gaze, she had averted her eyes and glanced down at the table, at the cigarette box. She saw that it was a gift, the box, inscribed under the open lid where there was a fulsome tribute composed by the giver. She saw that the cigarette box was a present from the English playwright, Noel Coward. Truly, her uncle Frank knew everyone.

Shyness, more than evasiveness, had compelled her to look away, because she intended to try. Natasha Smollen loved her mother and would do everything she could to make her mother as proud of her as she was proud of her mother.

ONE

The life inside her didn't yet show. She was blossoming in that way he'd observed in the past that pregnant women sometimes did. But she was early in her term and thin anyway and there was no bump to speak of, no belly yet for her to fold her hands across and seek some kind of comfort from. Her condition had brought a flush of colour to her cheeks and her lips were blood-filled and her eyes were bright. But all this somehow emphasized the grief, rather than disguising it. Bill had seen grief before, was an expert in grief, had watched his first wife die amid its desolation. And despite that hectic flush above her cheekbones, he knew that Julia Smollen was desolate now.

He pushed her coffee across their table to her, pushed the bowl of brown sugar after it and watched as her thin smile briefly signalled thanks. But she didn't move to take it. So he spooned sugar into the coffee and added cream and stirred it for her.

'I don't have it white.'

'Today you do. You need the nourishment.' He nodded at where the bump would grow. 'Both of you.'

She had slid a book onto the café table as soon as they had found a table in the shade from the sun and sat down there. One hand hovered over the book with the fingers spread, and then retreated into her lap. It was something she kept doing. He noticed that the fingers trembled when she did it and that her nails were badly bitten. He suspected that the shaking was something she would have to endure, would have to live with, for a while. He wondered at the toll her condition would take on the unborn baby. He wondered, more idly, at the contents of the book on the tabletop.

She was dressed indifferently in clothes for which he had wired her the money. She sat pale-skinned in a plain white cotton shirt and black, calf-length skirt. The skirt was the bottom half of a suit and its jacket hung over the back of her chair. She had only very recently escaped the fugitive cold of occupied Europe and it was very hot here and of course she was not acclimatised yet. Unless the damp of her forehead was a symptom of nausea. She might have morning sickness, he thought. It might be the effects of the pregnancy. Certainly she had not yet touched her coffee.

'How well did you know him?' Her eyes were searching. Had been ever since they had met in the hotel lobby and walked the short, sunlit walk to the café and sat down here. Actually, he thought, her eyes were pleading.

'Well,' he said. But not well enough to do what those eyes were imploring him to do and bring his dead friend back to life.

She blinked. She tried and failed to smile. He thought her very brave. Her hand hovered over the book again, fingertips raw and quicks bitten pink, and disappeared. 'A horrible shock, his death?'

Bill thought about this. He wanted to be honest with her. It was tempting for him to slip into that easy, avuncular self who would soothe and insist she drank her sweet, creamed coffee. The role required no effort or thought and he did it all the time. But Julia Smollen merited more. He watched a tramcar take the corner outside the café. Two policemen in white gloves orchestrated limp traffic. Aboard the tramcar, Latin women in mantillas made from Spanish lace protected the skin of their shoulders and their modesty under splashes of floral silk. The European woman opposite him waited for a reply. She was really quite beautiful. She was nothing like he had imagined she would be. Mourning became her. It was a cynical observation. But it was one he couldn't avoid.

'Not a shock.' Bill took a deep breath. The loss was terrible and he did not trust himself to talk about it without tears for his dead friend betraying his true feelings. He did not know this woman, though he knew he had very probably saved her life. 'Martin flirted with death for as long as I knew him,' he said. 'He did that in the mountains, when he climbed. And then he did it more when he chose to make soldiering his career. It was combat he wanted, as a soldier, I always believed. It wasn't ceremony. Or advancement. He was a man who invited physical risk. So I wasn't shocked when I learned of his death. Only by the manner of it.'

He was silent a moment. They both were.

'And the means by which I came to learn of it.'

He had met Martin Hamer on the Riviera one summer, honeymooning with his wife, Lillian. Bill had been with his own wife, Lucy. Actually he and Lucy had met Lillian first, plimsolls kicking over the red clay of the tennis courts where they encountered one another as the opening, halting, half-stalled sentences were exchanged, in the breeze from the sea, under the hot July sun. They had asked Lillian to bring her new husband for a day aboard the boat they had rented to fish. It had been Lucy's typically impulsive, generous invitation.

'They don't know anybody on the Côte,' his wife had said to Bill by way of justification. 'They're here because they've read a novel about it, for God's sake.'

He had gotten to know Martin Hamer over beers cooled in a tub of ice on the deck as the skin of their shoulders burnt on the stern and the lines from their rods hung redundantly before them. That was after he had gotten over what Martin Hamer looked like. If you ever did. As if anyone ever could.

Lillian and Lucy were both dead, now. And Hamer was dead, too. If the woman in front of him was to be believed, she carried Martin's child in her belly. Bill did believe her. Had believed her from the first. He watched her as she tried to cope with the heat and the light of the southern hemisphere at a table outside a Mexican café. And her grief, of course. The heat and the light and the insurmountable obstacle of grief. He believed her. But in spite of what he'd just said to her, it was barely credible to him to think of Martin Hamer dead.

He'd known for almost two weeks now.

'What's the book about?'

'The what?'

'The book on the table. The one you keep almost touching. But never do, quite.'

'Oh,' she said, 'it's nothing. Of no significance.'

She smiled down at the book. She was nauseous, he saw, or feeling the heat. A trickle of sweat ran from her hairline at the temple down the side of her face. It was tear-sized. Smaller than a tear. She would never, he knew, acclimatize to Mexico. But she would not need to.

'The book?'

'*The Pilgrim's Progress.*' She picked it up. It was cloth covered, a cheap, mass-produced edition. He saw now from the title on the spine that the book was written in French. 'I stole it from the public library in Lucerne. I needed a vehicle, to transport something.' She allowed the book to fall open in her palm and took from where it parted a sealed envelope. When she held the envelope out, he saw his name on it, written in blue ink in a once familiar hand. He hadn't received a letter from Martin Hamer since the letter of condolence sent to him and Lucy after their daughter's

11

death from scarlet fever. The war had interrupted their friendship, severed their correspondence.

'Dear Christ,' Bill said. 'Oh, Jesus.' It was true, then. Martin Hamer was dead. All their cherished history together was gone. He swallowed.

'Take it,' Julia Smollen said.

Bill took the letter and put it into a pocket. Julia snapped shut the book and put it back on the table. But there was something else between its pages, some faint troubling at the book's centre. He reached for the book and opened it and a wild flower fell, dusty, ochre with pollen, onto the sun-bleached table-cloth.

'I prised that from his palm in the meadow where he died,' Julia Smollen said, looking down at the flower. 'I took it from him before I took the money and maps and papers and the wristwatch from his corpse.'

Breath shuddered out of Bill and a motorcycle backfired and birds flapped from balcony rails on the corner buildings around the café and took, black and reluctant, to the sky.

She unbuttoned her cuff and folded back the sleeve. Bill recognized the shockproof watch Martin had saved for and bought for his failed attempt in the Alps, on the Eigerwand. Shockproof, all right. It had apparently survived the Blitzkrieg assault on the East. Martin had campaigned in Russia, had been wounded and decorated there, according to the woman in front of him. Had fought through the cellars and street rubble and survived the battle of Stalingrad. Had played some crucial role in the German army's counter-offensive with the Dnepre River at their backs after the trudged, frozen retreat. The strap of the watch wore a fresh and clumsy puncture wound where the woman had pierced the leather so that the watch would buckle around her own narrow wrist.

Bill sat back in his chair. He gestured vaguely for the tab and blinked against the sunlight. The birds had settled again under tarry feathers on balcony rails and roof gutterings and even vacant tables all around the square. Guitar music squawked from somewhere, flamenco, distorted by amplification on a wireless, playing from the café kitchen.

'You looted his corpse?'

Julia Smollen smiled. 'He told me you were a lawyer.'

'Martin was my friend.' There was nothing avuncular, now, in Bill's tone. 'You looted his corpse?'

'I took nothing he did not give me, sir. He gave me everything. And then he died.'

Bill knew now that driving here had been a mistake. He could have, should have chartered a plane to Guadalajara or Mexico City itself. But he hadn't known how much danger Julia Smollen might still face from vindictive pursuers. Their communication had been cryptic, distant and necessarily brief. Three or four intimate and shockingly redolent phrases had served, over a long-distance telephone line, as proof of her intimacy with his dead friend. She had given her location and spelled out her predicament in stark telegraphese. He had then applied the lawyerly part of his mind to plotting the painstaking logistics of her escape.

13

And he had driven to their rendezvous because there was time and because the chartering of a plane was a conspicuous act for a Beverly Hills-based movie lawyer in a community always rife with gossip. But anyone could hire a Ford and fill the tank and nobody cared. So that was what Bill did, figuring his Jaguar, with its wire wheels and low-slung, English curves would fail to pass unnoticed on its route through a succession of flyblown Mexican towns.

But driving there had been a mistake. The vast distance had made him weary and stale and its endless, featureless monotony had revived his thirst for a drink. He had driven along the coast to San Diego and then headed east towards the fringes of the Sonoran Desert. Then he'd taken a route southward roughly parallel with the coast, with the waters of the Gulf of California occasionally glittering to his right and the foothills of the Sierra Madre undulating through heat haze to his left. There was no radio in the car. He drove to the sound of the big Ford engine labouring noisily under the hood and the spatter of occasional insects against the windshield. He reached Culiacan with the fine sand that was blown from the roads in his hair and under his eyelids and in his throat. By the time he got to Mazatlan, the engine of the Ford sounded as thirsty as he felt.

Bill pressed on towards Guadalajara and the mountains and the sight of the bruise-coloured peaks in the distance saddened and depressed him. He had never been here before. Mexico was where Gable and Wayne came, it was said, for nights with dark-blooded women. And he had heard that Flynn crossed the border sometimes for boys. Bill had never been to Mexico before. But he had been to Colorado with Martin and Lillian Hamer before the war. And being close to the mountains brought back memories of happy times he would visit again only ever in memory. He drove and he thought of the past. And the grit under the lids made his eyes water and forced him to take one hand from the wheel and wipe them.

After his first day of driving he stopped for the night at a fishing village about fifty miles south of Hermosillo. The village was a stumble of dark shacks at the edge of the sea with its boats pulled up on the sand above the tide line. Exhausted, he was reconciled to sleeping in the car. But there was enough light coming from one of the larger buildings to give him the optimism to investigate.

The cantina was four clapboard walls under a roof made from corrugated steel. The glow of light he'd seen from the road came from a pair of hurricane lamps. Their wicks were thick and filled the one room with a damp, paraffin smell that forced a brief, bitter nostalgia into Bill's mind before he banished it to take a look around. Three tables. No customers. A bar made from nailed-together pieces of driftwood timber atop a row of oil drums. The drums were rust coloured. On one of them, Bill could make out the ghost of the Shell symbol in faded yellow paint. The proprietress sat knitting in an armchair beside the bar. She was an old woman, knitting something for a child. When

15

she rose and put the work down on her chair, he saw that her knuckles were purple and arthritic. But the knitting was very neat work. He doubted, over the decades, whether many of the fish enmeshed in them escaped the nets that had ruined her hands in their making.

He asked in Spanish if he could buy anything to eat.

She replied in English that he could.

'A room?'

She shrugged. 'Not much of a room,' she said.

'Worse than sleeping in the car?'

She smiled, without showing her teeth. 'A bed, at least,' she said.

He ate fish stew spiced with searing peppers and served with a flat, sour bread. He drank two bottles of cold Mexican beer and cradled his exhaustion, watching the beads of condensation form on the cold glass and dribble down the sides of the bottles, with their unfamiliar labels. He listened to the sea break in ponderous night waves a few feet away. The woman resumed her knitting. Other than for the sound of the sea and the clack of bone needles, the village was silent.

It was camping that he remembered the paraffin smell from. It was being snug under canvas at Thanksgiving or Easter with his wife and daughter, with his family in Yosemite, or Banff, or pitched on the cool pine carpet of a Maine forest.

Bill called for Mescal and the old woman jumped and he apologized in his flawless Spanish for startling her. She brought the bottle and a glass to his table and he complimented her on the excellence of the food. Truly, he could not remember when he had eaten better.

She bowed stiffly at the compliment, obviously pleased, the fright he'd given her forgotten. She cleared away the debris of his meal. He was a big man. He had always been a big man and so his size and strength were natural to him and sometimes he was careless of the effect he could have on strangers. Most of the time he was gentle, too. Most of the time, anyway.

Bill looked at the Mescal bottle and the thick little shot glass on his table. The glass was scored with a million infinitesimal scratches, opaque with wear, with time, with use. He'd just have one, he told himself. He had to get away from the smell of those wicks. He was very tired. He'd just have one, and then he'd find his bed.

His second night on the road was spent inland, in the city of Guadalajara. Here, there were more hints than he was used to seeing that a large part of the world was at war. Mexico was no more involved in the war than was the United States. But the city still seemed full, to Bill, of heavily armed police foot patrols. And twice, from a seat at the same pavement café, he saw convoys of troop lorries rumble by. The fact that they travelled, portentous, bristling, in opposite directions from one another, seemed slightly farcical to Bill. But the expressions on the faces of the soldiers did not encourage laughter. They had that light, empty look of young men eager to pick a fight.

He thought that Guadalajara was what travel writers would be inclined to term a vibrant or exotic place. Bill thought it frenetic, loud and probably pretty dangerous. He hated the blare of the maharachi bands and the constant hoot of car horns and found the sight everywhere of wild dogs in scabrous, whining packs depressing. He didn't fear dogs and the thought of rabies never truthfully occurred to him. But watching them, with a drink in his hand, seeing their pack hierarchy determined and enforced by the endless snarls and scuffles among vicious and mangy animals, he found himself uncomfortably reminded of many of the people he had met and knew in Hollywood.

Uncomfortable on the street, unwilling to retire for the night to his room at a perfectly acceptable hotel, Bill eventually found a bar whose cavernous depths were cool and dark. Discrete lights were strung along its length. The furniture was made of some dense hardwood carved and polished in black and amber whorls. Several brands of tequila competed in jewelled bottles for the palate and there were cigars on display in humidors with plate glass lids. Best of all, though, it was a refuge from the gaudy chaos of the streets outside. Bill bought a drink and sat down at a vacant table. He sat alone with his thoughts and his fatigue. The concierge at the hotel had been tipped – with the promise of more later – to garage the car somewhere they could be trusted to change the oil and water, wash and wax the body and fill the almost empty tank. He would drive the remainder of his journey to Mexico City in the morning.

All he had to think about, to trouble over, was his encounter with Julia Smollen. And so he pondered on that, reclining at his solitary table in a leather chair, looking at the oily yellow liquid in his glass. He tried and failed to picture the woman, unable to put a face to the fraught voice he had heard only over a long-distance telephone line. His only confident speculation was that she would be dark. He imagined dark, straight hair falling lifelessly to her shoulders. He saw thin, carmine lips. And her eyes were a brown in his mind, so dense they were almost black. Fierce and unreadable, her eyes, he thought; furious, lightless jewels.

Anger was all he had got from her. No fear, just anger. Anger at what had happened to her and the predicament it had put her in. It occurred to Bill there, in Guadalajara, that maybe Julia was angry, too, about what had happened to Martin Hamer. But he didn't know whether she was or she wasn't. Maybe she'd been simply indignant, inconvenienced by a death badly timed. He studied the viscous surface of his drink in the scant light from the bar and saw no point in giving Julia the benefit of any doubt until he met her and was able to come to an accurate judgement. He hadn't liked the sound of her. But maybe that was only because what she'd had to say had been such horribly unwelcome news.

He looked around the bar he was in, trying to determine what it was that made the place so foreign. Except that maybe foreign wasn't exactly the right term. Hollywood successfully achieved foreign all the time, and not just in the plasterboard exoticism of the studio back-lots. The scope and scale and story of film demanded a cast from all over the world and the money and the glamour – or at least the promise of these – delivered them. Pockets of LA were cosmopolitan enough. And if you had the money, you could eat in France and you could eat in Tahiti or London in southern California. But none of that felt foreign. The foreignness of Hollywood came in familiar clichés a person could feel comfortable with. But Guadalajara wasn't like that at all.

It was the temperature, for one thing, which even in this subterranean tunnel of leather and wood, forced sweat to ooze from his skin. It was the decor, too. Bill saw skulls etched everywhere on glass and bottles and table-tops, carved deeply into the pillars supporting the roof. At once Catholic and pagan and piratical, the skulls were, he knew, a crucial part of the culture of Mexico. But despite his excellent Spanish, it was a culture of which he was entirely ignorant.

And the skulls reminded him of Germany. They reminded him of the grinning SS troops he'd seen in movie newsreels and in pictures in the newspapers. They wore the same death's head symbol. It was part of their insignia, on the collars of their uniforms. Its intention in Germany was to chill and intimidate. Whatever the intention in Mexico, the effect on Bill was the same.

It was the clientele. There was a table full of South Americans to his left. He guessed from their sleek and haughty manner and their tailored, European clothes, that they were from Argentina. They had the sallow, smooth look on the skin that only a cut-throat razor could achieve in a shave. They spoke Spanish and wore their hair carefully brilliantined and parted and shouted aggressive toasts and there seemed to Bill more challenge and threat than honest amusement in their laughter.

It was the danger. There was a volatility about Mexico, about Guadalajara, anyway. There was a trigger-happy mood of something unexpected and dreadful just about to happen. It was a place of feral pack dogs and truckloads of sullen soldiers and the tireless, insistent beat of the maharachi band. Bill had not disliked a place so much since visiting Germany in 1937 to attend the funeral of his best friend's wife. He had buried the friendship, too, on that visit, after what he had seen there. Maybe it wasn't Mexico at all, he thought, looking into the yellow residue that was all there was left of his drink. Maybe it was the news about Martin, afflicting his mood and souring his senses. Maybe that was all it was.

Just then a man carefully attired in a black lounge suit and tie approached his table and requested on behalf of the establishment that Bill finish his drink and leave. The request was made in careful, accented English. But it was firmly put. They weren't about to serve him up a complimentary dinner and crack a vintage bottle in his honour. They wanted him out of the place, now.

But Bill wasn't really in the mood to co-operate. Events had put him in a frame of mind bad enough to border on mean. And Bill was a man very capable of being mean. At

Yale, he'd compiled a tackle record on the football team so formidable that, to this day, it remained unbroken. At Fort Bragg, training for the war in which he never got to fight, he had become army heavyweight champion, winning the title by stoppage over eight brutal rounds. That was better than twenty years ago, of course. But he had not exactly allowed himself to run to fat. He'd been good enough in recent years to hold his own sparring with Martin Hamer. And Hamer had been a force of nature, had possessed a big cat's attributes of strength and lethal speed.

Bill got to his feet. He stood six-four and two hundred and twenty pounds in the lightweight suit he had taken from the overnight bag in the trunk of the Ford and changed into in his Guadalajara hotel room. He faced the man who had asked him to leave and, behind the man, the bar. Tables and chairs would clutter the path of anyone trying to rush him from left or right and he could cover the approach from his rear in the big mirror behind the bar. He was obscurely glad he had left his pistol at the bottom of the bag on the hotel room bed. He held a firearms licence and was comfortable enough with guns. But he didn't habitually carry one and considered this a country in which things could very easily escalate.

'I'll leave when I'm good and ready,' Bill said.

'Please,' the man in the black suit said. He smiled. His manner was deferential and hostile at the same time, a combination Bill could not remember having encountered before.

Bill shrugged. 'Give me a reason to go.'

The man's eyes flicked towards the well-barbered quartet seated to Bill's right, a couple of tables away. They were quiet now. There was a lull in their laughter and toasts. 'It is rude in this country to stare,' the man said. 'You are making other customers feel uncomfortable.'

Bill knew this to be bullshit on two counts. If it was rude to stare in Mexico, he had been on the receiving end of some appalling etiquette ever since he crossed the border. And he had not stared at the Argentine party. He was a very observant man. But looking without being seen to do so was a necessary skill in a lawyer, one he had long honed and mastered in the courtroom. He looked over at the Argentines; they did not look directly back. He grinned at them and raised his glass; none of them chose to meet his eyes. Part of him wanted to go over there and haul them out of their leather chairs and decorate the place with them. He was drunk and angry and upset and wanted to break bones and splash blood because, Christ, he'd feel better after doing some honest damage.

Yeah, for about five minutes, the sane and sober part of his mind insisted. And you'll wake up with raw knuckles and a sore head in a Mexican jail cell with the Polish woman stranded and pregnant and conspicuous and here illegally and by now probably broke. And wouldn't that be fucking clever?

He placed his almost empty glass carefully on his table and turned and walked out of the place, onto the hot, lurid emptiness of the street. He gathered his bearings breathing Guadalajara's exhausted air and then walked back in the direction of his hotel. It would be something to do with the war, he supposed. The further south you went in the continent of America, the more sympathetic became the people to the Axis cause. Opinion at home had been pretty cut and dried since Pearl Harbor. Everyone except maybe Joe Kennedy and a few Chicago beer and frankfurter barons knew and pretty much accepted they were fighting for a just and necessary cause. But that wasn't a point of view popular in Buenos Aires. It had been about the war. The Argentines had scented an enemy and hadn't liked the smell.

In his room, awake in bed, Bill was pretty sure he had been followed back to his hotel. The altercation, the possibility of violence, had entirely sobered him. In truth, he hadn't really been able to surrender to proper drunkenness since hearing the news of Martin Hamer's death. He'd been alert, on the walk back, to the footfalls, to the odd, clandestine rhythm of pursuit. In an odd sort of way, he'd enjoyed it. It had dissipated his anger, given him something else to think about. Now, he lay in bed and thought about the mechanics of tomorrow and his meeting with the Polish woman with the black eyes and the carmine lips and his friend's child growing in her belly. Thirty-five. Hamer would have been thirty-four or thirty-five, by Bill's reckoning. It was no age to be killed, was his last conscious thought, before sleep claimed him.

★

She had green eyes. They were sun-smitten, her eyes, with the sparkle of dew. Her hair was short and shaggy, growing out from a crop exacted as punishment in the camp where she'd been held. Her lips were red, blood-bitten. And she was missing an ear lobe. The wound had scabbed where the lobe had been roughly severed. The lobe had been taken as a trophy, she explained to him, by a man Martin Hamer had subsequently fought with and killed.

'He was an accomplished killer,' Julia said. 'It was something he was practised at. It came easily to him.'

'He had other accomplishments.'

'I'm sure he did, sir. I didn't have the luxury of spending sufficient time with him to discover them.'

'Please don't call me sir,' Bill said. 'What did Martin call me?'

'Bill. Always my friend Bill.'

Bill swallowed. 'And that's what you call me.'

She smiled.

'What's funny?'

'The land of the brave and the home of the free,' she said. 'Where everyone is equal.'

'Except that we aren't in the land of the brave and the home of the free. Not yet, we're not. We've got to get there.'

'More running,' she said. And he saw in the hard sunlight then how tired the grief had made her.

'Are you up to it, Julia?'

25

'I have to be,' she said. She looked at Bill. 'We're being watched, you know.'

He nodded. 'I know.'

'I have to be up to it,' she said. 'For the baby.' Her fingers rose and skated the cheap cloth surface of the book on the table. 'And for him.'

She made him feel crude, lumbering, hapless. She had escaped a labour camp in an occupied country and out-witted her Nazi pursuers. He'd arrived here full of churlish suspicion and unleavened grief and come face to face with Julia Smollen, with her torn ear and chopped hair. With her beauty and great sorrow and resolution.

'Come on,' Bill said. He said it gently. He got up from the table and held a hand out to her. The gesture was courtly. But anyone watching closely would have considered the effect spoiled by the way his eyes searched the windows and balconies and roofs around the square rather than resting on the comely woman who was his companion.

'Where are we going?'

'To the home of the brave,' Bill said. 'To the land of the free.'

Out of Mexico City, he drove a route that skirted Guadalajara, heading for the coast. They reached sight of the Pacific slightly north of Puerto Vallarta, Bill averaging fifty despite the roads, nothing in his mirrors except dust, fairly sure they were not being tailed after eighteen straight hours of driving, his passenger asleep across the back seat for much of the journey under a plaid picnic blanket he'd taken from the trunk.

When finally they stopped, it was at the fishing village with the oil drum-and-driftwood bar in its tin-roofed cantina, the same elderly woman still knitting the same child's garment in the same chair beside it. She's slow, Bill thought, dully, or she has many grandchildren. His eyes and head and body ached from driving. He was forty years old and feeling every day of it. He asked the woman was there any fish stew to be had.

Always, she said.

He awoke Julia Smollen, half expecting her to leap out of some skittish nightmare off the back seat of the car. But she just rubbed her eyes with her knuckles and blinked and looked up at him and through the dust-caked rear window, at the gauzy sky.

'Are we there?'

'Halfway. Better than, actually. Are you hungry?'

She yawned and sat up and nodded.

After they had eaten and darkness had properly come, she took to the bed he had slept in on his outward journey. Bill returned to the car and sat with the windows open, the oiled weight of his gun heavy and reassuring in his right fist, waiting for the glow of headlamps on the flat horizon or, more likely, the hum of an approaching motor, closer, along the road. He waited calmly. He had never been a coward in the physical sense of the word. He would kill, if he needed to, to protect the woman and the carried child. But nothing came and there came the moment when he knew that nothing would. He looked at the sky, which was starlit and

27

clear. No moon, but enough silver twinkling in the black abyss above him to read by, he thought. He put the infantry issue .45 into the holster he'd strapped under his left arm and reached into his jacket pocket. The letter from Martin was there. He would take it down to the beach and read it. By starlight and phosphorescence glowing from the sea, he would hear the voice of his dead friend talk to him for the last time.

Dear Bill,

If you are reading this, then I feel obliged to begin by saying farewell. We never did take the opportunity to say a proper goodbye to one another. That was a pity and a mistake. Much in recent years has been pitiful and mistaken. But there is neither the time nor the need to dwell on how anything might have been different.

So I will say my goodbye to you now. I sit and write this unable to help myself thinking of how you were in those days when we met. It seems long ago in years, further in memory, with many sadnesses and much loss intervening between then and now. But I remember you as you were then, old friend. You and your lovely wife, Lucy, the dazzling continental Americans; you like Gatsby, golden, or like Dick Diver raking his beach in his jockey cap and his Riviera tan. We were dreamers, weren't we, Lillian and myself? We were romantic and impossibly naïve.

But it was a more romantic time, wasn't it? It was

how we saw you then. And you never lost the lustre, in the way those fictive characters were fated to do. It's how I see you now, Bill, just as I saw you then, in your generosity and your hospitality and grace.

I walked away from the war, Bill, which is an act of treason in a soldier. I write this a fugitive, wearing civilian clothes. Men I would until recently have called comrades have been dispatched to capture me. When they try to do so I will kill them in order to secure my escape and win the freedom of the woman who has delivered this note. The fact that you have it in your hand means that I will at least have half succeeded.

My pride and vanity oblige me to tell you, truthfully, that I fought with distinction. But there came a time, eventually, when there seemed no worthwhile point to the fighting. This war is being prosecuted by my country. I still love my country. But I could not find it in me any longer to believe we have a cause.

Julia Smollen is a part of it.

I have not sacrificed honour on the altar of love. I do, with all my heart, love her. But the circumstances in which I first encountered her simply helped prove to me that I had no honour to sacrifice.

Over recent months I have been forced to confront some hard truths. My hope and consolation has been the lovely, noble woman bearing this note. I want to thank you for your gift of friendship, Bill. An only child, I could have wished for no finer or truer brother and felt happy and grateful in my heart to know you. In recent years, you have lived only in my memories. I have cherished them.

I ask you, please, help this woman if you can. I love her. She carries my child.

Martin

Bill took the letter to the edge of the sea where the breeze caused the pages to flutter in his fingers. The sand was heavy and hard at the edge of the water with its weight of brine. Seaweed in glossy clusters bobbed and bowed in the ceaseless back and forth of the waves. Bubbles of foam burst on the sand in those intervals when the sea briefly receded. Some solitary beast of the sea broke the night silence with occasional cries that sounded distant and mournful. A seal, perhaps. Perhaps even a whale, searching for some forgotten latitude or mate butchered by hunters in boats. Bill listened to the sea. Far out, he thought he saw its surface briefly stippled by a shoal of flying fish. Light from the stars smoothed and gilded the water. He breathed a long breath through his nostrils and smelled the metallic perfume of the oil he'd used to clean his gun earlier in the evening, as the weapon creaked, heavy in its leather holster. And he heard the footsteps approach on the sand behind him until they stopped. And he did not turn.

'Hello, Julia.'

'How did you know it was me?'

'The weight of your steps. The length of your stride.'

'Are you all right?'

He cleared his throat. 'You should worry about yourself.'

The cry came again, mournful, from the sea.

'What was that?'

Bill didn't answer. He still had not turned to face her.

'He said you were a remarkable man. That was the word he used.'

One of his current clients was the actor Errol Flynn. More accurately, he had been engaged by the studio currently employing Flynn to troubleshoot on Flynn's behalf until the movie wrapped. It was a war movie.

In the picture, Flynn played some kind of intrepid English jungle fighter, fighting the Japs. Before the real war, Flynn had been very pally with the English actor David Niven. But Flynn was a star who could carry a picture. Niven was more of a support player who skated along on a veneer of English charm. At the outbreak of war, Niven had gone back to England and trained to be part of some kind of elite combat unit. Bill had heard that he'd been involved in heavy infantry fighting before the fall of France. He'd come close to being killed. Now, he was in the thick of it in Italy. Meanwhile, Flynn pulled the pins from fake grenades with his teeth, wearing Max Factor as the lead player in a Hollywood feature. And Bill did what he could to stop the actor indulging his appetite for the young flesh of both sexes.

Bill didn't personally chaperone Errol Flynn. That task was punctiliously endured by a young, teetotal intern from his office. And the rolling contract he had with the studio was one of the many retainers that had provided him, for nearly twenty years, with an increasingly lucrative career and an enviably comfortable life.

Bill had met Niven at a number of dinners and receptions and dreary rounds of cocktail parties before the war. He had thought the English actor a man who had to work extremely hard to compensate for his lack of skill and impact on the screen. But Niven was a man, it seemed, with remarkable qualities. And Martin Hamer was Bill's idea of a remarkable man.

'What do you do, Julia?' Finally, he turned to face her. 'Before the war, I mean. What did you do before the war? Did you have a profession?'

'I was a librarian.'

He nodded. 'Do you read English as well as you speak it?'

'Yes.'

'Then we'll find you something. We'll take care of you.'

If Julia wondered at that plural, she didn't question it. 'Come here,' she said. He did. 'Hold me,' she said. And he held her. They held one another in the night at the edge of the sea.

TWO

America never seemed to Julia Smollen like a country at war. It lacked battlefields and their desolate aftermath. There were no trains of desperate refugees. There were camps, apparently, out in the desert in New Mexico, where Americans of Japanese extraction were held for the duration. But she never felt the dread vibration of artillery shells or the drone of approaching bomber squadrons.

America fought its war at a remove. In the streets, in the shops and the schoolrooms and cafés, there was no fear abroad; there wasn't even the need for the rationing of power or food. Mostly absent was the rumour of defeat that spread among a panicked people with the debilitating symptoms of a disease. The Americans were confident of victory. They were going to win this war that never threatened their soil.

But she read the newspapers and she saw the newsreels at the cinema. She saw footage of the landing at Normandy and the marine assault on Okinawa in the bloody campaign in the Pacific. And she came to appreciate the courage of the American soldiers and the resolve of their leadership. America fought its war with a professionalism almost comically absent from what she had witnessed in the tragedy of Poland's conquest. She thought of her poor, dead brother and the clumsy espionage attempt that had led to his torture and execution. She thought of the Germans who had killed him; the bullish swagger of their victory and the dull, routine cruelty of occupation. They were not swaggering now, the Germans, she thought, reading about an American general called Patton. With his pearl-handled pistols and riding crop, George Patton seemed like some character from the pages of a comic book. But in battles and skirmishes with tanks, he was destroying crack German divisions on the fields and in the forests of northern Europe.

She thought, of course, about the German who had fathered the child she carried. As her belly swelled and the baby grew and kicked with incipient life, she thought tenderly of its father. He had been a soldier hero, decorated by Hitler himself amid much ceremony at the Reich Chancellery. She had seen him kill a man with his hands in the rain at night in a camp in Poland with no more hesitation than a peasant might register before twisting a chicken's neck or banging the head of a rabbit against a fence post. Martin Hamer had been a brave and ruthless patriot. She could imagine no more purely forged example of the steel in the storm that had spread from Germany and engulfed a continent. But he had been kind and tender and good, also. He had sacrificed his rank and renounced his country and saved her life out of love. And she grieved for him. And she was bitterly sorry that he had not lived to share the joy of their child.

Bill, who had been his friend, did his best, now, to make himself hers. He used his influential contacts to get her American citizenship, the papers stamped and passport supplied within weeks of their flight from Mexico. He got her a comfortable apartment in San Francisco with more amenities than she had ever seen in a home and paid the rent for a year and charged the utilities to an account he set up and put money into, a separate checking account he opened for her at a San Francisco bank.

'I can't take this,' she said, looking at the balance on the account.

'Just until you get yourself established,' he said.

'I can't take this amount of money from you, Bill.'

'If only my ex-wife shared your Polish scruples,' he said, laughing.

'Bill—'

'Call it a loan, Julia,' he said.

She looked around the apartment. The walls were freshly painted and the sunlight slatted through blue blinds and splashed yellow bars on the floor. She could hear the hum in the kitchen of the big American refrigerator. The lambent bars of light on the floor trembled when the blinds moved in the breeze from the ocean. The apartment was near to a flower market and she could smell flowers, freshly cut, through her windows above the street. Azaleas, orchids, lilies, lavender. In a tall pine bookcase she saw titles by Conrad and the Brothers Grimm and Flaubert and Thomas Hardy. They had discussed her love of books, her favourite authors, after their rest stop on the long drive out of Mexico. And there were pictures on the walls. She recognized Dufy's painted summer boats.

'You must have loved him.'

'Oh, you know,' Bill said. 'We had some times. We sure had some times. But I'm not doing this for him.'

He was there when her daughter was delivered. Born frail, the baby spent her first week, when not being fed, in an incubator at the side of Julia's hospital bed. Bill tapped the glass of the incubator and the baby gazed up at him with her open-eyed look of newborn wonder.

'You okay, kid?'

'I'm sad,' Julia said. Her face was in her pillow.

'I know. I know you are.'

There was a silence then, for which Julia was grateful. She wanted him there and she didn't.

Bill waved to the baby through the glass.

'She's beautiful. Have you decided on a name?'

'Natasha,' Julia said.

'Natasha isn't a Polish name.'

'I don't feel very Polish.' And she didn't. Her parents were dead. Her brother had been killed. Her last three years in the country of her birth had been spent as an inmate of a labour camp a few miles outside Poznan. Her job had been washing laundry, when it hadn't been servicing camp guards. She was an American now. She had the papers and the passport to prove it. She had given birth to a daughter here.

When Bill became godfather to Natasha a week after the baby left the hospital, it was at a Catholic baptism at an Italian church in the Bay area. His hands shook at the ceremony and his face was pale and there was sweat in a sheen under his sallow skin. The area beneath his eyes seemed almost bruised by shadow and there were cracks of dryness at the corners of his mouth. He had been drinking, she knew, and drinking heavily. He was not precisely drunk. But he did not look as though he had been properly sober for a week. His movements were clumsy with absence of sleep and he seemed smaller, somehow, diminished by guilt and delicacy. She had grown up in a country of hard liquor consumed relentlessly by Poland's drinking classes. But she had never seen anyone brought so low in spirit by drink as Bill appeared. As soon as they left the cool, marble sanctity of the church, he fumbled on his sunglasses. In the light, his suit looked slept in and she saw that one of his shoes had scuffed, raw leather scabbing the polished toecap.

These details had eluded her when he had picked her up, preoccupied as she was by the baby in her christening shawl, distracted by the sight of the car at the kerb with its chauffeur and ivory satin ribbons stretching back from the figurehead on its hood.

'You look unhappy, Bill,' she said, the baby across her lap, dozing, as they were driven back to her apartment.

'Everyone is entitled to a little unhappiness, Julia,' he said. His voice was mock grave.

'Is it written into the constitution?'

'If it isn't, it should be. Perhaps I'll raise the matter with the Supreme Court. Suggest the constitution is amended to guarantee the interests of the morose and the gloomy. Champion the cause of our melancholy minority. We have an inalienable right to our unhappiness.'

She smiled and kissed the baby's head and ruffled her halo of fluffy blonde hair. He was putting a brave face on things. But he'd been wallowing in booze for days. And it wasn't over nothing.

'I'm happy for you, today,' he said. He looked at Natasha. 'She has her father's eyes.'

'I pray hers never see what his did.'

'Amen to that,' Bill said. He sank back into the plush leather seat. A fog had descended around the bay and car headlamps loomed through it pale and amoebic, like creatures from deep under the sea. Julia leant into Bill, her head on the width of his shoulder. She did it for comfort. But the gesture was more about giving than it was about receiving. She had her comfort. Her comfort slept the sleep of the innocent, wrapped in a christening shawl in her lap.

Later that night, after Bill had gone, Julia was awoken by the lunar wail of sirens. She rubbed her eyes and looked at Natasha's crib. The baby slept. For a moment panic coiled her insides at the thought of her child's exposure to an air raid. There were no shelters. There was no drill, no provision. But it couldn't be bombs, could it? She climbed out of bed and pulled up the blinds and saw searchlights out in the bay, cleaving pale avenues of light through the fog. Boats were out: tugs and police launches, from the small, pugnacious sound of their engines. She heard the cackle of a loudhailer out over the water. Fog and waves distorted the amplified sound into something whispery and inhuman.

'I hope you get away,' Julia said. 'I hope you get away, whatever you've done.'

They said that nobody escaped from Alcatraz. She often looked towards the island, to that small patch of confinement and misery squatting in the sea. And she wondered if the inmates were tortured by a view between bars of the lush, proud sweep of San Francisco Bay. The boats bobbing in its harbour; the splendours of Nob Hill; the tramcars twinkling under coach paint and polish as they toiled up its picturesque city ascents. Al Capone had died in there. It was a place peopled by the bad and the mad, the infamous and probably the innocent too; but they were all equally damned, weren't they?

She looked at the face of Martin Hamer's watch. It was three-fifteen in the morning, the water cold and deep and unforgiving under the fog in the bay. She had called Bill a cab at midnight, after any number of Martinis from the jug she had mixed that morning and left to chill in the big chrome refrigerator. He'd cheered up a bit after a few drinks, become more loquacious in that clubby, conspira-torial manner he used to keep people at a safe distance. She played jazz records on the stereogram he had bought her in furnishing the apartment. She had played them quietly, so as not to wake the baby in her crib. They even danced a little, which Julia could not remember having done for years. She didn't know what had wounded him. He was a kind, wounded man. But it was a time when there were a great many wounded people in the world. On the battlefields, in the bombed cities, the world itself wore wounds. On leaving he had hugged her tight and thanked her for the great compliment of asking him to act as godfather to her child. He had pulled a small black box wrapped in silk ribbon from his pocket and presented it to her. After he left, she had taken a bracelet of fine, beaten silver from the box. Natasha wore it now around one deliciously chubby ankle.

In the bay, the searchlights continued to carve spectral, vigilant beams.

'I hope you get away,' said Julia, who had once been rescued from confinement in a place she had been certain would habour her grave. She shut the blind, took a last look at her sleeping daughter in her crib and went back to bed.

In the limited, contingent manner of the survivor, Julia came to enjoy her life in California. She lived in a beautiful city and the people were more generous in their welcoming of strangers than she ever could have imagined or wished. She got a job as the librarian at a large and lavishly equipped co-educational college.

Natasha grew into a clever and demanding girl, first at kindergarten and then at infant school. The Californians had an endless appetite for recreation. There were sailing and rowing clubs and people played tennis. Julia had been a member of a cycling club before the war and she bought herself a bicycle and rode the deserted lanes of the Nappa Valley when a neighbour she had befriended could babysit. Cycling was a European sport and the only Americans she saw on bikes were boys in the mornings hurling newspapers from the saddle at suburban porches. But if her cycling was considered eccentric, nobody commented on it. She learned to drive a car. She began to save, so that one day she would be able to pay back Bill the money he had so generously lent her. Berlin fell. America won the war in the Pacific. With everyone else, Julia Smollen celebrated in the streets. Many young American men had lost their lives in the war. But it seemed to her that they celebrated peace more than they celebrated victory. She sensed no gloating with the end of war in the celebrations on the streets of San Francisco.

She thought she came to understand the reason for this attitude to victory a few months after the peace when she was asked to help supervise a history trip the school at which she worked took to the battlefield of Gettysburg. She was asked only because a flu bug had left the history department short-staffed. But she agreed happily enough to a change of routine that would show her some more of the country she now called home.

Watching the teenage students tour the battlefield under caps and hats and sunshades, it was impossible not to think of the soldiers of both opposing armies, clothed in rough wool uniforms, bearing the weight of clumsy rifles, toiling in their thousands in the stifling July heat. Murderous courage and the tactics of attrition had made this an engagement in which more men died than had before or since on American soil. But it wasn't the casualty figures that distinguished Gettysburg from other Civil War battles, appalling though the losses were. It was what Gettysburg had come to represent as the word itself resonated through the tender history of this still youthful nation.

Julia watched their young history teacher talk to his students. He didn't look much older than they did, with his swatch of reddish-blond hair and spread of freckles and suit of blue and white seersucker. Enthusiasm for his subject seemed to energize him in the wilting humidity as he pointed to features in the distance on the heat-glazed landscape and worked to bring the conflict back to life.

Julia knew about the power of myth. Already the exploits of the exiled Polish pilots in the war just ended were becoming mythic. Their lunatic courage as they fought the Battle of Britain over the chalk hills of sedate counties called Kent and Sussex. Their suicidal raids launched over the English Channel on the German fortified French ports before the Normandy landings. Poles were not strangers to martial legend. Theirs was a history that demanded and craved the consolation of glory.

But this was different. Flies plagued their party and the

contours of the land sagged in the dripping heat. The children, though, remained respectfully attentive, the way children might at some solemn ceremony in a great building or at a service in a church. And Julia listened at Gettysburg to the litany of place names and the deeds they represented: Cemetery Hill, Seminary Ridge, Peach Orchard, the Wheatfield and Plum Run. And the names of the commanders: Meade, Sickles, Longstreet, Warren. And Pickett, of course. And Pickett's Charge. And there was a stir as one of the students found something and approached the teacher and showed him a thin, rust-mottled fragment of what Julia thought was probably bayonet blade. And the teacher calculated the battlefield disposition and speculated that here, on this spot, the bayonet might have belonged to a soldier of the 6th Wisconsin, mustered into the United States Army in the early part of 1861 and under the command, at Gettysburg, of Captain Rufus Dawes. Dawes had arrived at the field from Mauston with two companies composed entirely of Italians and Germans from Milwaukee. Then the teacher told the boy to put the relic back exactly where he had discovered it on the hallowed ground.

Julia understood, then, something about the Americans. She understood why they had not crowed in their street celebrations after the surrender of Japan. This was a nation birthed in blood, in Revolution and Civil War. Its freedoms had been hard won at intimate cost. Victory in war was not something to gloat over. And at that moment, on that sweltering field, she felt, for the first time, that she could come to love America and to be an American and to call this country home.

It was a feeling from which she was not remotely deflected that evening, when the freckled teacher turned up at her motel room door, having swapped the seersucker for a double-breasted blazer with a jaunty crest sewn onto the pocket. He wore a cravat and carried a pack of Pall Malls. She declined his offer of dinner, not wanting to give him a misleading impression. But he looked so crestfallen at her refusal that she softened, saying that the heat had tired her but she would join him for a single drink. In the event she drank three glasses of beer and, to his evident delight, smoked two of his cigarettes. She mentioned his apparent reverence earlier in the day for the battlefield relic.

'The war dead are deserving of our respect,' he told her, a grave look on his young face. She wondered was it some patriotic value instilled in him at college. It transpired he had served under Patton, had commanded a tank and fought in the war in the forests of France and Germany. And he hadn't just meant the American dead.

Julia Smollen did not date in this period of her life. She did not establish, discounting Bill, any authentic, lasting friendships. She raised her infant child and she assimilated herself into the patterns and rhythms and lesser intricacies of American life.

She dreamed, often, of Martin Hamer.

He had been sent to the camp where she was held, apparently to recover from a wound suffered in the German counter-offensive in the East, after the retreat from Stalingrad. The medal ceremony in which he had been decorated for his valour in that action had been turned into a propaganda coup. He had been given a nominal job in the camp outside Poznan, it transpired, for two reasons. One was to encourage, by example, German pioneers to settle in the conquered territory they termed the General Government. The other was to avoid the risk of his being killed back at the front. Germany had plenty of dead heroes to remind its people of the mortality rate in the East. What they needed were some live ones whose valour they could less morosely celebrate.

The first time she saw Hamer, she was measuring out what she was certain were the last days or even hours of her three years of incarceration. Forced to join the camp's small Joy Division, she had tolerated the attentions of the guards until driven beyond endurance by a sexual sadist called Hans Rolfe, an NCO who treated the camp as his fiefdom. She insulted Rolfe, goading him before an audience of his comrades. She saw Hamer for the first time moments after, as she pegged washing out. He was walking the perimeter of the camp. She noticed him because he looked so out of place amid the combat dodgers and Party die-hards, the thugs and carpetbaggers of Germany's new empire. He was one of the breed that had done the conquering that brought the scum that fucked her nightly in his wake. A moment after Hamer had passed, Rolfe let slip an attack dog trained to rip out groins and armpits and throats. She was losing the

Francis Cottam

fight to keep it off her when Martin Hamer ran back and
wrestled off and shot the beast. She looked into his eyes for
the first time, then. And she saw that he would shoot Hans
Rolfe with the same total absence of compunction.

'It's your fault,' she wanted to say to him, to scream and
spit into his handsome, troubled face. 'You did it,' she
wanted to say. Because he and his type had turned her
country, and her life with it, into a kind of hell.

Sometimes, she dreamed of that first encounter. And as
the Dobermann tore muscle and tendons and wrenched her
defending arm from its socket, Hamer walked blithely on.
His hands were linked loosely at his back and his head was
tilted to examine the wire in its dense coil at the top of the
perimeter fence. And as the teeth of the dog ripped her
neck in a spray of arterial blood, she saw his wedding band
glint dully under the light of the Polish winter.

Sometimes she dreamed of his death. In this dream he
perished in the snow, in his uniform, the snowflakes falling
mournfully around him and gathering in his lap as he sat
and died, his face sad and uncomprehending; she pulling at
his epaulettes and tugging fistfuls of his hair as though he
were some petulant child she could bait back into indignant, obstreperous life.

Waking was always the same. She would climb out of bed
and creep over to Natasha's cot and touch her daughter's
cheek with the back of her hand and then bend and smell
her hair and kiss her head. Then she would make herself tea
and sit and drink it, black, watching the night bay through

46

her window. She would weep, which she had trained herself to do too quietly to awaken her little girl. And she would wait for the pain and despondency of missing him to become once again something she could accommodate well enough for sleep to return to her. Sometimes it did.

She told Bill over the telephone about the visit to Gettysburg.

'And then that fellow from the *Superman* comic books knocked on my motel room door.'

'Clark Kent?'

'No. Not Clark Kent.'

'Lex Luther? Julia, honey. Jesus. You should have called the cops.'

She was laughing. 'Jimmy Olsen. He was Jimmy Olsen,' she said.

'I hope you were suitably underwhelmed.'

She held the receiver close to her face. It was always so good to talk to Bill when he sounded this sober and well. When he sounded this happy.

The fugitive from Alcatraz had not escaped the cold clutches of the bay. She read about him. His failed bid for freedom made page three of the *San Francisco Chronicle*. That was the headline: 'Rock Lifer in Fatal Freedom Bid'. She read the story on a Saturday morning at a table outside a coffee shop near the harbour. She chose places with seats outside because other patrons objected to the presence of a baby. It was one of the differences between here and

Europe. Between here and the Europe she remembered, anyway. Poland was a part of Russia now. And 'Tasha wasn't crying and spoiling the customers' coffee and pastries. She was gurgling and staring at the sky, at the silver fuselage of a passenger aircraft rumbling through the blue air.

Cold had killed the Alcatraz fugitive. Cold had guaranteed, also, that the poor man hadn't been a fugitive for very long. His blood had stopped circulating, the story said, as he clung to a wooden pallet in the water. He'd been twenty-three, two years into a life sentence earned when he carried out an armed robbery on a liquor store. The storeowner suffered a stroke in the attack and his inept assailant used a payphone on the liquor store wall to call an ambulance before running away. The victim died on his way to hospital and the man the paper called the perpetrator was caught cowering in an unfamiliar doorway a few blocks away from the scene of the crime.

'The kid was an amateur,' the arresting officer recalled. 'He didn't know the neighbourhood, had no modus operandi. Typical street punk.'

An editorial in the paper wondered what America was coming to. The streets weren't safe from acts of banditry. Organized crime was spreading its tentacles from New York and Chicago to Nevada and New Orleans. There were protection rackets and something called numbers running. There was an organization called the Cosa Nostra, or the Mafia. It was a secret brotherhood of Sicilians, driven out before the war by Mussolini only to resurface in the United

States. The country was caught between the crime wave and the Red Peril, warned the *San Francisco Chronicle*. Now a hapless street punk had breached security at Frank Lloyd Wright's impregnable island prison. The outlook was decidedly bleak.

'Not so bleak as for that boy who died of cold,' Julia said, surprising herself, because she'd said the words in her own half-forgotten tongue. She was so fluent in this version of English America spoke and wrote, she even thought in the language now.

Shading her eyes with her hand, she peered out over the bay, where the outlook was decidedly sunny. Her stomach was filled with coffee and Danish pastry. In her pram, her baby gurgled with infant glee. But Julia felt troubled, somehow. She felt, obscurely, that there had to be some point to all the trauma and the sacrifice that had delivered her here. It was Hamer's sacrifice, Hamer's life, which had delivered her. That had been the true cost of her own escape. And her own life could not be just about bringing up the child he had fathered, no matter how loving and conscientious a mother she wanted to be. Her freedom had not been earned, she felt. She needed to find its justification. It wasn't so much that she felt guilty or indebted. It was more that she felt the compunction to live a life she could respect.

'What am I doing?' she asked rhetorically, once, of Bill in a phone conversation during her San Francisco interlude.

Bill was silent. Until finally, he spoke. 'You're convalescing,' he said. And later, when she thought about it, she realized that this must have been true. Because one day in 1950, everything began to change for Julia Smollen.

It was Easter. Natasha was a bright six-year-old, a slender, serious girl who had read fluently from the age of three. It was the school holidays and it was coming up to Bill's birthday. Julia booked vacation time from the college and Bill took them up to Yosemite, where they camped and he taught Natasha his boy scout survival skills.

'Your boy scout survival skills must be somewhat rusty,' Julia said. 'You'd probably survive about ten minutes in a real wilderness before gibbering for room service.'

'Kid,' Bill said, 'I'm obliged to correct you, there. It so happens I've read every story Jack London ever wrote.'

'Have you read *The Call of the Wild*?' Natasha asked, and her mother could see she was impressed.

'Read it? I can recite it,' Bill said.

And despite the jokes, he was a skilled outdoorsman. He taught Natasha how to tie a fly and cast for trout. He taught her how to make fire without matches and when her kindling finally caught, on a wet day after much painstaking effort, she squealed in pure delight.

'She adores you,' Julia said, as her daughter slept on the cot between theirs one night in their tent.

'I'm having a party at my house and I want you to come,' Bill said. 'A grown-ups party. It wouldn't do for Natasha.'

'Heavy-hitters?'

'Heavy-hitters.'

It was what he called the important people in Hollywood.

'I'll be out of place.'

'Of course you will. As the most beautiful and best educated woman there—'

'I'm serious, Bill.'

'—and as my escort, you're bound to feel conspicuous. And envied.'

But this was important to him. Rain began to patter on the taut canvas over their heads. Their trip had been pestered by rain.

'Good for the fishing, though,' said Bill, who could sometimes read her thoughts.

'Shut up,' she said. 'I'm thinking.'

'I've booked you into the Montmorency,' Bill said. 'They have a babysitting service that comes highly recommended. The girls are trained and vetted. You can meet the sitter and have Natasha meet her and play with her all afternoon, if you wish.'

'I'll do it on two conditions,' Julia said.

Bill's weight creaked on his cot. 'Only the two?'

'You're forbidden to buy me a ludicrously expensive dress. And I won't wear rented jewellery.'

'Done,' Bill said.

She would buy herself a new dress. She wanted to look her best. She wanted the evening to be a success for him. Rain began to drum heavier between squalls of wind on the fabric roof. Bill's breaths deepened and regulated as he descended into sleep. It had been a happy trip. She heard wind soughing between the wet leaves and branches of trees. They had camped close to a scree slope and high above she thought she heard the bellow and crash of a bear. She heard his cot creak as Bill tensed at the sound in his sleep and then relaxed again when it was not repeated. Out here, his was a vigilant sort of sleep. In the little time Martin had had to tell her about his friend, he had mentioned that Bill was a skilled and lethal hunter. They had hunted together before the war. He was a formidable man in the wild, his Jack London joke being exactly that. Apparently he was an expert rifle shot. He had made another joke, when the two of them were tying fishing flies, about teaching Natasha to shoot.

'She's too young,' Julia protested.

'Annie Oakley probably started young,' Bill said.

Julia shuddered and shook her head. She wanted her daughter to have nothing to do with rifles and the bullets fired from them.

But she felt safe, in the tent, in this wilderness, with Bill. And she felt Natasha was safe. He was a bear himself, a man of colossal, wasting strength, absurdly constructed, really, for someone whose occupation was the law. She didn't doubt the courtroom could be a bear pit. America was a country ferocious for litigation. But most of Bill's work seemed to be done behind the scenes, over the telephone, in bars and across secluded tables in the lush country clubs of Southern California. Maybe it was to his advantage that he looked built like a prizefighter when he squeezed himself into a suit. Maybe it lulled adversaries into thinking they were dealing with a brain full of brawn. They weren't. When he was sober, Bill's intelligence was rumoured to be as deadly as his instinct for the pursuit of prey. Certainly he made a very comfortable living at the law.

But she worried about him. When he was hurt, or troubled, he had this way of hiding behind his own bluff size and jocularity. The jokes came ever thicker and faster. But Bill's jokes, in Julia's mind, were very much subject to the law of diminishing returns. He adopted a tone, in these moods. It was like listening to a skilful mimic, sometimes, impersonating Bill. His face took on a vacant cast and he responded to what you said to him with a bland, avuncular energy. He was Good Old Bill in these moods, and what made it all the more insulting was that he seemed to think nobody noticed. When it was so obvious! Julia thought that even Natasha saw it, and she was only six years old. 'Tasha did adore Bill, she truly adored him, and Julia thought she could see disappointment eclipse the joy in her daughter's face on those occasions when she would open the door to the godfather she loved and instead greeted Good Old Bill. The persona, the use of it, troubled Julia deeply. She sensed it was nothing more than a bandage wrapping and, at the same time, concealing a wound that refused to heal.

His house was in Laurel Canyon. It was built in the modern style from slabs of concrete and huge panels of opaque glass. The floors were polished wood, softened by the occasional rug. The furniture was all of a theme and the theme was coldly modernist. Bill had not taken a single artefact from the home he had shared with his first wife, Lucy, after her death. He had had the place razed and donated the land to a hospital trust. Everything from the home he had left for the one in Laurel Canyon belonged to the ex-wife who still lived there, in some splendour, on the beach at Malibu. I didn't like the beach anyway, Bill would joke, at the loss of real estate and expensively accumulated art. I never wholly trusted the tides, he would say. And he would wink.

So now he lived here. Water cascaded through the artful tiers of his garden and tonight it was lit by a procession of paper lanterns placed on either side of a meandering path. Guests mingled inside and out. The volume of talk, the abundant laughter, suggested the night was a success. Julia thought it was. At first she had been blind to all but the sparkle of Cartier necklaces and Balenciaga gowns and the drowning exclusivity of scents by master perfumiers spreading in aromatic waves from warm and wealthy flesh. The men wore their money more discreetly, in Rolex watches on gold bracelets and cufflinks set with diamonds and emeralds and studded with occasional pearls. She saw lizard-skin shoes and, on one man, the silver belt buckle of the Lone Star State. There were familiar faces there, of course: movie star faces she had disciplined herself before arriving not to gawk at like the popcorn-munching matinee fan she sometimes was. Bill's guests were an eclectic mix, the one common denominator among them being success.

'You look gorgeous,' Bill told her, for the eleventh or maybe for the twelfth time, and she noted, perhaps surprised, that he was entirely sober. 'I know you hate all this. But I'm immensely grateful that you came.'

'I don't hate it,' she said. She put her hand on his chest and reached up and kissed him on the cheek. 'It's a marvellous party,' she said. Which was true.

There were inevitable, minor dramas. A drunken starlet locked herself in a lavatory and a guest from Chicago earned a bashful round of applause when he picked the lock with the pin of a borrowed brooch. Two good-looking young men vying for the lead role in a prison thriller fought in the garden for at least ten uninterrupted minutes without either landing a telling blow.

'Stop it, for Christ's sakes,' implored a man in a white tuxedo with shoulders like Bill's and a nose almost flat to his face. 'They're killing one another!'

The fight petered out in the laughter that followed as Julia absorbed the surprising knowledge that the heavyweight champion of the world possessed a sense of humour.

She thought of Martin Hamer, then. But then, she thought of Martin Hamer all the time. Hamer had met Gene Tunney in America and Tunney had been the heavyweight champion, once. Bill had been there, too, that sunlit day in an American gymnasium. In Martin's heartbreakingly short life, this encounter had been one of the riches bestowed. He had lived very intensely. But very little of his life could have been measured in anything but terrible cost.

'Don't be sad, kid,' Bill said. And it was Bill. It was not Good Old Bill. He must have read her thoughts.

'You're a lovely man,' she said.

'Then please try to love me,' he said.

Did he really say that? She watched his broad back retreat through the throng and wondered whether to believe her ears. Their words had needed to be half shouted and cupped against the frenetic noise of a jazz quartet performing from an upstairs balcony. She had misheard him, surely, she decided, the squeal of an alto-saxophone solo forcing its tempo into her brain and tapping feet.

By five in the morning all but a reluctant caucus of guests had departed. A pretty blonde Julia knew as a singer of ballads played the piano from the open door of the den with astonishing skill. Her repertoire seemed limited to Sartie and Debussy, but Julia had never heard either composer played with such subtlety and finesse. Beyond Bill's glass and concrete walls, the dawn was slowly arriving, subdued by a light but persistent falling of rain. A fan of candlelight splayed and flickered out from the den into Bill's sitting room. The remaining guest sat there, sharing a table with Bill and Julia and explaining the problem he faced.

'My dilemma is this,' he said. He was a director in his late twenties with thinning hair that made him look older and he had Bill on retainer because a wunderkind reputation brought problems only experience could successfully deal with in Hollywood. 'My dilemma is this.'

He'd done one thing right, in hiring Bill, Julia thought.

But his dilemma was pretty depressing. He had been offered a three-picture deal by a cash-rich producer on the basis that the first feature reviewed well and at least broke even at the box office. Get the first one right, and he got carte blanche on the second and third. The problem was the specifics of the first picture. The story was formulaic. It was a Civil War drama with the usual, humdrum amalgam of death and heroism. And Audie Murphy had been chosen by the producer to play the lead. Murphy had been gifted Hollywood stardom by becoming the most highly decorated American soldier to fight in World War II. He had clearly been some kind of phenomenon on the battlefield. But he could not act. Any correlation between real and celluloid heroism existed only in the minds of movie people. Murphy, a sharecropper's son from North Texas, seemed to sense this himself, in performances so stilted there was almost something poignant about their failure. He'd been brilliant in the one movie in which he simulated himself. But otherwise he was lost.

And Murphy wasn't even the problem.

The producer had stormed into Hollywood with the usual gatecrasher credentials of money and energy and philistinism. His wealth came from the profits his auto-parts company was making from the reconstruction of Europe. He had met a beautiful nineteen-year-old girl in Milan and promised to make her a movie star. She had never acted in her life. She did not possess a word of English. She was sweet and heartbreakingly beautiful. And she was the balding director's problem as the man sat and sulked and dawn reluctantly broke over the debris of Bill's birthday party on an Easter morning in Laurel Canyon.

Julia was bored by it all. They were smoking cigars, the men, and she had loathed the smell of cigars since a series of forced encounters with a German doctor called Buckner in the labour camp outside the Polish city of Poznan a few years and a lifetime earlier. She had been up all night and was tired. She did not want to resort to the bottle of Benzedrine upstairs in Bill's bathroom cabinet to restore her alertness. She wanted to be there when her daughter awoke in a couple of hours in a strange hotel bed. She wanted to be showered and changed by then into soft pyjamas, to brush her teeth and get into bed and cuddle Natasha awake. There was a car outside for her with a driver waiting at its wheel and the hotel was a forty-minute drive away on deserted dawn roads. But she could not leave without saying a proper goodbye to Bill, who was engrossed in his cigar and the dilemma faced in his debut feature by the balding director. Self-obsessed, the director, Julia thought. But then they all were, the successful ones. And the ones who wanted properly to succeed.

In the den, the pretty blonde had fallen asleep over the piano lid. The only soundtrack now was the gurgle of water from the tiered stream in the garden. Julia took a Dunhill from a marble cigarette box on a table and lit it.

'The scene where he departs for the war is the problem,' the director was saying. 'We need to see it through his eyes.

He just doesn't have the gravity for us to see him through hers and anyway, it throws the balance off. It's more noble, his departure, seen from her perspective.'

'Can she cry?' This from Bill.

'Anyone can cry with glycerine.'

'Then you'll just have to dub her.'

'I know. Jesus.'

'Why will you have to dub her?' Julia said. 'Is it not plausible for a soldier in 1860 to take an immigrant wife?'

'Sure,' the director said. He laughed. 'It's a nice take on the turbulent demographic of the period.'

Someone had been at the Benzedrine bottle.

'Then what's the problem?'

'The problem is that she speaks no fucking English.'

Bill stiffened at the obscenity. Julia squeezed his shoulder. The director seemed not to notice. There were flecks of white, dried saliva at the corners of his mouth.

'She wants him to go?'

'Of course she doesn't. But she sees the need. She appreciates his calling. Knows the crusade is just and so on.'

'Then she could buy him some martial parting gift,' Julia said. 'Not say anything. Just give him some keepsake that demonstrates her approval of the cause and his part in it. He's a cavalry officer?'

'Yes.'

'Perhaps a pair of field glasses.'

'They're in officers' quarters in a Texas fort,' the director said. 'Where's she gonna get fucking binoculars from? The fucking Sears and Roebuck catalogue?'

'You're a valued client, Tommy,' Bill said. 'But Julia is my guest. If you use language like that again in my house, you will be climbing out of the canyon.'

Julia sat down with them. She scrubbed out the last of her cigarette in their ashtray. The director had grown very pale. Bill was not, she knew, a casual maker of threats. 'They're in officers' quarters?'

'Yes.'

'They have a scullery?'

He shrugged. 'Yes.'

'After he has gone to sleep on the night before his departure for the war, she takes his sword from its scabbard where he has left it, tied by his sword belt, to the bedpost. He awakens, but he does not stir. She takes the whetstone from the cutlery drawer in the kitchen and she sits and sharpens the sword. And then she very carefully, almost tenderly, puts it back. And surreptitiously, he watches her.'

'No dialogue?'

'Not a syllable.'

The director cleared his throat. 'What do you do for a living, Julia?'

'I'm a school librarian.'

'Not anymore, you're not.'

Bill dismissed her car and driver and drove her back to the Montmorency himself, through the quiet undulations of the canyon, then through the flat, mesa and cactus landscape, through the parched lake bed and arroyo-pitted earth. But for the odd, trundling truck, they had the roads to themselves. Bill had put the air conditioning on and Julia wrapped herself in the passenger seat in her short astrakhan coat. They were all the rage that season. She had spent a lot on her dress and her accessories. She had wanted to look elegant and graceful for him. He had done so much for her. And for Natasha. For both of them. Perhaps it was the terrain, but she was reminded of the first time she had shared a car journey with Bill, coming back from Mexico, bearing her child in her belly and her burden of grief. So much had changed since then. And so much would never alter.

'What are you thinking?'

'You usually know.'

'Not today.'

'That you're much better like this, sober, Bill. That drink diminishes you.'

He smiled. She suspected very strongly that she was the only one who dared say this to him. She suspected, in a darker part of her, that she might be the only one who really cared. The party had been a big success and Bill was evidently very popular. But Hollywood struck Julia as a loveless place.

They pulled up outside the hotel. It was still very early on a bright morning. The pavement outside the hotel entrance had just been washed and smelled of Lysol. Young men in white tunics with blue piping and epaulettes rushed around

61

the entrance with pails and brushes and mops and polishing cloths. It was a very energetic scene, full of American colour, Julia thought, and urgency. Bill wound down his window and already she could here the busy pop of ball on catgut from the tennis courts. There would be industrious swimmers, too, completing lengths of the hotel pool.

'Drink doesn't diminish people,' Bill said. 'It's life that does that. Life diminishes us all.'

'You stayed sober last night.'

'Last night I felt undiminished. Relatively speaking, I mean. I did have a couple of drinks. But they were drinks of very modest dimensions.'

'Don't make fun of me.'

'Maybe that's the secret,' he said. 'Drink small drinks and you stay the same size.'

'Don't be angry, Bill.'

'You'd better go in,' he said, looking towards the hotel. 'You have an appointment with someone very precious. If diminutive.'

'Will you answer me something honestly?'

'If I can. I'm a lawyer, remember.' But then he seemed all at once to weary of his own forced levity. He looked at her and his expression was absolutely sincere. It could have been a special effort made out of gratitude for her help with the party. She didn't want to think it was the obvious thing, the emotion most likely to compel his honesty.

'Go ahead, kid,' he said, gently. 'What is it you want to know?'

It seemed odd to be asking him this, here. They had turned the hotel sprinklers on now and the rhythmic swish of water washed over the hoots of horns from the car port and the percussive sounds from the tennis courts and the pealing telephone bells in the Montmorency lobby.

'Six years ago. When you came to Natasha's christening. Do you remember?'

'Barely.'

'You'd been drunk for a week, hadn't you?'

'Longer,' he said. 'Three, I think.'

'Why?'

He was silent for a moment. Then he said, 'The first time I saw my daughter, it was in the hospital. She was in one of those glass cases they put Natasha into when she was born. The last time I saw her, to say goodbye, was also in the hospital. And it was under the glass of an incubator then, also. Hannah wasn't quite two and a half when scarlet fever took her from us.'

'Oh, Bill—'

Bill looked at Julia. 'We were very grateful for her life. But within eighteen months her death had taken her mother, too.' He took one huge hand off the wheel and made it into a fist and looked at it. 'We keep those things we're not equipped to deal with hidden,' he said. Then he laughed and reached across where Julia sat and pushed open the passenger door. 'I didn't realize how diminished I'd be, seeing the inside of a children's hospital again. That's all.'

He kissed her on the cheek, then, and said, 'You should

consider Tom Sweeney's offer. That was his instinct talking, not the uppers. I don't think he's ever going to give Houston or Welles sleepless nights. But he's right about you. You could do very nicely here.'

Julia got out of the car and closed the door.

'Thanks for making it a swell party,' Bill said to her through the open window. He started up the engine and he drove away.

THREE

He was in the port of Danzig when the end came, when the surrender was declared and the world descended on Germany in judgement and its righteous hunger for retribution. He no longer wore a uniform by then. Only boys by then wore uniform. And the streets of the port were full of them. They lay everywhere, the corpses. Hitler Youth diehards killed in patriotic clusters manning obsolete guns. In some places their bodies had been scattered and burnt by the allied firebombs, or shattered by the Soviet artillery assault that had levelled the city. Some were not uniformed but naked, stripped of everything by the conquering Russian troops. For perhaps the first time in his life, Landau was glad that he wasn't a better specimen of German manhood. Unprepossessing and thin, he wandered through the port with an impunity by no means guaranteed by a suit of civilian rags and tatters. He saw the executed bodies in Danzig of dozens, scores of German non-combatants. It was enough provocation for the Red Army for their victim to be a capitalist, a German, and even, Landau supposed, a male. You needed luck and timing and an appearance so wretched it couldn't provoke anger or greed. He had mastered this. You also needed never to come across the Russians when they were drunk. This was mostly where the luck came into the art and craft of survival.

He had chosen a port as soon as he had made the decision to desert. But any ideas he had about escape from Germany had proven to be hopelessly naïve. He'd stayed off the roads and walked the shattered railway tracks by night to get to his destination. Pillars of smoke over the city, rising to a mournful pall, hinted at what to expect when he got there as he rested up by day in hides in the embankments and cuttings and beside the broken canal bridges along the route. He survived during this time on what scant supplies he could unearth from the defeated land. From the defeated dead. And he stole what there was to steal when he came across refugees weaker than he was. He took no pride in doing this, but neither did he feel ashamed. Like his country he was numbed, inured to feeling. He was stripped, like certain scavenging animals, of all the senses and sensibilities but for those upon which self-preservation depended.

For two days of his journey he feasted on black bread and rabbit stew when he fell in with a giant madman who had lived rough, so he claimed, for ten years. The man reminisced fondly about the happy times when all the other vagrants, the ones they caught, were rounded up by the Gestapo and shot in the forest.

Too much competition again, the tramp grumbled. The

good days are gone forever, he said, sucking meat from soft little bones, chewing his food between hard, toothless gums.

And Landau nodded his head. It was a philosophy he had his own good reasons for agreeing with.

He was grateful, relieved, when the morphine he had laced the vagrant's meal with finally took effect and the man dropped into a heavy stupor. Landau wasn't at all sure of the provenance of the rabbit in his bowl. Rabbits did not have fingernails. He sifted through the various horrors in his new friend's pockets and found only a clasp knife worth taking. So he took it. And he progressed on his way.

The land was black with corpses, black with the cinders of fires, scowling with defeat, sown everywhere with fear, sullen with accusation. The very air was heavy and impending with the hatred of the world. Landau saw the lights from Russian camps and heard their singing. He saw the dust churn and rise over fallow fields as the grind of their mechanized columns squared and quartered their prize portion of his fatherland. He hid from their aeroplanes and watched as the hammer and sickle insignia cavorted on painted wingtips through German skies.

He made his way to Danzig and when he got there, he sneaked and stole close enough to see the port. He saw the sandbag-and-gun, bristle-and-wire cumulus and watchtowers of its new fortifications. Searchlights carved through the ash in the air in vigilant sweeps. And Landau almost wept with laughter. It was the familiarity. And the irony of it, too. They were constructing an empire here, the Russians. They needed a workforce for their empire and had taken, already, determined steps to prevent that workforce from leaving. Danzig under the Russians had taken on the characteristics familiar to him from the industry-rich parts of Poland he had seen under his own army's occupation.

Beyond this dock perimeter, he could just make out the harbour. He studied it through the telescopic sight that was all that remained of his precious, lamented rifle. And what he saw did not give him hope. The superstructures of several scuttled warships he supposed were from the North Sea Fleet, blockaded the port. Through his sight they looked crenellated, in their grey massiveness like so many castles rising, listing, from the sea. Some of them were smoking and wore the tattered damage of attempts, presumably, to blow them out of the water from above. But they had been skilfully sunk. They were too low in the water for a bomb or an air-launched torpedo to strike their flooded ammunition magazines. Divers would have to do that with explosives and timers. And the task would be painstaking and fraught with danger. The naval wrecks were sure to have been booby trapped by their bereft captains and banished crews. There were other sunk craft. The assorted hulls of tankers and freight vessels canted at mad angles out of lapping, oily water. One object he couldn't make sense of at all, thinking at first it might be the corpse of a whale. Then he saw the pattern of rivets on the hull and realized it was in fact a capsized U-boat. It wobbled in the water, full of ballast and poisoned air, bobbed with the grotesque motion of a child's toy in a giant bathtub.

Landau knew that even given the fearful efficiency of the Russians, it would be months before this carnage was properly cleared. To escape undetected, he needed a working port with a volume of traffic busy enough to divert its custodians, overwork them, make them tired or nonchalant. That wasn't Danzig. With no food in his belly and no money in his pockets, he would need to formulate another strategy entirely. He didn't have much hope. He had never set great store by hope; he had never been a sentimental man. But he set considerable store by cunning. And he was more desperate than he had ever been in his thin, inconsequential life.

Landau had married, as everyone had who practically could, because there was no way to prosper in Germany under Hitler unless you conformed to the imperatives of the state and its breeding programme. He had wed a fat girl from a village a few miles from his Dresden barracks. In her League of German Maidens uniform, she had looked fecund, if not comely. She was undemanding of him. And she had produced two fat, apple-cheeked children in three years of fertile industry. Though there was no doubt he was their biological father, he had never really taken to either child. Nevertheless, the family was photogenic enough and as a family man, he swiftly won the kind of military preferment that had been his motive for spawning in the first place.

He learned to socialize. He learned to do this with his wife's parents, with the local pastor and, as they grew up, with his little angels too. He found it easy enough. He watched other people doing it and if they were generally adjudged to do it well, he copied them. His children loved him. He was a considerate and patient father. He never smacked them. It became an indulgence remarked upon.

He imagined that his wife and children were dead now. Certainly he would never see them again. But they had served a purpose, provided him with a skill the absence of which might have proved a fatal handicap in his efforts to escape and assimilate himself into the new world order. The experience of his family had given him the ability to communicate with other people. He would never be a garrulous, life and soul sort. But he had mastered the basics. He could get by.

Some were alert, of course, to his true nature. Some men possessed the preternatural instincts of the hunter and were aware, he supposed, of the danger he might represent. One such man had been Martin Hamer. He had met many impressive men during the course of the war. Hamer had been the only one he had truly feared. But he was dead, wasn't he? Landau was almost certain that Hamer was dead. He had seen the bullet strike home in the traitor's one faltering step in the snow as he carried his whore in his arms to Switzerland over the pass.

Landau liked to think it was destiny that had put him in the position to take that fateful shot. But it had been luck, really, hadn't it? Nevertheless, the skill to execute it had been his, seated in the lower branches of the pine tree he had climbed to achieve the angle, the soap from an incomplete shave drying as grey scum on his cheeks and his throat, even as he had taken aim. It had not been an easy shot, either. Hamer was a formidable adversary. He had butchered the man who had led their mission to bring him back with no weapon other than his hands. You felt a sense of foreboding when you saw him. You felt fear even looking at his broad back through a telescopic gun sight.

Landau put that gun sight into the breast pocket of his civilian suit. The rifle it had served, its lethal barrel and action and lovingly polished walnut stock, were decaying now, weighted by a net bag of road spoil at the bottom of a canal. In some ways, that rifle had defined him. But he was forced now to be someone else. And he was forced to find that person somewhere other than Danzig.

The city had been German through six years of Nazi rule. Now it was in Soviet hands. But the talk was of it being handed over to the Poles, renamed, and the very speaking of the German language outlawed here. It was a ruin anyway, a place of waste and rubble, not much more than a vindictive memory.

He needed to get to the American zone, he knew. The Americans were building an empire in Germany, too. But theirs was a metaphysical empire constructed from hearts and minds. He had heard the refugees, in their sad processions, whisper as much as they had passed his various hides on the journey to the port. He did not want to be broken on the wheel of Soviet industry. Who did? He would get to the American zone, where those social skills he had so studiously acquired would surely serve him in much better stead.

But then the winter came to Germany and, with its bleak arrival, there was no comfort. Landau's new plan had been to stick to the limit of the land, to skirt the edge of the Baltic Sea. Hamburg was a port in American hands. He could work his way to Hamburg without having to endure a march across his country's scorched hinterland. Most of those fleeing the East were stampeding through Russian-held Germany to Berlin. It was flight rather than strategy and made no sense to Landau. They would scour the land in their hundreds of thousands and starve. There was no provision for them. The Red Army had many qualities but compassion and pity for defeated invaders were not among them. Emotion drove the German exodus to Berlin. Berlin was the heart of Mother Germany. But those that got there would find neither comfort nor even recognition. The heart of the country was riven and burnt.

His own survival logic lay in fish. The Russians could not burn or deplete the sea. One day their trawlers would empty the Baltic of fish stocks in pursuance of one of their mad, five-year plans, he was sure. But he was equally sure that the war had left the fishing grounds to grow rich and heavy in neglect. The proof of this was evident in the spoil left by those who did possess the expertise and the presence of mind to harvest the sea in the chaos. Landau came eventually on his escape west from Danzig to a small natural inlet with a wooden dock a little past Kolberg. And he saw the gulls in a mad clutter above a pile of some stinking matter a few feet proud of the tide line. Sensing something edible, he took a driftwood spar from the debris washed up there and scattered the scavenging birds. They left a mound of fish guts and heads and eels still writhing; as birds pecked, they struggled to eat the entrails of herring and flounder and cod.

Landau, sat on the scree of pebbles and amid the slime of scales and stink of fish blood, feasted on the discard, raw. He retched with the age and unaccustomed richness of the feast at first, throwing up. His body had become a stranger to such nourishment. But after the one bout of stomach cramps and vomit, he was able to discipline himself to keep the matter down. When he could eat no more, he crawled off to a building higher on the beach. When he got there he saw that it was a smokehouse, abandoned by war. He inhaled the salt aroma of the smokehouse, present even under the threat of snow on a chill wind.

Someone had netted the stuff he had found. But whatever industry had trawled the sea here once was a ghost of itself. Subsistence, Landau thought. The old tidal rituals abandoned to women and girls. Thus the waste. He was glad then, as nourishment leaked into his deprived body, of the Führer's blind faith in the earth as the larder of the fatherland. The Führer's breadbasket philosophy had made

73

an almost mystical faith of barley and corn; of the scythe and the harvest, the ancient pattern of fields sown and crops nurtured and reaped. His hunger for fertile land had been principal among their reasons for conquest. The fishermen, by contrast, had been conscripted for war. They stoked the boilers on battleships and perished in submarines. And the sea had grown rich and fertile in their absence.

There was a heavy padlock on the smokehouse door. It was still strong, but had long rusted and seized. His instinct was right, he felt. There were no men here. There was no industry. Women had taken out the boat that had netted his meal. There was no danger here from people. There was only the biting hazard of the cold. It had got colder in the last few minutes, he felt. The food should have warmed him, but the cold wind pulled and teased at his layers of stinking rags, and his toes were growing numb in the leather boots he had peeled off the feet of his tramp. He looked out towards the water. The Baltic Sea was the same metallic blue-grey as the sky. White fronds of icy water capped sluggish waves. There was a still, bitter emptiness to the sky that he knew was the prelude to a storm. In this tempera-ture, in this exposure, that storm would be a blizzard. With desperate hands, he prised a loose plank from the smoke-house wall and slithered inside through the gap. He replaced the plank as best he could and looked around inside.

There were charred racks on the walls where once the people from here had flavoured the fish. There was a storm lantern suspended from a beam and when he shook it, a

sump of paraffin and rust gurgled in its base. But he had not
the means to light the lamp and did not anyway dare draw
attention to himself by risking either light or the heat of a
fire. He saw a wooden wheelbarrow heaped high with
beech shavings. The shavings were dry, dessicated; had been
there probably since before the war. He tipped the barrow's
contents into a pile on the wooden floor and lay in them.
He gathered the shavings around him, making a burrow.
The walls of the smokehouse were shuddering now with
the force of the wind and, through a narrow window, he
could see the light had turned sullen under a lead-coloured
sky. He shivered. He knew that it was a weakness to hanker
after the past, but sometimes he was honestly nostalgic for
the camp. For the good days at the camp. For the time
before Hamer came and everything turned bad and was
destroyed.

Ariel Buckner, a doctor and a geneticist with a fondness
for the ether bottle had official charge of the camp. He'd
administered it carelessly, under the benign authority of his
cousin Wilhelm Buckner, an important figure in Poznan in
the organization of the General Government. But Hans
Rolfe had to all intents and purposes run the place. Rolfe
was a veteran of the Bier Keller Putsch, a proud bearer
through the street-fighting years of the blood banners. He
sang the table-thumping songs with party pride threatening
to burst the blood vessels in his thick neck most nights;
claimed to have known Horst Wessell, to have been there
when Wessell's anthem aired for the first time, earning a

beery accolade in some cobbled cavern with straw on the floor under the Munich streets. He had been a bully, had Rolfe. He had been as mighty a pain in the arse as any man who ever strutted under party colours. But he had made the camp a profitable enterprise. The Poles inside it laboured and Rolfe sold off the bulk of what they produced. He hired inmates out as labour to the pioneer farmers paid generous Berlin subsidies to try to grow crops on Polish soil. Everyone in the camp benefited. And then Hamer arrived.

He had come, it was said, to recover from a war wound. His duties were light, nominal. Lousy timing had to take some of the blame. But he was one of those officers, like Rommel, later like Von Stauffenberg, Landau believed, one of those aristocratic types who thought themselves above the squalor and self-interest indivisible from war. And he had happened to be there when Rolfe set one of Buckner's dogs on the woman for goading him about the size of his dick.

Landau had seen the whole thing from the vantage point of his watchtower. Hamer had strutted by. The woman was pegging out washing. Rolfe had looked the worse for wear from drink, truthfully, struggling on his boot heels for traction behind the ether doctor's Dobermanns, exercising them. The woman had held out a peg in her fist and pushed it down till only an inch of it showed. And Rolfe had blushed and glowered and set one of the dogs on her.

Hamer hadn't been content merely with killing the

doctor's dog. He insisted on putting Rolfe on a charge. Landau hadn't seen the subsequent fight between the two men. It took place in the stables, late. And Rolfe was beaten and humbled. Landau and others tried to tell him there was no disgrace in that. Hamer had fought hand to hand in the cellars under Stalingrad. It was rumoured he had bitten out a Cossack's throat in the pitch blackness of night fighting where you identified friend and foe by the smell of the rations on their breath and in their sweat. There was no dishonour, surely, in losing a fight to such a man. Better to take pride in having survived it. So Landau and others argued with Rolfe. But there was no reasoning with him. He wanted revenge on the girl and saw Hamer as her protector. He had to discourage Hamer so that he could have a free hand in dealing with the taunting Polish whore. So he ambushed Hamer with a pick handle at night in the rain. And Landau did see this fight, on the porch of Hamer's camp quarters. Indeed, he gave the waiting Rolfe the nod when Hamer approached after one of his evenings over Buckner's chess table. And Hamer disarmed and held Hans Rolfe and spoke to him. And Landau, who had a sniper's eyes, saw the stain spread across the sergeant's groin in the sweep of a searchlight as he struggled to get free and pissed himself, knowing that he never would. And then Landau heard the neck of Hans Rolfe snap as Hamer twisted the sergeant's head in his hands. It was a small, sudden sound of shocking finality.

Hamer left the corpse in the rain on his porch as a

warning, or a reproach. Or maybe he left it there just as a trophy. In six years of war, Landau had never seen a man with anything close to the facility for killing other men that Martin Hamer possessed.

He survived the ice storm. After two days of shelter in the smokehouse, the wind cursing the land from the Baltic Sea lifted and vanished. The sun emerged from a streak of red, petrified cloud with the dawn and ascended into a cold blue sky. When the air grew warm enough, swaddled in his rags, Landau left his sanctuary of wood shavings and fish odour for the white enormity of the world. Even the sea held snow, he saw to his astonishment. It heaved in a briny crust at the edge of the land with the lap and stir of the water underneath.

And he found more fish. The cold made them torpid in the slushy water. Sometimes he would trawl from a jetty with a tatter of discarded net. Sometimes he would bait a hook and fish with a line. Once he stole a boat and snatched a dozing cod from the sea with his hands alone. But then he saw Russians around an oil drum brazier guarding a solitary building on a promontory and he knew that he would need to be more careful and less greedy if he were to survive his solitary march. West, he trudged, to Swinemunde. He passed through Wolgast and Greifswald, where he sat and rested and sucked the brains from the eels that were the last of his precious rations as his route took him inland and away from the sea.

Because he was careless and tired, because his eyes were red-rimmed and raw with snow-blindness, the Americans saw him before he saw them. They were in a Jeep and the vehicle had a heavy machine gun mounted on its rear. They were half a mile away when they consolidated into something more significant than a black smudge on the undulating whiteness of the snow. He knew they had seen him. The machine gun appeared unmanned and motionless. But the long barrel of a sharpshooter's rifle moved as he did, covering him, between the hands of the soldier in the passenger seat. It took him an age to reach them. Once he stumbled and, recovering himself, lost them completely against the blank vastness of the plain. Then they were there again. With the extravagance of Americans, they were going nowhere with the engine running. He thought the warm idling of their engine a wonderful sound after all the wind screech and silence he had been forced to listen to. It sounded civilized. It was, somehow, a hospitable sound.

He thought he might celebrate with a piece of the eel tied curing in the belt loops of his trousers. But then he thought that if he moved his hands from his sides, the sharpshooter with the long rifle would probably err on the side of caution and put a round in him that would take out most of his chest. The man with the rifle did move then, climbing out of his seat and manning the machine gun, spinning the weapon on its swivel base so that it covered Landau. Landau raised his hands above his head and tried to smile through the cracks and scabs of his frozen lips. He

79

estimated he was somewhere east of Lubeck and Hamburg and must have escaped the Russian zone as he swung south, inland, at Wismar. Unless the Americans were lost. He didn't know how bad a complication that would be for them. On paper the Americans and Russians were allies. But wars were not fought on paper. Wars were fought in the snow with rifles that possessed a lethal range of a kilometre or more. They were fought with machine guns like the .50 calibre Browning mounted and manned on the back of the American Jeep.

He had not been this close to Americans before and he was impressed. They possessed a fantastic quantity of equipment. There was a field radio in the Jeep. A pick and a shovel and a water canister with something like a sixty-litre capacity were neatly mounted on its side. Both of the Americans in the Jeep had side arms and he could see that the pistols were large-calibre automatics. Their personal kit included grenades, knives and abundant ammunition pouches. The men themselves looked clean and fit and well fed. They were very alert. There was something else about them, though, that puzzled him. Given the lack of threat or provocation he represented, they looked inexplicably furious. Landau was not concerned about the corporal squatting behind the machine gun. He was worried about the man behind the wheel. The corporal wouldn't kill him unless the sergeant gave the order to fire. The sergeant, though, looked like a man comfortable with issuing commands. Now, he looked appraisingly at Landau. He was blond and freckled and heavily built. He spat a green stain into the snow near Landau's ragged feet and the air was assaulted by the stench of chewing tobacco.

'Easy, pilgrim,' the American said. 'Any sudden moves will severely diminish your chances of surviving the next few minutes. Keep your hands where they are. Get over here.'

The words were spoken in fluent German. Landau thought the accent from Hanover. He did as he was told. When he got there he saw something the bulk of the Jeep had hidden during his approach. The torso of a third soldier rested upright in the snow about thirty feet away. He was holding a rifle equipped with a bayonet in his right hand. The stock was resting on the snow. His blood was fresh but already congealed in a thick puddle on the snow around him. There was nothing of him at all below the waist. About sixty feet further on from the corpse, a metal hatch stood open on the ground. It looked like a tank hatch, had the same sort of mechanism that would securely lock it from the underside. But it was bigger than a tank hatch and there was nothing underneath it but flat terrain.

'Sir, how far does the minefield extend?'

'Speak when I fucking tell you to,' the sergeant said. Snow was falling carelessly out of the sky in odd flakes and drifts. But the tracks of the Jeep were still clear. They could reverse the Jeep out of there to safety. The dead comrade they were so upset about had not opened the hatch. He had not even reached it. It struck Landau as odd that it was open. But then war was a very odd state of affairs

81

altogether. Still, he thought he knew what was going to happen next.

'Here's how it's going to play, pilgrim,' the sergeant said. 'You're going to walk from here to that hatch over there and back. You're going to plant your feet very firmly in the snow along the way. Imagine your footfalls are stepping-stones across a stream. That's how you are going to do it. If you don't start now, the corporal will send you to Valhalla, or wherever the fuck it is you people think you go when you die. He'll also kill you if you stop walking. Or if you try to run away.'

Landau licked his lips. 'You'd kill an unarmed civilian?'

'Oh, pilgrim, I'd kill any fucker,' the sergeant said. He spat again. 'You people didn't worry overmuch about who was armed and who wasn't, did you? When you were killing half the world?'

Landau, no philosopher, nevertheless thought this a point well made. He knew he'd made a mistake, though, in his claim to be a civilian.

'Move,' the sergeant said. 'I suggest you take a route different to the one attempted by our late friend and colleague.'

Landau went. He consoled himself with the thought that they were going to kill him anyway. He hoped they would spare a bullet for him if he tripped a mine and survived the detonation. Probably they would. They had such an extravagance of kit. They would not weigh the cost of a bullet against the opportunity to silence the noise of his screams. He progressed through the minefield on his numb and ragged feet. He was afraid, dry mouthed with dread. But he was not as frightened as he had been in his life. Buckner, the ether doctor, had made him follow Martin Hamer to a wood near the camp where Hamer sometimes went for the solitude. And Hamer had of course discovered his surveillance. There had only been the two of them that day in the Polish wood. And Hamer knew how to frighten a man. That had been fear. Christ, that had been fear.

He had reached the hatch. He looked down into a circular cylinder of concrete with further hatched openings on its sides. It was guarded by a dead officer in an SS uniform who, judging by his green, glassy expression, had bitten down on his cyanide pill. It was the opening to somewhere that didn't concern Landau and he had no curiosity at all about where or to what it would lead.

'You can come back here now, pilgrim.'

Probably the dead officer stank. But he would be competing with the smell of the eels knotted to the belt loops of Landau's trousers. They weren't curing, the eels. They were rotting. There was no point in kidding himself, he thought, despondently. His field rations were a long way past their best.

'I'm a soldier, just like you,' he said to the sergeant, when he reached the Jeep.

'He's lying, Sarge,' the corporal behind the machine gun said. His voice was filled with a bland menace Landau remembered having heard before on occasions involving death. He allowed nothing on his face to register the fact that he understood their language. His appeals were spoken in German and to the sergeant.

'I have a mother. A wife and children waiting for me in Hamburg. Infants. The war is over. Please.'

The sergeant seemed to consider him, drumming the fingers of his big hands in a heavy tattoo on the metal steering wheel of the Jeep. He reached over and took a rifle from its bracket on the side of the vehicle and took an eight-round clip from one of his pockets. He loaded a single bullet from the clip into the rifle. Then he threw the weapon to Landau.

'Shoot something, soldier,' he said.

The rifle was a Garand, the M1 .30 carbine, the mass-produced weapon of the American infantry. It was a short, comparatively light rifle with a small, almost abbreviated stock. It seemed like a toy compared to the Springfield sniper rifle the corporal had covered him with on his approach to this strange encounter. That leant now on the Jeep's passenger seat, a wonderful weapon of awesome range and calibre and killing accuracy.

But the Garand would do. He was a man of no great stature and the Garand suited his dimensions better.

Landau chambered his single round and held the un-familiar gun between both hands across his chest with his finger testing the trigger tension. There was a joy thrilling through him at the having of a weapon in his hands again that came as a wonderful surprise. All capacity for emotion he had thought bled and wearied out of him. He looked up, at the low sky, raising the rifle as he did so to his shoulder.

'He's got to be fucking kidding,' the corporal said.

The distance was about four hundred metres. It was nowhere near the limit of Landau's shooting skill or even the Garand's effective range, but the bird was a finch, fast moving, erratic in the swoops and dips of its flight. It was a challenging shot. There was no other target in that white wilderness. And he sensed the sergeant would not be patient long in waiting for one. So Landau aimed and squeezed the trigger and the report of the rifle was a compressed sound in the cold as the recoil thumped its stock into his shoulder and the bird tumbled in small pieces of flesh and feathers out of the air.

'I'll be blowed,' the corporal said.

Landau tried not to let his reluctance show on his face as he handed the weapon back.

'Your lucky day, pilgrim,' the sergeant said. 'If you'd missed, I'd have killed you.'

Landau nodded. He knew this was true.

'Follow our tyre tracks. That'll put you on the road to Hamburg about seven miles back. I'd offer you a ride, but we're going to be a little tied up here for a while.' He looked back at the trail of footprints Landau had left as their safe path to whatever secret it was the mines and SS corpse were guarding.

'Besides,' the corporal said, 'you fucking stink.' He laughed. 'Who'd you serve with? The fish unit?'

The sergeant smiled briefly at that and jerked his head in the direction Landau now knew was where Hamburg lay. 'Beat it, pilgrim,' he said.

With German such as he spoke it, his father or his mother must have come from Altmark or Gifhorn or Wolfsburg. Somewhere in that region. It was remarkable. He had almost been curious enough to ask about it, but that would have been dangerous. The sergeant seemed a very angry man. Angry about his comrade's death, about matters generally.

Landau had never met Americans before. On the whole, he had enjoyed the experience. Walking away from them in the rags on his ruined feet, he began to think America a place where he might thrive.

He had expected plaudits, a citation, perhaps a medal and a promotion too, after killing Martin Hamer. But the pursuit had been a grim and bloody catastrophe, all told. And they had wanted proof of the traitor's death.

They sent a squadron of mountain troops with an SS man and a guide and found a blood trail leading over the pass. There was much blood in the snow and they looked for his body optimistic that he might have bled to death soon after being shot. But he was strong. He was quite unbelievably strong. They were still following in the steady footfalls of the tracks he made as he carried his whore in his arms over the mountains when the weather closed in. The guide was forced to bring them down. The white-out lasted three days and brought a metre of snow and obliterated all trace of Hamer's wound and the escape. Worse, they wanted to know why Landau had taken only a single shot.

The answer was a mixture of fastidiousness and foolish pride. He had been bested, twice, by Hamer at the camp. The single shot was his vindication. It was the proof to himself of his confidence in his defining skill. Of course, he could not tell his interrogators that. And he had plenty of time to regret his hubris in the years after, consigned to a shit hole training camp in Vilnius to teach loyal Lithuanians how to shoot Soviet infantry with a bullet ration that seemed to grow scarcer by the week. In Vilnius, under seeping Lithuanian skies, he could feel the breath of the Russians on his neck. And he wished bitterly that he had riddled them both with bullets; killed the whore, left her and Hamer bundled and cold on the high pass clutching one another in death.

He was thinking this as he stumbled into the charred ruin of Hamburg. It was something he had thought about a lot. It was a therapeutic thought, one that took his mind off the cold and the hunger in his belly and the grotesque stink of the decomposing eels flapping around his midriff. It was a thought that cheered him. He would speculate on what he should have done and picturing it would excite him in a way and renew his energy. Was hatred fuelling him? He didn't care. Certainly he hated the Polish woman. Sparing her, with his fastidious marksmanship, had been a terrible mistake. Its nagging consequence was that he could not take the pride in having killed Hamer he knew he was entitled to.

He walked into Hamburg. And he felt a sudden, overwhelming shame about his smell and his appearance. He shuffled towards the rousing aroma of an American soup kitchen. And he realized that everyone in the queue for soup and bread looked just as he did. Steam rose from tureens of nourishing soup and great pots of simmering coffee and Landau heard the juices in his empty stomach boil in expectation. What did they call it? The land of the brave? The home of the free? A cheerful American volunteer put a tin cup in his hand and gave him an enamel dish. He would go to America, Landau decided. Germany was spent. They had spent Germany. He would go to America. He would give himself a fresh start in life. He had earned it.

It was six years before Landau gathered the means to emigrate to America. He took with him three hundred dollars, laboured English, his skill with a rifle and a violent antipathy to fish of any sort. He worked as a pump jockey at a gas station and lived in a sort of village comprising old Airstream trailers mounted on concrete blocks. That was in Connecticut. When he tired of the work, he moved west and juggled shifts as a short-order cook in a roadside diner with bartending in a tavern half a mile along the turnpike. But the Americans were willing slaves to soap, he discovered. And what was seen as his indifferent attitude to hygiene got him fired from the diner. He was not a natural at the bar work, either, lacking the smalltalk to cheer the huddle of thirsty losers who gathered each night to drink.

He worked next as a garage mechanic, but found the American automobile too irksomely reliable to earn him anything like a decent income. He squandered most of his savings on a hot-dog and soda concession that failed to provide any but a meagre return. And so he was forced into a shiftless life of petty theft, living out of a suitcase in a succession of featureless motels, increasingly aware that the forces of law and order in his new country were shrewd and energetic opponents with far greater resources than he would ever have at his disposal. There were no friends during this period. And there were no women. He was relieved, to be honest, that he was no longer obliged to be involved with a woman. In the old Germany, a family had been a necessary accoutrement. Here, nobody cared. And nobody could have cared less than Landau did.

He got a job eventually, servicing and selling guns at a Colorado hunting resort. He saw the advertisement for the job among the classifieds in a newspaper left on the seat of an Oldsmobile he stole from outside a Denver barbershop. He was obliged to try to sell the Remington brand. But he considered Remington a fine manufacturer of mass-produced rifles. He was of the view that underestimating American factory output had probably cost Germany the war. The Americans made good hunting rifles. They made good radios and refrigerators, too. His own, hand-tooled rifle, he fashioned himself. He made it to the exact specifications of the weapon that had killed Hamer, even to the burr on the walnut stock. And, of course, he made his own bullets. The evening in his workshop was very satisfying when he attached to his new rifle the old sight through which he had taken aim at the traitor in the mountains above Landeck.

He thrived in Colorado, at the lodge, where they took his rudeness and taciturnity to be aspects of what they called character.

'What sort of ammo should I be buying, Pete?' he would be asked by an executive from General Motors in a ridiculous plaid jacket.

'It doesn't matter. You'll be too drunk to shoot straight,' he would say. 'Too drunk or too hungover.'

And the executive and his friends would roar with the good-natured laughter of men enjoying themselves at play and he'd be thumped on the back or subjected to a friendly headlock by someone dressed like the hunter in the Bugs Bunny cartoons he watched sometimes on the television.

The ruder he was, the more they apparently liked it. Old Pete, they called him. And he knew that his status at the lodge in Colorado, despite his acknowledged expertise, was that of a grumpy and reluctant clown. And so he thrived, despising the misapprehension and ignorance that bolstered his growing popularity.

He would watch glorious sunsets over the mountains and as the day disappeared in a purple flush, creeping across the rocks above the tree line, a part of him would ache with nostalgia for the great days outside Poznan in the camp. The days of Rolfe's munificent reign, when the very uniform ruled a ripe and fearful world. It was the woman, he came to realize, pondering those sunsets, thinking of those times. Hamer would have come and then gone again back to his murderous war in the east, had it not been for the intervention of the Polish whore.

And then one day, he saw her. She was in a photograph on the front of a newspaper discarded by one of the lodge guests on a counter in the gun shop. A smear of gun oil had been absorbed by the newsprint, staining it. But the picture was clear enough. She was svelte and handsome in a tailored suit and her hair was long and she had gained weight and hardly aged at all. She was pictured with the young senator from Massachusetts, the one tipped to get the Democratic nomination for the presidency. The caption explained that Mr Kennedy had been present with his aides at a picnic fundraiser in Hollywood. But it was someone else in the picture that most shocked and fascinated Landau. It was a girl, blonde, at the edge of the frame, too young to be employed as an aide to anyone.

'You have your father's eyes,' Landau whispered to the picture.

He wondered did the girl know who her father was. He wondered did the girl have any notion of the cause her late father had served and the things, in that service, that her late father had done. Then his eye was dragged back to Kennedy, the figure at the centre of the picture, his charismatic smile wrinkling the skin around his eyes in the California sun. And he wondered what the young senator knew about the past of the handsome woman described in the caption as his aide.

FOUR

Bill was surprised when Julia became involved in American political life. When he thought about it later, it was with the sense that some strong element of fate or inevitability had played a part. It was as though it were something not so much decided, as pre-determined. She had shown little prior sign of interest in politics and no sign of political allegiance. She could have been responding to the charismatic pull of the man who asked for her help. Much of the country eventually did. But Bill thought it went deeper than that. Because her participation brought to the fore profound questions about who she was and what she had done. The beacon on the hill was bound to shed a little of its light on the darkness of her secret past.

During her first couple of years in the industry she had energy, it seemed, only for her career and for her daughter. She moved to a pleasant town in Orange County. She got Natasha into a good school and she employed a house-keeper. She worked meticulously as a script editor, first on a series of abortive projects for Tommy Sweeney. The Civil

War picture was abandoned after the girl from Milan revealed herself five months pregnant by the auto-parts mogul financing the project and Audie Murphy got cold feet about playing a character in a costume drama who did not survive until the final credits. Bill thought this no great loss to commerce or to art. Events before the eventual cancellation of the picture provided Julia with a valuable apprenticeship, a working insight into the way that things functioned in the industry. Or, more often, didn't.

She outgrew Sweeney pretty fast. He found his vocation in television, directing a cop series that made his fortune while ruining his health. She outgrew Sweeney because she possessed qualities that he did not. She didn't strike Bill as particularly ruthless or ambitious. But she was disciplined and intelligent and given to a sort of patient, diplomatic tact when she dealt with the more infantile and egocentric film people she encountered. It didn't hurt, either, that she was so attractive. She had this European style, this dark sophistication that seemed almost mysterious. She wore Chanel suits to work and smoked Gauloise and left the lingering scent of Joy perfume behind when she vacated a room. She guarded her privacy, protected her daughter and had no appetite for gossip.

Bill heard it whispered that Julia Smollen might be one of those gorgeous, ball-breaking dykes. The only evidence he heard supporting this theory was that she wore a man's wristwatch. At first her looks and that unconscious quality of exoticism caused a certain amount of confusion. She would arrive for a meeting only to be told that she had missed the casting, or that auditions were taking place in a different part of the building or on a different day. But as she became more successful, she became respected and better known and the misassumptions about who she was grew rare. Bill took a sort of pride in her smooth progress to sought-after script consultant. He was very irritated with himself for feeling this. The pride felt almost paternal. His feelings for Julia Smollen were a complexity beyond his heart, let alone his mind. But since they were not in the slightest fatherly, he thought this flush of pride in her achievements might mean he was becoming middle-aged.

She retained what he thought of as some endearing eccentricities. Principal among these was her passion for cycling. He tried to interest her in equestrianism. Learning to ride was a rite of passage in the industry. All of the lead players had to ride at least competently because horses were ubiquitous in films. Outside of the westerns and the period dramas, in what passed in southern California for real life, ownership and mastery of a horse was a reflection of social status. So there were lots of riding schools in their part of the world. There was much faux Englishness about the riding culture, with hacking jackets and stables featuring fake Tudor beams. More than compensating for the pretensions, though, were the wildernesses of coast and country open to riders.

But Julia stuck stubbornly to her bike, with its light-weight frame forged from English steel in Coventry. And its two aluminium drink canisters mounted on the racing handlebars. And the horrendously ugly shoes she wore to pedal it. What was wrong with a western saddle and a pair of hand–stitched riding boots?

'Riding is so much more elegant,' Bill said.

'I am riding when I ride my bike. You don't need to feed a bicycle. You don't have to pay to have somebody stable and groom it.'

Bill shook his head. 'You can take the peasant out of Poland,' he said.

'If you finish that sentence out loud, Bill, I shall punch you with my Polish fist.'

She was a voracious reader of newspapers and periodicals and took an intellectual interest in what was going on in the country. But she was as likely to read about European matters as she was about the domestic dramas occurring in Washington or New York.

Or in the South.

In 1954, the Supreme Court ruled racially segregated schools illegal. The papers had been full of nothing but the bloody implications of this landmark decision when, a few weeks after it, Bill drove over to visit Julia at her home. It was a beautiful day in high summer. Her house had a painted wooden balcony on the first floor, facing south. She waved down to Bill, who went up. She poured him a glass of lemonade from an iced pitcher on a table under a gingham cloth. Sunlight bathed the balcony. Newspapers and magazines were spread across the table, loosely anchored at the centre by the weight of a glass ashtray. Natasha was on a school trip to Niagara Falls. A picture on a newspaper front page, distorted by the angular glass of the ashtray, showed a black man with a bloodied face trying to shield himself with a broken banner demanding his civil rights. Julia had sat back down after pouring Bill's drink. There was a French newspaper across her lap. Bill sipped cold lemonade. He could smell newsprint warming and yellowing in the strength of the sun. Julia was relaxed in a floral summer dress and espadrilles. She rested her feet on the balcony rail. Her hair was scrunched up under a sun hat. She looked about as beautiful as he had ever seen her look.

He nodded at the French newspaper. 'What are you reading about?'

'About the tour.'

'The what?'

'The Tour de France. It's a bicycle race.'

'I know what it is.'

'I'm rooting for Fausto Coppi,' she said. 'He's so brave in his attacking in the mountains. But you need to be a pragmatist to win the tour. So Louisan Bobet will probably ride down the Champs Elysees in the yellow jersey. Again.'

Bill spoke quietly. 'Go, Coppi,' he said. He sipped lemonade.

'I know what you're thinking,' she said.

'You do? It's normally the other way around.'

'It isn't fiddling while Rome burns, Bill. It isn't the same as saying, let them eat cake.' She gestured at the paper

97

weighted by the glass ashtray, at the cruel picture distorted across the table under it. 'Events in Georgia and Mississippi will not be affected either way by my reading about a bike race.'

'Do you even care what happens?'

Julia dropped her French newspaper and folded her hands across her lap. She squinted up at the sun. Bill thought that the question had made her furious. When she answered, her words were very deliberate. 'I'll tell you what I think, Bill, from the luxury of my balcony, on this lovely, unsullied day.' She was momentarily silent.

'I'm glad the Union won your American Civil War. I think it tragic for what followed that President Lincoln was killed. Slavery is an abomination and segregation its abominable consequence. But I bore a child to a man who helped his nation enslave mine.' She smiled. 'I'm too ashamed to tell my daughter who her father was. I am in no position to judge others. If I pontificate, it won't be about the situation in the South. I'd prefer to discuss the injustices of a bicycle race.'

'I'm sorry, Julia.'

'No need to be.'

He was silent himself for a moment, stunned by the implications of what she had told him. 'Will you never tell Natasha who her father was?'

'I don't know.' She picked her newspaper up off the balcony floor and then put it down again without unfolding it. 'I don't know that I could forgive myself for burdening her with that. But if I don't tell her, I break the promise I made to him in the moment before he closed his eyes and died.'

Bill didn't say anything.

'It's what one terms a dilemma, Bill. And the older she gets, the more urgent a dilemma it becomes.'

'He was the best man I ever met, Julia.'

She met his eyes. 'I know. I know what kind of man he was. I loved him.'

Bill rose from his chair. He would drag his elephantine bulk and bottomless stupidity elsewhere. It was still early. He was confident there was plenty of further crass damage he could do on his Saturday stampede through Orange County.

'I'm sorry,' he said, reaching for his hat.

'Don't leave, Bill,' she said. 'I need you to stay.' She smiled again. 'Now that you have depressed me so thoroughly I need to have you to stay and cheer me up.'

These were the years, also, of the McCarthy witch-hunt. Bill thought America generally more alarmed by atom bombs in Russia than by the supposed threat of communist sympathizers in Hollywood. He was surprised at the energy and spite of the accusations. He was distressed, too, at the livelihoods lost. The gloom and panic became endemic. He had friends who were frightened and depressed. He went on the march to Washington, on the HUAC protest bravely led by Humphrey Bogart. But then Bogart was forced into his humiliating climb-down, his capitulation, confronted by the threat of a wrecked career. Bill himself lost wealthy clients when they saw his picture in the papers and saw him on the newsreels in the press coverage of the march.

Everyone knew that McCarthy was just a crude opportunist on the make, that his list of supposed influential communist sympathizers was so much paranoid fiction. Bill thought of him as a snake-oil salesman in a suit behind a microphone. He was a tub-thumper. A rabble-rouser. He was all that was least defensible about democracy. He was a dismal paradox of a man; exploiting what he condemned, denying those he accused of the very right to the free speech he said they threatened. He was also the subject of the first political argument between Natasha and Julia that Bill ever witnessed.

They were camping in Colorado, the three of them. Bill had gone to gather kindling and wood for their fire. There were wolves in the mountains that year in packs and he had decided as a precaution to build the fire to last right through until dawn. He had cut the dead wood to lengths with an axe where it had lain and then gathered it in his arms and carried it back. He walked lightly because that was the best way to carry a heavy load. If you had the strength, it was. Bill did. He had probably eighty pounds of wood aboard. They didn't hear him approach. Good job I'm not a wolf, he thought. He bent down and put the wood on the ground and still they didn't hear him. Their voices were low and urgent and emphatic and, of all things, they were talking about Joe McCarthy. They were on the other side of their tent from him. Their shapes were bathed in the diffuse glow of a lantern through the canvas. They were sitting so close together, mother and daughter, that he could not tell where one figure ended and the other began. He could not even tell which of them was which. He felt guilty about eavesdropping, so he started to build the fire, methodically, to tactfully alert them to his return. Their response to this was to raise their voices. Natasha sounded excited. Her mother enunciated what she said with a sort of cold disdain. And Bill was party to every word the two of them exchanged.

Natasha said, 'I don't think rich people, people like us, can imagine what it is like to be really poor. Poor people don't have any hope. It's why they turn to communism, isn't it?'

Julia spoke carefully. 'I've had experience of both wealth and poverty,' she said. 'I've seen both extremes.'

'But you always had hope,' Natasha said. 'You were never in a hopeless situation.'

Julia said, 'When you live without freedom, hope becomes very difficult to sustain.'

'Everything is personal with you,' Natasha said. 'I'm talking about people here, in America, so downtrodden—'

'America? I've seen worse.'

'Two wrongs don't make a right, Mother. America wouldn't be the worst place to start.'

'You could start at that school I pay for you to attend,' Julia said. 'There must be kids devastated they didn't get to

Europe on vacation this year. Don't their parents know equality is a fundamental human right?'

If this were a prizefight, you'd be begging the referee to step between them and stop it, Bill thought. If it were a dogfight, you'd have to have a veterinarian put Natasha down. He took a match and struck it and watched flames curl around dry kindling.

'McCarthy is a dangerous and disgusting person,' the girl said.

'Disgusting, certainly,' her mother said. 'But a danger to whom, precisely?'

'Those people he's persecuting.'

'Persecution is ten thousand Polish soldiers taken into the Katyn Forest at the point of Russian guns and murdered on Stalin's orders,' Julia said.

There was a silence. Bill thought Natasha might be crying. 'It's impossible to talk to you about anything,' she said. Go, Coppi, he thought. He rose and one of his knees cracked as he went to intervene.

Natasha had this particular way of introducing some outrageous claim. She owed it to one of her teachers at the school she attended. The school always referred to itself as an academy and its recruitment policy was a reflection of its pretensions. The staff was unconventional. The standard of scholarship and rate of exam success were high, but the teachers tended to be egocentric and flamboyant types. Natasha's English literature professor was a Boston Irishman who had shown great promise as a juvenile poet. The consensus among publishers since then was that his youthful muse had departed abruptly carrying all her bags, since which point she'd never sent so much as a postcard home. His opinion was that he was the victim of a nationwide literary conspiracy. But he thought it had spread from the South, where his third collection earned its first poisonous review in an Atlanta literary journal.

'There are towns in the southern states of North America,' he would begin, 'where the residents are known to eat their own young.' Or, 'There are towns in the southern states of this august nation, which have banned shoes with elasticated gussets on the grounds that they provoke sexual desire.'

Bill was driving the three of them back from Colorado, the route vast and panoramic on the way towards Los Angeles across the Utah badlands. It was three days since the argument he had heard and the chill between the woman and the girl had not lessened by a single discernible degree. Bill had Hank Williams playing on the car radio. When Hank had come on, he had turned the volume up. He thought Hank's weary vocals went well with the endless landscape and if the mood of his songs was melancholy, that was quite all right with Bill, who was melancholy more often than he should have been himself. Then Natasha giggled from the back seat.

'There are towns in the southern states of North America,' she said, 'where my mother would be welcomed as a bleeding-heart liberal.'

There was a silence in the car. Bill did not turn to look at Julia's expression. Hank yodelled on the radio and twanged at his guitar. Bill cleared his throat. 'There are towns in the southern states of this august nation,' he said, 'where your mother would be welcome.'

He actually heard the pause as they waited for him to continue. Then they knew he wasn't going to. They both laughed, amused and then relieved, he thought, their laughter in the thaw between them much more generous than the joke deserved. He relaxed at the wheel. It was more than a decade, now, since his flight with Julia Smollen in the big Ford from Mexico. He thought of the grief and the thirst, the enormous, raging sensations that had governed him then; Julia a still, spectral presence with her hands over her belly, the veins blue in their backs through her translucent skin, the nails bitten and gnawed, the tyres slewing under them and the engine roaring as they fled Mexico over terrible roads. What did he feel for that time? Was it fondness? A sort of nostalgia? He smiled to himself. He had lost his best friend and gained a hopeless affliction. That's what it was, wasn't it? He loved Julia Smollen with all his heart and it was an affliction he had not the strength or the courage to fight.

A few miles on at dusk they found a lonely diner wrapped in blue neon and extruded aluminium and they stopped there for something to eat. Julia went to use the rest room and when she had gone Natasha put her arms around his neck and kissed him on the cheek and said, 'You're the best, Bill. You are. You're the best.'

And he smiled at the compliment and thought of what he wouldn't pay, at that moment, for a good, straight shot of honest southern bourbon.

Later, at the wheel and bolstered not by booze but by two cups of thick black coffee, he confronted Julia about the row. Natasha slept heavily under a picnic rug across the back seat of the car. He thought the feuding had worn her out.

'Julia?'

'Bill.'

'I know from recent, painful experience that I should confine my political observations to the Tour de France.'

'But you're not going to, are you?'

'You were right, of course. Coppi was valiant in the mountains. But Bobet won the race.'

She sighed. 'Sometimes being right is not at all the point.' She wound down the window and lit one of her French cigarettes.

'You need to go easier on the kid, Julia. She's only eleven years old, for Christ's sakes.'

The road unwound in front of them. It was yellow in the pool of their headlights and then it was nothing at all. Julia smoked and picked tobacco from her teeth with a fingernail. Her hands were beautiful now, the nails neat, lacquered ovals pearly in the light from the dashboard instruments. 'I was a radical myself, once. I was almost hanged for my defiance, made an example of, confined in a camp.'

'None of which is your daughter's fault.'

'What irritates me about the young is that they always pick the fashionable causes. It's more to do with peer group competition and crushes on rebellious writers and actors than it is to do with principles.'

'She's eleven years old, Julia.'

'And I'll be putting up with it until she's twenty and decides that children of her own are a more alluring prospect than slogans and street barricades.'

'She may not come to that conclusion,' Bill said. 'If she starts to believe what you say about her.'

Julia watched the road. She threw her cigarette out of the window and settled back in her seat. 'You're right, of course. I'm much too hard on her. I love her more than anything. I want so desperately what's best for her. I want her to turn out right.'

'Valedictorian prom queen?'

She twisted and looked at her sleeping daughter and smiled. 'Healthy,' she said. 'Happy.' She turned back again and leant against Bill's arm and put her head on his shoulder. 'I do try.'

'You know what I always say, Honey.'

'What do you always say, Bill?'

'You don't try, you don't fail.'

They laughed together, comfortable with each other and with their old cliché, the car steadily devouring the road, Bill glad that he had said what he thought needed to be said. But he couldn't help a song lyric nagging at his mind, and it wasn't one of Hank Williams' lost, plaintive appeals to fate. It was a song from a Fred Astaire musical from the years before the war. It was the Irving Berlin song, 'Let's Face the Music and Dance', and it was the first line that insinuated itself, in Fred's familiar voice, over and over again into his mind. *There may be trouble ahead,* Fred sang. And Bill thought there almost certainly would be.

The years following the war were not what Bill would have called dignified or hopeful years in American political life. This was true even though the history of the Republic had always featured its share of corruption and injustice. Johnson and Harding had only been the most indiscreet of the several dishonest incumbents to embarrass the office of the Presidency. Government integrity had frequently been sullied by treaties solemnly sworn and swiftly reneged on out of nothing other than naked greed. And there were always people possessed of sufficient hate and prejudice to make populist demagogues a danger. Before McCarthy there had been Huey Long and bigot and radio star Father Charles Coughlin.

But something was different now. America should have emerged from the war with pride. The cause was noble and the victory unambiguous. War output and technologies had made the economy strong and confident. The trouble was that the new balance of world power was such an uneasy one. Russia was volatile and its communist ideology aggressive and expansionist. Winston Churchill had coined the term the Cold War. And that had generated its own lexicon with American foreign policy experts talking about such dangerous phenomena as spheres of influence and the domino effect.

And the missile gap.

It was the bomb, of course, that made the outlook so sombre. It was the bomb that cast its horrible pall over the hopes of the world. And while Russia schemed and scientists toiled to turn deposits of uranium into deadlier payloads, buses were burnt in the South because coloured children were permitted to take them to integrated schools. And in the senate a bully banged a gavel with a mallet and spewed paranoid lies about the threat from within. No, Bill did not think the years of McCarthy and Little Rock a happy or optimistic time in American political life. The period lacked dignity. It lacked hope. And if Julia was disdainful of it, wasn't that her perfect right?

In criticizing her daughter, Julia had condemned Natasha's radicalism as a chic choice rather than a choice of intellect or conscience. Bill thought the judgement harsh but probably true. Natasha was a precocious kid and teen rebellion had come early to her, as most things did. But he had trouble, if he was honest, thinking any kind of politics chic. Certainly the subject was seen to possess no glamour in Hollywood. In the year Bill argued with Julia on her balcony, *On the Waterfront* and *Carmen Jones* were among that year's major film releases. It could be argued that one dealt with union corruption and the other brought coloured lead actors into the mainstream for the first time. Bill would have thought both those claims disingenuous. The first of the two films was far more revolutionary for the style of acting Brando brought to the lead role than for anything it said about work practices on the New York docks. The second, when all was said and done about Harry Belafonte and Dorothy Dandridge, was a musical. And the big box-office performers that year were *Rear Window* and the smash hit *20,000 Leagues Under the Sea*. What the audience most wanted on their screens wasn't Brando's washed-up boxer fighting graft. It was Kirk Douglas grappling bravely with a giant rubber squid.

Bill would remember 1954 as the year that Natasha Smollen first became interested in the issues and ideas that would come later to consume her. But he also saw the first signs that Julia wanted to both give and get more from life than the comfortable living she was earning.

She had been drafted in to do some emergency surgery for Billy Wilder on his movie *Sabrina* after Cary Grant abruptly pulled out of the project and was replaced by Humphrey Bogart.

Watching the movie in later years, Bill suspected that Bogart was already ill by the time of the *Sabrina* shoot. Certainly he was tired and his tired performance reflected the fact. Julia was more withering in her criticism. They saw the finished cut in a preview hosted by Wilder and the applause that followed the final fade seemed spontaneous and genuine enough. But afterwards, over drinks, Julia said that her work on the picture had been like bandaging up a patient who was already dead.

'Holden was okay,' Bill said.

'Callow,' Julia said. 'Under-rehearsed. Bill Holden is having an affair with Audrey Hepburn. If he thought sleeping with her was a practical substitute for working on their lines together, he was wrong.'

'Bogart?'

She shrugged. 'Bogart is Bogart. But he is a mature leading man and Hepburn is an ingénue. He looked more like her grandfather than a realistic suitor.' She looked around the bar they were in. It was filled with firm-bodied, flawless young women out for an evening with men who looked like their grandfathers.

'It's this town, I suppose. For a particular type of girl, the men who are powerful here have a particular allure. It doesn't matter what they look like or even what they say. But it isn't like that in the rest of the country.'

'You think a romantic comedy the right vehicle for exploring the demographics of modern dating?' Bill was fifty-four, the same age as the century, and Julia was thirty-seven. And he was touchily aware of the fact.

Perhaps she guessed his thoughts. It wouldn't have been the first time. 'Maybe it's the genre that's the problem,' she said. 'I don't find romantic comedy very convincing.'

'You think it trivial. You think working on trivia demeaning.' He sipped at his Martini. It was dry and strong in a properly chilled glass and his fourth since their arrival.

He wondered why it wasn't hitting the spot. 'You want to work in theatre?'

'It isn't the work, Bill,' she said. She looked restless. Her eyes went again around the room and she shrugged her shoulders under her velvet stole like someone struggling slightly for air. 'I'm very fortunate. It isn't the work.'

The bar they were in was a cocktail lounge on Hollywood Boulevard. They were seated four or five tables away from a raised dias with a pianist who tried to play in the style popularized by Oscar Peterson. There were cigarette girls behind trays of their wares lit by neon tubes that cast a ghoulish light on their made-up, smiling faces. For no obvious reason they were trussed in red bodices with corset laces up the back and berets like the one sometimes favoured by the actress Veronica Lake. There were mirrors on the walls in frames sculpted from fruit in wax or plaster or painted papier mâché so that your reflection stared back at you out of plaits of bananas and pineapples. They had chosen it because of its proximity to the preview theatre in which they had endured the movie together.

'What are we doing in here, Bill?'

'Having a good time.' He winked. 'Waiting for the cabaret.'

They waited for the cabaret. And it was terrible.

And then in 1957 Julia found her cause, and with it, her calling.

He'd seen the Kennedy book, *Profiles in Courage*, in her book case, the single volume of political philosophy jostled and cramped and very likely depressed by all the gloomy, pessimistic nineteenth-century novels she seemed to like to read. He took it out and flicked through it. He had heard little about the Catholic senator with the millionaire father except that he had been some kind of war hero and had gone into politics as a surrogate for his dead brother.

'Have you read this?'

'Yes.'

'Why?'

'Because the author interests me.'

'Is it any good?'

'Up to a point,' she said. 'But I think what he has to say about the future is more interesting than the way he pontificates on the past.'

'He hasn't exactly set the senate alight.'

'I met him at the weekend. And he had plenty to say.'

It had been at a barbecue hosted by Peter Lawford. Bill had been invited too but had been away that weekend. He'd been fishing, which was his shorthand, or code, for trawling the red-neck bars of Arizona, quenching an insatiable thirst for beer and rye chasers and sometimes getting into trouble with those locals resentful of anyone to whom they weren't linked by a defective gene pool. He'd recently bought a Jeep to facilitate these fishing trips. But even with his telescopic rods strapped to the sides of the Jeep in their expensive cases, he wondered just how secret his real destination could be. He came back from his fishing trips reeking of booze, raw knuckled, layered in desert dust and bar-room bruises.

He was too old for this shit, he kept telling himself. Much too old. But he didn't know where else to go with his anger and frustration at the things about his life he so despised. It was demeaning, truly demeaning in the way that Julia had meant it, criticizing the three-week drunk he'd gone on all those years ago. And his drunken, delinquent desert odysseys had become addictive of late. He no longer kidded himself it was just letting off steam. There was more to it than that. But he hadn't worked out what. And until he did, he wouldn't be able to work out how to stop. Besides, he wasn't hurting anyone except himself. Other than himself, it wasn't as though he was really letting anybody down.

Julia had her own independent, abundant life. She did not need old Bill. The Peter Lawford party at which she had met Jack Kennedy was convincing evidence of that.

She hadn't dated much during her years in Hollywood, he knew. Her romantic life was not much discussed between them. He would not have been comfortable with the subject and she was far too discreet. But he guessed from how often she was alone and odd remarks made by Natasha that there was no significant man in her life. She hadn't lacked for suitors once the dyke rumours were dismissed. He did not honestly know why she had failed to meet someone she could care for. Her years of convalescence were surely over. He did not think she was a hard person to find attractive, or to love. She only really talked about it once with him, when she stopped dating an actor she had been seeing. He was a spectacularly handsome man, athletic and about as popular as any man could be who inspired, without effort, the envy he did in other men. He pursued Julia with charm and persistence and flowers. But she never seemed more than lukewarm about the mention of him. And their relationship petered out almost before it properly started. Bill didn't ask, but on this occasion, Julia told him anyway.

'He always plays the hero,' she said. 'His problem, where I'm concerned, is that I have encountered the real thing.'

'And he doesn't measure up?'

She smiled. 'Only in the pictures. In the pictures, he does.'

But she had friends who were men. There were facets to her that most men found alluring. He asked Sinatra, once, what it was he so much liked about her.

'If I tell you, Bill, you're sworn to secrecy,' he said.

'You can trust me, Frank.'

'You're a lawyer, Bill. I can't. That's why you have to swear.'

'I swear.'

'She never flirts with me,' Sinatra said.

'Come on, Frank.'

'Never,' he said. 'That's what I like about her, Bill. She's unique.'

She went to the Lawford party and Frank and Sammy were there and Leonard Bernstein and Mailer and Hepburn and Monroe and others, most of them in a marquee Lawford had thankfully thought to have pitched, because rain hissed out of a pewter sky that showed no sign of clearing. The guests were enjoying themselves anyway. At a table at one end of the marquee, Sinatra had organized what he called children's activities, which basically meant a high-stakes poker game. At the other end of the tent, Sammy Davis taught dance routines and conjuring tricks to the children their famous parents had brought along. Outside, a few people braved the rain in scattered groups while table umbrellas dripped a fringe of droplets onto them. Julia said hello to people and commiserated with the already tipsy host about the rain. Then she helped herself to a glass of rum punch and looked for a vacant table outside. There was the odour of cigar smoke in the tent. It was not strong, but it was persistent and a smell Julia habitually avoided for the dark memories it kindled in her. She found a table and sat and sipped her drink, squinting, for a hint of light, at the sky. There was none.

'And that's when he came over,' she told Bill.

He was alone. Rain darkened the shoulders and lapels of his grey sack suit. He had his hands thrust into the coat pockets in a gesture that to Julia looked awkward and shy. He was tall and thin and had poor posture and a dense thicket of reddish brown hair brushed too low across his forehead. He was not handsome. He was not handsome the way you saw men every day in the business she was in. But it was hard to take your eyes away from him. He was compelling, particularly when he smiled, which he did quickly, as though doing so made him self-conscious so that he had to get the smiling business over with. He shook hands formally and introduced himself and asked her permission to join her at her table.

'I've read your book,' she told him.

He said he was flattered. And they talked for half an hour before Sinatra and Lawford came over and took him away to introduce some casino people keen to meet him from Las Vegas.

'He's going to be president, Bill.'

'There's a surprising number of guys in very softly up-holstered rooms.'

'What?'

'Think they're Napoleon.'

'He is, though.'

'An Irish Catholic president?'

'Meet him and see. He's marked for something. I think for greatness.'

Bill had never seen her like this. 'I bet he was tough on Russia. Talking to a Pole?'

'He isn't cynical at all.'

'He's a politician.'

'He has strength, Bill. I don't mean the physical kind. He's quite hesitant in his movements and much too thin. But he has steel in him. And he has grace.'

And he sure as hell has your vote, thought Bill, who had never seen Julia so alive to any subject outside Natasha. He didn't know what to make of it. It had come so unexpectedly. It was like some kinds of religious conversion he had read about. It was like she had been exposed to the power of revelation. He didn't know whether to be happy or alarmed for her. He didn't know Kennedy, had never met him, although he supposed they must belong to some of the same clubs. Then again Kennedy had been a Harvard man and Bill had gone to Yale.

'I want to do this,' Julia said. 'I want to do something worthwhile.'

'Do what, exactly?'

'He gave a short speech at the Lawford house. He delivered it in the marquee and had to contend with bored children, confined by the rain, bickering at his feet. Also Lawford, who was drunk, interrupted a couple of times with what he thought were witticisms. Kennedy laughed off the noise and the interruptions. But the speech itself was poor. If he could get the passion of his conversation into his speechmaking, then his speeches would be wonderful. And I think I can help him achieve that.'

'You're going to work for him?' Bill was incredulous.

Julia nodded. 'Voluntarily. Someone from his office is going to call me.'

'Don't hold your breath,' Bill said.

But somebody did call. Ted Sorensen called the following week and Julia was invited to Hyannis Port to discuss the collaboration further. By this time Bill had done some research on Kennedy. It was preliminary stuff, but the one constant that kept coming up was the presidential hopeful's track record with women. Bill felt obliged to caution Julia. She was a grown-up girl and tough, but he didn't want her savagely disabused of her new ideals at the compound owned by the Kennedy family on the seashore in the East.

'I've heard all that stuff too,' she said. 'But he's invited Natasha along. This is an opportunity for me to do something I can be proud of. I'm going, Bill. Natasha too. We're going.'

She rang off, then, called away to help Natasha with an essay her daughter had to complete before their departure for Massachusetts. Natasha was fifteen now and the precocity had not dulled. But her mother had a gift for languages and could help her with her French assignments and Bill thought help with homework was one way in which Julia ensured she stayed close to her sometimes wilful and secretive girl. Bill was in his den. He still had the phone in his hand. He would, habitually, have held a drink in the other, were it not holding a copy of the Kennedy book, which he had now read himself. *Profiles in Courage* had earned its author a Pulitzer Prize. Well, it had earned Jack Kennedy a Pulitzer Prize. There was a widely held belief that the book had been written on his behalf, probably by the loyal and erudite Sorensen. Or maybe the book was the work of the loyal and erudite Arthur Schlesinger. When it came to aides, Kennedy certainly had a following among the loyal and the erudite.

Bill put the book down. He lowered the telephone receiver back onto its cradle. He walked over to the bureau in his den and took the stopper from a decanter and poured himself two fingers of Scotch. There was music playing in the den. Bill had been listening to the Sinatra album, *Come Fly With Me*, when he had made the call to Julia. He'd turned the volume down. The music was almost inaudible. Frank would have been scandalized, would have thrown things, stormed out of the place. He smiled and went across to the stereo and turned the record back up again. He still hadn't touched his drink. He could smell the warm Scotch in its glass. It was familiar, like Frank's voice, like the evening sunlight slanting through his blinds onto the furniture.

He opened a drawer in the bureau and took out some photographs, snapshots, a cascade of abstract black and white patterns as they fell from the envelope where he had half filed and half hidden them from his own eyes, onto a table top. Then he sat with his drink beside him and started to sort through them, touching each image with gentle fingertips, remembering their golden light and fading foliage and baked earth and ripples dappling and fixed forever in their streams and ponds and on their broad, unceasing rivers and the people he had loved in them. These people, he had loved. Lucy, he thought. Hannah, my darling. He touched their smiling faces with his fingertips and closed his eyes and his heart filled with a fondness he had thought lost to him. And he remembered them.

Sinatra rebuked him, wise-guy optimistic, jaunty from the speakers of his absurdly expensive stereo. Bill was no stranger to self-pity or nostalgia. But when he wallowed, he wallowed in bars, not at his home. Tonight he was supposed to go to see a Joey Bishop routine at some new club off the

Boulevard. He wouldn't go. He thought Bishop a nice enough fellow but his jokes weren't funny and he had no gift anyway for telling them. But he didn't plan to sit here, either, getting slowly drunker and more maudlin in front of old photographs growing blurry because he was staring at them through tears. No. He had taken the pictures out because there was one among them, he knew, of Martin Hamer. It was over twenty years old, taken on a hunting trip in the forests on the border with Canada. Taken by a local hunter, it showed them both. Martin, eight years his junior, would have been about twenty-seven.

Bill shared the composite memory everyone shares of people who are gone and like everyone's, it was made up of the way they moved and sounded and gesticulated and the smell and weight and mood and presence of them. He had not looked at a picture of Martin since discovering his friend was dead. And so doing so, now, made him gasp as he recognized the eyes of Natasha Smollen gazing coolly out of the photograph from under her flaxen hair, cropped here, cut short and severe.

Julia had sworn a vow to a dying man. Natasha had grown up believing herself the consequence of some anonymous rape carried out in a Polish labour camp. Bill wondered would the mother ever keep her promise and tell her daughter the truth. His own conviction was that two people, one of them dead, very much deserved for her to know it. And he felt that Julia very much needed to tell it. Secrets of this enormity were corrosive to the soul. But this secret looked likely to remain a secret, now. Particularly, now.

Bill remembered his drink and picked it up off the table. He raised it, and prismatic light glittered through crystal in the sunshine between the blinds.

'Go, Coppi,' he said.

FIVE

Some of the girls were smoking a reefer at the back of the bus. Even though it was bone cold on the bus and the air frigid, they had a window cracked back there. She could smell the smell, familiar enough, if still illicit. She'd smelled it in boho coffee bars and on the porch outside sorority parties and even once in one of the dorms. One of the boarders at school, Alice Dorne, was said to be heavily into the stuff. Alice was a pale, thin girl from Philadelphia who'd had to give up ballet over stage fright and stayed in her room a lot, listening to Rod McKuen. She'd even tried it herself once, but once had been enough for Natasha Smollen. It had made her nauseous and edgily paranoiac. She thought it was probably more common among her mother's friends than hers. That was pretty ironic, really. Or it would have been, had she grown up in Salt Lake City, or some steel town in Pennsylvania. People her mom knew used it. But they were consenting adults. And they had far too much class and money to smoke the stuff at the back of a freezing bus.

There are towns and cities in the southern states of this great nation, she thought, where possession of dope is a felony crime punishable by public execution.

He was back there with them now, Professor O'Brien, his nose in the air and his head in *Ulysses*. Probably it wasn't *Ulysses* at all. He always appeared to read the same book on trips, claiming it to be the only novel ever written worthy of his enlightened attention. But Natasha had sneaked a peak and though the dust jacket was suitably dog-eared and ragged, the pages were pristine. Probably a pulp western by Louis L'Amour. Or something featuring a hard-boiled private dick. Was there such a thing as a soft-boiled private dick? Or maybe he was reading wham-bam sex stories. There are towns and cities in the southern states of this august republic, she thought, where pornographic books are a prize beyond all measure. And she smiled to herself, because that was probably true. But Prof O'Brien wasn't reading smut. He was the Celtic cowboy, heading into town for a shot of red eye and a shoot-out. It was Louis L'Amour and not James Joyce at all the old fraud was reading. It was a wasted opportunity. With what he was unknowingly inhaling back there, *Ulysses* would probably have made a lot more sense. More sense, that was, than Natasha ever thought it normally did.

She had reading of her own. She had a net book-bag full of Kerouac and Ferlinghetti and Camus to muse over. But she was too excited to read. She was travelling to Europe for the first time and was so thrilled about it that she couldn't even think about mundane requirements like eating or sleeping or the reading of books. It was December and bitterly cold and she was aboard a bus churning and wheezing over snowy roads on the way to New York Harbour and a boat to France. From there they would take the train to Austria. She was going to the Alps on a school ski trip. She would have preferred something cultural, like Paris or London or Rome. But her mother had made the perfectly valid point that she was only seventeen. She might have no patience. She had plenty of future. Paris and Rome were places best seen in May or September, not December. Besides, she was a good skier and there was likely to be plenty of snow. You can see Innsbruck if you want culture, her mother had said, and a look had passed over her mother's face that she did not recognize. They have a crystal museum at Innsbruck, she said, and she shivered and goose bumps rose on the flesh of her arms, perhaps, Natasha thought, at the memory of snow.

Natasha almost hadn't made the trip. Her mother hadn't wanted her to come. There was often conflict between them, and fines and confiscations were her mother's favoured methods of imposing discipline. Natasha had been rude on the telephone to someone calling from Hyannis Port. More accurately, she had been rude back. The aides were endlessly civil when they called. They understood her mother had a career. They understood that she couldn't always be pacing the carpet, waiting for the call, as some of them were paid to be. Natasha sometimes fielded her mother's calls. Ted Sorensen nicknamed her Bush Baby. She didn't know where the endearment came from. But even when she could hear how hard pressed he was in the tone of his voice, Sorensen was kind and courtly. Kennedy himself was kind of old fashioned, on the two occasions she had spoken to him on the telephone. He called her 'Tasha, which he must have overheard her mother do. He was apparently unaware of just how intimate the contraction was, because he was so polite and formal and, though it sounded crazy to say it, almost shy. Jack's brother Bobby, though, was a complete jerk on the phone.

'Julia?'

'No.'

'She there?'

'Yes.'

'Get her.'

Or:

'Julia?'

'No.'

'She there?'

'No.'

'Shit.'

Usually he hung up then. Sometimes he demanded numbers at which her mother could be contacted. You would have thought he was the one running for office by the urgency and temper of him. He always sounded in an absolutely foul mood.

She'd seen him at Hyannis Port, usually at the heart of a

huddle of cronies, their ties and tight shirt collars incongruous on bleached decks and against the picturesque sand and boat-sails backdrop of the village. He was good-looking and boyish in repose, but you never caught the man without a frown creasing his features. Unless he was with his older brother. He seemed to relax around Jack. Jack could make him laugh out loud with a joke you could never hear, no matter how close or still you were. He had that knack, that gift of witty confidentiality his younger brother so woefully lacked.

On the infamous occasion of the rudeness, Natasha had been tired and pretty grumpy on her own account. She struggled maintaining her maths grade. She wasn't bad at maths, but everything was relative. She didn't enjoy calculus or algebra. She didn't respond to their cold abstraction. When she looked at an equation, she didn't see elegance, she saw hard labour. Everything else came more easily to her, nothing else so unrewardingly. The fact that it was a Friday probably exacerbated her existing misery. But she wanted to get her maths assignment out of the way to have the weekend free. So she had struggled that evening over sines and co-sines, her feet already feeling the sway of fresh powder under her skis, her lungs filling with the unfamiliar air of an alpine adventure. It was October. Semester-end and Europe were only weeks away.

It was about eleven-fifteen when her mother arrived home from one of her dates. She walked into their sitting room putting her car keys into her clutch bag. She was dressed in a belted, calf-length skirt tailored to her slim hips. She wore it with a white shirt with a single string of black pearls at the open throat. Her skirt was a deep red and her jacket, slung across her shoulders, was a pale grey. She looked chic and beautiful and unhappy. Natasha could tell she was unhappy by the set of her mouth under her lipstick. There were blue shadows on the pale skin under her eyes.

Natasha felt sorry for her mother at times like this. She thought forty-three a tragic age for a woman to be dating. She was in before midnight, so the date had been unsuccessful.

'You should be in bed, darling.'

She only ever called Natasha that when she was in one of her remote, withdrawn moods, preoccupied and uninvolved. And 'Tasha hated it.

'Calculus,' she said. She yawned. 'I'm going to make some hot chocolate to take to bed. Would you like some?'

Her mother breathed out through her mouth and shook her head and started up the stairs. The telephone began to ring, then. But her mother didn't respond.

'Hello?'

'She there?'

Natasha looked up at the empty staircase. She could hear her mother moving around her bedroom, taking things off. Could hear a tap running and then water splashing.

'She's not available.'

There was a pause. 'What?'

'I don't want to disturb her.'

'Let me get this right. She is there?'

'Yes.'

'Then get her. Now.'

'You really need a lesson in manners, mister,' Natasha said. And so she gave it to him. She hung up.

But of course, he had rung back. And her mother had come down in her dressing gown with her hair wet around her shoulders and had taken the call. And when she finished the call, after forty minutes for Natasha of purgatory under the covers in her room with the light switched off, her mother came in and sat on the edge of her bed.

'I don't need to tell you never to pull a stunt like that again.'

'No.'

'You're not a little girl. And I don't need to tell you what's at stake here.'

She meant Jack Kennedy's election. Natasha thought it was already in the bag. Not even the boorish antics of his brother could sabotage that.

Her mother was quiet. 'I'm not going to pay for the trip to Europe, Natasha. I need to do something to discourage this spoiled behaviour.'

Natasha sat up in bed. She didn't deserve this. 'I'll ask my godfather to lend me the money. I'll go down and phone him and ask him right now.'

'Fine,' Julia said. She stood, wearily. 'Phone him. But it's after midnight, now. And he'll be far too drunk to speak to you.'

The phone was a very busy instrument in the Smollen household that evening. And though her uncle Bill might have been too drunk to speak, he was capable of listening.

Bill slalomed over in his dust-caked Jeep. He was wearing a pair of combat fatigues and sneakers and a white singlet and a frown. The muscles bulged with red-neck belligerence in his upper arms and massive chest and neck. Natasha hadn't realized just how big he was. He looked a little like Clark Kent in the telephone booth in mid transition. In their living room, in this outfit, he was that big. Except that his hair was not blue, the way Clark Kent's was in the comic books. And he was staggeringly drunk. He waved his arms around to no effect except perhaps maintaining balance. Natasha hugged her uncle Bill. He had come. That was the important thing. The important thing was that he had come.

Her mother had come down. She wore her silk dressing gown and slippers and a sardonic expression and watched his flailing from the sofa. Natasha thought her mother secretly amused. There was something noble, Herculean, about Bill's struggle to appear sober. It was a performance possessing that tragic dimension of always being predestined to fail. Her mother sat and watched and lit a cigarette and tried not to smile. She was glad Bill was here, Natasha realized. Even in this condition, in these circumstances, she was happy to see him.

Bill extricated himself from Natasha's embrace. 'Julia, hon, gotta drink?'

129

'You know where it's kept. But you can't have anything if you're planning to drive home.'

'Tickle a cab,' Bill said. 'Cab. Tickle.'

'In Orange County? At two in the morning? Godparents are supposed to give spiritual guidance,' she said. 'It's not at all the same thing as guidance in spirits.'

Natasha could see that her mom was enjoying herself. Stripped of make up, with her hair splashed darkly over her shoulders, she looked much younger than she had on returning from her date.

Bill fetched himself a beer from the refrigerator and sat nursing it between both hands. He was a lawyer. Tonight, though, his self-appointed function seemed to be to play both judge and jury. He had what he probably thought was a sage and judicious expression on his face. To Natasha, he just looked constipated. He asked her to reiterate what she had told him on the phone. She did so.

'Julia?'

But her mother refused to testify.

'Taking the fifth,' Bill said. 'A pragmatic choice.' He pulled a thick roll of bills from a pocket in his fatigues and leant across and put it into Natasha's lap.

'Ask me, Bobby Kennedy sounds like an asshole.'

'Bill!'

'Sorry, Julia, but he does.' He winked at Natasha. 'Enjoy the trip, kiddo.' And he stood. 'I may retire to the spare bedroom, if that's acceptable,' he said. 'These judicial proceedings have taken their toll on my stamina.'

Natasha and her mother sat in the room for a while after Bill had left it and the radio comedy of his ablutions had ceased and they heard the bedsprings stop groaning as his dormant weight settled into slumber in the spare room. Natasha shifted the roll of bills off her lap and put it on the table between where mother and daughter sat. It was hundreds, a tight cylinder held by a rubber band.

'We'll give it back to him in the morning.'

'There must be five thousand dollars there.'

Her mother shrugged. 'I don't think he would have counted it. I don't think he ever does. I think five grand is chump change to Bill.'

'And I'm the chump.'

'No, 'Tasha. You're not a chump at all.'

'I'm sorry, Mom.'

'Come here.'

They sat and held one another and her mother stroked her hair. 'I'm sorry too. We were both at fault. Of course you are going to Europe.'

'I worry about Uncle Bill. I love him so much and he's so unkind to himself.'

'He's kind to you, though.'

'He'd be much better if he took things more seriously.'

Her mother stroked her hair. 'I think that just the opposite is true,' she said. 'But then if we didn't disagree all the time, you and I, what would we be?'

'Well, I don't know the answer to that. What would we be?'

'Imposters,' her mother said.

It had been a very late night for Natasha and when she got up the next morning, she could hear Bill and her mother breakfasting already on the balcony. She went down to the kitchen and passed a packed overnight bag at the bottom of the stairs. It meant a flight to Cape Cod. It was what the call had been about. She would take advantage of the situation by making herself a peanut butter and jelly sandwich and washing it down with a Coke. This was not a breakfast her mother would have allowed her. But she gambled on having the time alone to prepare and eat it. The key to a contented life with a parent as puritanical as her mother could be was never letting an opportunity slip.

They sounded pretty engrossed in their conversation. They were talking about Kennedy's campaign for the presidency. Her mother had been with him in West Virginia, which he had not been expected to carry. His wealth was a problem with electors there. His Catholic faith was an even bigger one. Kennedy had been shocked at the deprivation he saw there, her mother said.

'A man with his background would be shocked by the deprivation at the Paris Ritz,' Bill said.

She heard her mother laugh. She never heard her mother laugh the way her mother laughed with Bill.

'Is that you, 'Tasha? Are you up?'

'Hi, you guys,' she said.

'What are you eating?'

'Rye toast,' she said. 'Yogurt. Grapefruit juice.' She took a sip of Coke. You could justify it in revolutionary terms. She took a bite of her sandwich and peanut butter and blackcurrant jelly oozed from between the layers of bread in her mouth. In revolutionary terms, she was liberating the kitchen.

Her mother's voice grew hushed again. 'It was the lack of hope that appalled him. He spoke to men of forty who think they will never work again because of their age. He spoke to men in their twenties who will have to leave young families and move elsewhere if they are to get jobs. He wants to help them. He doesn't just want change, he has a vision of change, a vision for America.'

'You should write his speeches.'

This time her mother didn't laugh. 'He writes his own speeches. He speaks a lot off the cuff. Schlesinger and Sorensen polish the phrases. I help with the structure, that's all. He wants rapprochement with Russia, Bill. He wants to bring the Cold War to an end. Can you think of another candidate with the brains and courage to accomplish that? With the will?'

There was a silence.

'What do you think of him?'

'I think he's the best hope we've got,' Bill said.

The bus ride to New York was easily the worst part of Natasha's journey to Europe. Salt rime from the frozen roads splashed and stuck halfway up the bus windows and above that was only a blear of dripping condensation on

133

cold glass. There wasn't enough light to read by. It was hard to doze against the stiff collar of her winter coat. Most of the interesting conversationalists in the party spent the ride zonked out on reefer at the rear of the bus. And the driver tuned to a series of stations that played exactly the same sorts of songs by a series of identical artists. So it was Elvis Presley and the Everly Brothers and Doris Day and Patsy Cline. Her own album of the moment was *Kind of Blue*, by Miles Davis. Jazz was big at her school, where the girls thought John Coltrane and Thelonius Monk infinitely cooler than Elvis crooning his way through '*I Ain't Got a Wooden Heart*'. She had a soft spot for Frank, of course. She'd grown up with him. Her favourite album of his was *Only the Lonely*, one of his gloomiest sets. It had this European feel that was in total contrast to the albums usually arranged for him by Nelson Riddle. She wouldn't have said so out loud, but there was something almost existential about the mood and atmosphere of *Only the Lonely*. You could not have said that about Bobby Darren or Little Richard or any of the rock and rollers. It had more in common with the Jacques Brel and Charles Aznavour recordings her mother listened to. She had school friends who thought Frank Sinatra was all golf slacks and corny Vegas schtick. But they hadn't met him. Natasha had. And if Frank wasn't cool, then the word didn't have any meaning.

They took the boat train from Le Havre to Paris and it was deeply thrilling, when they changed for the sleeper, just to hear the porters on the platform shouting and gesticulating at one another in French. They walked in a file through the streets between stations. Everything smelled different and the scents of tobacco and coffee and baking bread seemed to give the light itself an antique quality. There was a burnish to Paris, a magic-lantern glow. Aboard the sleeper, she watched the city disappear into its own suburbs, transfixed by just how foreign everything looked. Then they were in a landscape of flat fields stunted by winter cloud and sheets of intermittent rain. Exhausted by the crossing and the excitement, Natasha crawled between laundered sheets and slept for ten solid hours. When she awoke, they were east of Zurich, approaching the Austrian border.

Bill drove her mother to the airport in his Jeep. It was a sunny day in October in California and so the Jeep wasn't that eccentric a choice. He'd changed into a fresh shirt from a duffel bag in the Jeep and didn't look like Clark Kent caught out anymore. He didn't appear in the slightest hungover. Her mother wore a headscarf and sunglasses for the trip, perhaps in stylistic homage to the woman bidding to become first lady, Natasha thought. But probably because the sun was reflecting off the road and the Jeep was roofless. Having seen her cycling attire, having seen her cycle, Natasha actually thought her mother one of the least vain people she knew. But she was tall and slim and possessed hauteur and she was beautiful. Her lack of vanity was an absence she could afford. As Bill drove and chatted to her

135

mother, Natasha sat behind them and pondered on the conversation she had overheard at breakfast.

She had been to the Kennedy compound and had seen first hand the properties people grew so excited about in Jack. Once, walking on the seashore, she had seen a shadow eclipsing hers and blinked into the light to see him smiling at her there, quite alone.

They had walked along the beach together and discussed sophomore subjects like music and film and fiction. Discussed them in the self-conscious, sophomore manner. She had found him knowledgeable and funny. But there was this other thing, too. You found yourself hanging on his every word and gesture and storing them as if in some archival memory of immense importance and impending value. She even inventoried what it was he was wearing (pale pleated shorts, white shirt with the sleeves precisely rolled, canvas boat shoes). And the whole process was something that seemed to dictate itself and its imperatives to her, as though she were helpless to prevent herself from logging every urgent detail of the encounter. Why am I doing this? she felt like screaming at herself. I'm not impressed with your voting record in the senate, Mr John Fitzgerald Kennedy. I'm angry that you stayed silent throughout the whole McCarthyite debacle. Your father was a Nazi appeaser. Yet as they reached the end of the strand and she watched his tall figure ripple and disappear into heat shimmer, she knew it was something she would boast about to her grandchildren. I met Jack

Kennedy. I knew him. I didn't know him very well, but yes, I knew him. I did.

They said goodbye to her mother at the terminal and Bill suggested he could take Natasha for a drive and maybe a picnic in the hills.

'No booze, Bill. No stopping off at wayside taverns.'

'No booze,' Bill said. 'I promise.'

'And she has to eat something nutritious for lunch. A peanut butter and jelly sandwich washed down with cola isn't a dietary regime she's going to thrive on.'

'How—'

'She's your mother, hon,' Bill said. 'She knows everything.'

But her mother looked sad again now, solitary with her overnight bag slung over her shoulder and her eyes hidden behind her sunglasses. Natasha listened to the Tannoy as it sent some piece of travel information echoing off the hard shapes and surfaces of the terminal building. She thought Tannoy announcements the bleakest of soundtracks. Her mother leant forward and they embraced. 'I love you, 'Tasha.'

With Bill, she watched her walk away towards her airplane. Off to join the Kennedy coterie of Lem Billings and Chuck Spalding and Grant Stockdale and Bob Troutman and Sarge Shriver. And Larry O'Brien and Kenny O'Donnell and Teddy and Bobby. And their father, Joe. Jesus, she thought. And people called Sinatra's friends the clan and the Rat Pack.

'Bandit country, kid,' Bill said. 'That's where we're

headed. Rattlesnakes. Prickly cactus. Mean varmints. Oh, my.'

But he was watching her mother, the humour expressed merely by rote, by tradition, a look of concern and impossible tenderness on his face.

She hurt her ankle on the sixth day of skiing, more out of ambition than ineptitude. Down at the ski station they were concerned to ferry her to a hospital and have the ankle X-rayed at enormous expense. They were thinking dollars and rich Americans, Natasha thought. The joint was bruised, the ligaments tender when she touched the area. But there was nothing torn or broken. She had gone up with a guide, skins on her skis for the climbing part, and descended too fast through a narrow, demanding chute. She'd fallen. She wasn't dead or even crippled. She had over-reached herself, that was all. A few days and it would be okay. But she didn't want to risk cabin fever sitting in their cuckoo-clock hotel and she couldn't settle down with Camus or Kerouac in the mountains. So she decided that she would take the bus to Innsbruck and visit the crystal museum her mother had recommended before their short-lived falling out.

She had taken the cable car to get high on their peak with the guide. And then they had walked, climbing sideways on, using the traction given by the skins attached to their skis. Then at a certain gradient, they had taken off their skis and strapped them to their small backpacks, kicking foot holes in the frozen snow and continuing upwards on all fours. They reached an elevation where they were higher than some of the surrounding mountains. She saw peaks subsumed by cloud and suddenly freed again. She saw scats of snow on granite peaks powder in the wind. The cluster of mountains around them seemed close enough to touch. She felt party to the secrets of their colossal height and strange contours. She felt strangely privileged, exalted, to be so high among them. But she was also gasping with the thin air of altitude and when she turned to look at him, her guide looked alarmed at the place they had achieved. He pointed down. The gesture was urgent. He had no English.

Natasha paused to look around. They were in the mountains between Innsbruck and Landeck, north of the Brenner Pass that crossed through the Alps to Italy. To the west, in Switzerland, rose the great peaks. Mont Blanc. The Matterhorn. The granite ramparts of the Jungfrau. She would like to climb them, one day, she thought. There was something vast and intimate about the challenge of the mountains. You didn't conquer them. That was a lazy fallacy. You clung for your life to their fissures and ledges and cracks and if they respected your skill and your nerve you survived them. It was something she would like to learn and accomplish. One day she would have to find somebody to teach her.

Her guide was gesturing frenziedly and then putting his finger to his lips so she wouldn't play the bellowing American. It was not a time of the year when avalanches were common. She had read that they occurred mostly in the spring. But as he pointed upwards, to heavy banks of snow rising in scalloped ridges on the steep plain above them, that was clearly his concern. The snow banks were wind sculpted and massive, like the piled grey hulls of gigantic boats. And they were creaking. She pointed her skis down and descended nimbly for a thousand metres before falling and hurting her ankle. She lay in the snow and could tell by the rueful expression on her guide's face and the relaxed way in which he shed his poles and removed his gloves and goggles that the danger was behind them. He nodded at the hurt ankle and said something in German. She didn't understand him. She thought the language harsh sounding. But then she could not easily separate spoken German from its harsh associations. Austria had been German. This had been Germany, then. It was less than twenty years since the whole of Europe answered to commands barked in the gutteral German tongue. She held a hand out for him to help her get to her feet so that she could test the damage to the ankle with her weight. Above her, the sky rumbled where cloud now concealed the heights of the slope they had achieved.

'A lucky escape,' she said to the guide, in French.

He shrugged, nonchalant.

Above them, the clouds tore and shuddered with hidden turmoil and abruptly stopped. It had been a lucky escape. But she wouldn't let it put her off. She had an attraction to such places. As her pulse slowed after the excitement of the descent, she could feel that attraction beating as if in her blood.

Bill seemed to know lots of desolate places. She had been to parties at his house in the canyon where all the men wore tuxedoes and the women wore the poise of handsome trophies mounted on revolving plinths. There, the water cascaded to command through pools descending the length of his garden. Ice blued crystal glasses in chilly toasts. Music found its own subtle volume beneath the chat among people gathered at his house to be famous and discreet together. But there was another side to his life and it involved the wilderness. She remembered, years earlier, his joke about Jack London made when they were camping near Yosemite. There were facets to Bill. Some glittered and some were dark, some were polished and others rough enough to cut yourself on. They were on their way to one of his desolate places and he was starting to show a different facet of himself. The journey had seen the arrival of Old Bill, the one face she and her mother hated. It wore the smooth equanimity of total preoccupation. And it was fucking rude.

'I want to go home, Bill.'

'Hmm?'

'I don't know why you even suggested this. We've been travelling for an hour and I've made three attempts to talk to you and you very obviously aren't interested in having a conversation with the only person here you've got to talk to right now. So maybe you're hungover or preoccupied about a case or a client or my mother or something. Anyway—'

'We're being followed,' Bill said. 'No. Don't look around.'

'Bill. You're kidding me.'

'Ford pickup. Kind of a mauve or a brown, depending on the light. Dented front bumper. Windshield's been treated with something so you can't see through it. Solarized, maybe. Three cars back and with us since the airport car park.'

'Three cars back? Does that mean he's a pro?'

Bill laughed. Given the circumstances, he seemed amazingly relaxed. 'First hon, don't start using dialogue from bad movies. It could cause me to crash. Secondly, amateurs don't generally spot professional surveillance. So I don't think it's the IRS or anything.'

Natasha was scared. They were driving along a highway in bright California sunshine and somebody was following them. She was quiet for a mile. During that time she caught sight of a battered fender on a mauve hood as the pickup swung out and swung back again three cars behind them.

'He just took a peek.'

'Don't be scared, Natasha,' Bill said.

'Do you have a gun?'

'Yeah, there's a loaded bazooka clipped to the side of the Jeep. I'm surprised you and your mother have never noticed it before.'

'Aren't you concerned?' He was concerned enough to

keep glancing in the rear view. The tenderness present on his face at the airport was completely absent now. The flesh looked bleached and taut across the bones and his eyes wore a dead expression.

'Not really,' he said. 'It's probably some creep who tails strangers for entertainment. Like a random phone pest. It's a sick world.' He swung left across oncoming traffic and accelerated along a dirt road before running the Jeep into a dense patch of scrub and switching off the engine. The engine ticked and cooled. Bill took a water bottle from his door panel and unscrewed the lid and offered it to Natasha. She hadn't realized how thirsty she was. He winked and got out of the Jeep and walked through the tunnel of leaves and branches it had left to where he could see the track they had taken. Dust was still descending from the churn of their tyres on the powdery ground. But the creepy mauve pickup had not followed them.

'Where do you think he went?' Natasha had climbed out of the Jeep and stood beside Bill now, staring through the billow of fading trail dust.

'Gone to find a phone booth to death-threat someone picked from the book with a pin and a blindfold,' Bill said. He put a hand on her shoulder. His hand was heavy and dry and immensely comforting. In the distance, very faint, she thought she could hear car wheels spinning by on the freeway.

'Who cares where he's gone?' Bill said. 'He's gone.'

They left the Jeep in its berth of scrub. It was cool and

dark in there and smelled sweetly of pine resin from the branches broken and needles crushed by their entry. They took the food they had bought at a grocery concession at the airport and walked up a hill to a plateau of orange groves where they found a shaded spot overlooking a small valley with a bright stream running through it. They had walked for an hour when they rested and most of it had been uphill. Hills undulated, brown and scorched on their higher slopes, into a hazy distance. It was a deceptive day. There was less light than there seemed and none of the residual heat with which the summer invests the earth. It was warm now because the sun was out. But it was October and it would grow chilly towards the evening and the dark.

Natasha had wanted Bill to take her home. She had been upset and scared by events on the freeway. But she didn't want her day to be sabotaged by the antics of some creep. She did not want to appear cowardly in front of Bill. And she felt terrible about her outburst in the Jeep. She had been peevish and rude. He'd come over to rescue her alpine trip with a roll of bills in his pocket. He had driven her mother to the airport. He had invited her on a picnic. And she had railed at him for some imaginary slight. The least she could do was provide entertaining company. But she found it hard.

They ate mouse cheese on Ritz crackers and pepper salami and sour autumnal apples and glossy, succulent plums. And Natasha found it difficult to talk and impossible to properly relax. She felt very vulnerable in the open, in the scorched glare of the hills. She knew that Bill would protect her, as she figured Bill had been doing in one way or another since about the day she'd been born. It felt like she'd known him that long. But she was spooked. She tried to put cheese on a cracker into her mouth and the cracker broke because her fingers were trembling and Ritz crumbs and cheese landed in her lap.

'Oops. Sorry, Bill.'

'Spooked?'

She nodded. She wanted to sound braver than she felt. 'Yep.'

'You know all that bullshit you've been hearing for years about me being a hunter?'

She was shocked. She knew Bill had a sometimes filthy mouth. But he didn't swear in front of her.

'Isn't bullshit, kid. I'm a pretty good hunter. And I have a pretty good instinct about the people I choose to hunt with.' He pulled back the zipper on his jacket and she saw the knurled grip of a large-calibre revolver in a snap holster in his armpit.

'When—'

'From the Jeep. When you were busy with the picnic food.'

Natasha licked her lips. 'Are we hunting now, Bill?'

'He's been watching us for the best part of an hour. I think it's time we found out what he wants,' Bill said. And he winked.

Bill made her take off her shoes and pull back her hair and tie it in a bun at the back of her head. He told her to

145

button her jacket. They retreated backwards on all fours through the orange grove to the lip of the valley. The valley was grassy and steep and Natasha was able to grip the moist grass on the sunless slope between her toes and prevent herself that way from slipping. Bill stayed above her, a shield between Natasha and whoever they were stalking. They climbed down until they got to the edge of the stream. The ground flattened there from erosion when the stream was swollen and broader than they saw it now. The stream was stippled and roped with current and it coursed loudly between its steep valley walls. It was one of Bill's desolate places. It was wilder and more remote than she could have imagined country being, only three or four miles from the road. She shivered with the chill and proximity of urgent water. There were dark pebbles mossy on the bed of the stream. Feathers fluttered around small bones at a spot on the bank a few feet away. The beak had gone. But the feet had not yet rotted. It was a very solitary place, she thought, in which to die. Even for a bird. She did not want to linger here. But Natasha felt much better now they were moving. And anger was starting to take the place of her fear.

It took an hour to find the place from which he had been watching them. They had to skirt around the high hills overlooking their picnic spot and ascend their rear slopes. They climbed in stealth and shade up the steep brown earth until Bill stopped and checked their progress with a raised hand. He looked around, for somewhere for her to hide, for cover for her, as he had been looking, she knew, all the way up this final part of their ascent. But there wasn't anywhere. He licked his lips and swallowed and gestured for her to lie flat on the ground. He pulled his gun free of its holster. He looked alert and worried and was breathing hard, though she could not hear his breathing. Sweat splashed from his forehead and he winked at her again and went. She thought he was very brave. She turned on her back because if anything came for her, she wanted to see it come. High above, in a sky the late October blue of infinite space, the shape of a bird with a giant wingspan wheeled and glided. An eagle? A condor? Probably a condor, she thought, in its graceful, vigilant search for carrion.

'He's gone.'

She turned her head. Bill was silhouetted in the last of the sun. The sun was descending, now, on the other side of the hill. It was on their side of the hill, on the side that sloped all the way down to their picnic spot in the orange grove.

There was nothing remaining of him when Bill showed her the spot. There were no cigarette ends near the loose cairn of stones Bill said he'd hidden watchfully behind. There were no gum wrappers. There were not even the crumbs to suggest a sandwich. There were no snapped twigs to give him away and he had not bruised the grass with his weight because there was no grass to bruise. Jesus, there wasn't a footprint. Was he a ghost? Natasha turned to Bill and shrugged. She was baffled.

'Cartridge cases,' Bill said. 'I picked up five or six of them. Luckily for us he's a terrible shot.'

The joke didn't make her feel any better. It must have shown on her face.

'Get down and smell the ground, hon. Close your eyes. Take your time.'

She got down and smelled the cooling stones of the cairn and the earth around them. Her sense of smell had always seemed to her a gift, sometimes appallingly acute. After a while she stood and brushed the dirt off her hands.

'Lanolin,' she said. 'He has greasy hair. He must have rested his head against the stones.'

Bill nodded. 'Anything else?'

'Aftershave. The guy wears Old Spice.'

She could see Bill trying to force himself into levity, but he couldn't, not on this occasion. He was sombre with the implications of what had taken place.

'What have you done, Uncle Bill?'

He shook his head.

'What on earth have you done?'

He shook his head. He looked at the sky. It was almost dusk and very quiet and the air was chilling with a creeping, autumnal cold.

'Have you made influential enemies?'

'Not as many as I've made influential friends.'

'How did you spot him?'

'A mistake. Just one. One flash of sunlight on glass.'

She thought about this. 'He was watching us through binoculars?'

Bill hesitated before he replied. 'I don't think so, Natasha. He was scoping us.'

'Doing what?'

'I think he was watching us through the telescopic sight of a rifle.'

He'd said he was particular about whom he hunted with, making a compliment out of a necessity. He hadn't dared leave her alone in the orange grove. And she did not feel like a predator. She felt like prey.

'You'll stay the night at our house?'

'Of course,' he said. 'I need you to take care of me.'

Natasha limped around the crystal museum at Innsbruck. She studied the exhibits. She scrutinized their dark, deeply etched regularity. And she could find not a single thing to admire there or to wonder at. It was all geometry and craft. The first quality she had never mastered and so it irritated her. The second seemed a labour too precise for modern times. What was the point of intricate decoration in a glass punch bowl or its fluted, impossible spoon, when the world was threatened by the atom bomb? This was, she knew, selective thinking. But she pleaded the mitigation that she was only seventeen years old in absolving herself of any blame in thinking it. She figured she would have plenty of opportunity as an adult for drawing conclusions that were humble and compromised and fair.

Bored and on a whim, she took a bus to Landeck. She went there walking on her bad ankle with the aid of a malacca cane with a silver handle. It was a fabulously valuable stick, apparently, if you believed the concierge at the hotel the school was staying at. They had lent it to her. It was light and rigid and black. It was the second stick she'd used. Sammy Davis had tossed a stick into the audience once at a private preview of one of his new routines and Natasha had caught it.

Luck be a lady, Sammy had said.

But he always said that. And the routine had been lousy. And the Sammy stick had gathered dust in the attic pretty much ever since. And of course, Sammy had altered his routine.

By most people's standards, Natasha knew that her life would appear to be pretty exotic and glamorous. From the outside, it certainly was. From the inside it was too, a lot of the time. She knew lots of rich kids at school who led lives more opulent than hers, indulged by wealthy parents careless about what they could buy. But she didn't know anyone who had heard Frank Sinatra dedicate a song to them on their seventeenth birthday. I mean, just how cool had that been? On those occasions when she felt in her life the absence she felt now, she almost always consoled herself with such thoughts. And in this way she could generally yank herself out of moods she tended to dismiss as at best self-absorbed and at worst self-pitying. But it was harder today, limping through snowy streets, abstracted from the day to day of the familiar, the recognizable and the routine. It was harder because she was in a foreign place where an avalanche had very recently come awfully close to claiming her life. The pain throbbing in her ankle was a persistent reminder of just how narrow her escape had been. The narrowness of the escape made her think of her own fragile mortality. It made her dwell on who she was. And so it obliged her to think, as she thought more and more these days, of how little the circumstances of her birth had left her knowing about herself. It forced her to think about the absence in her life her father had left.

It would have been a small funeral. The song at the Sands and the stick in the attic would not have swelled the numbers at her graveside. It would have been her bereft mother and Bill, raw-eyed and stoical. Maybe Professor O'Brien representing the school. One or two classmates whose wardrobes ran to sufficiently stylish black to meet the formalities of grief played out in public. Someone from Hyannis Port, of course, where they were big on protocol and felt the sacramental obligations of their Catholic faith. No father, though. She didn't have a father. Natasha had never had a father.

Mostly, this was a fact that went unremarked upon. She had lived the earlier and less mature part of her life pretty much unaware of it herself. Hollywood had more than the average share of broken marriages, of paternal absentees. And then there were the dead ones. Alice Dorne, for example, had a stepfather. Her real dad had died in the war, on the beach at Normandy, when his daughter had still been a cooing innocent in her Philadelphia crib. There was

an album of photos, though, a cache of treasured memen-
toes. Alice at least had a glass frame full of medals and her
mother's cherished memories to fall back on. To anchor
her identity, Natasha thought, now, limping on her stick
through snow. To help her understand where she came from
and who she was.

Natasha did not and would never have that. She had never
discussed her paternity with her mother. And she could not
really imagine herself doing so, now. What she did know
about her mother's history, she had dragged out of a
reluctant and tight-lipped Bill. Her mother had been
confined in a labour camp. She had escaped it pregnant. You
could draw what conclusions you liked about the circumstances in which the pregnancy occurred. But the tenderness
and heroism so fulsomely present in the Dorne bequest were
not going to be its distinguishing characteristics, were they?
Natasha suspected she had been conceived amid fear and a
desperate pragmatism she didn't want her mother forcibly
reminded of. It was why she didn't ask. It was why she would
never ask.

It was why she would never know.

She rested on her stick and smiled to herself. She had not
exactly craved a father. She had Bill, after all. She thought of
the stereotypical dad of the movies and magazine advertise-
ments with his plaid sportscoat and his pipe at the wheel of
one of those shooting brakes with enough timber glued to
its body to build a fair-sized dog kennel. Like a suburban
version of Gregory Peck, those idealized fathers were. Not

so outrageously good-looking as Greg Peck was, but the same type, sharing the same solid decency and those American virtues of sobriety, steady employment and the safe assurance that adultery was what French people did. No, she did not miss the father of cosy stereotype. She didn't miss his strictures, his standards, the tedious banalities of his fireside lectures whenever she strayed from the path of righteous conformity. She had Bill, who was capable of cosiness but so far from stereotypical the thought of it turned her smile into a grin. She would have liked to know who she was, that was all. She would like to have known a little about her father. At seventeen, she had come close to dying without ever having had herself properly explained. She breathed deeply and saw her breath bloom on the cold. She looked around.

Landeck was a pretty town at the base of steep hills covered in conifers with snow in clumps burdening their branches. The town was Tyrolean and picturesque and smelled of woodsmoke and pine needles. Wind from the mountains stirred the trees and chilled the cobbled streets in cold gusts. The pavements were slippery with ice and Natasha walked carefully on her malacca stick in her new winter coat. She found an inn and sat at a table next to a window and ordered Glühwein. And she felt exotic and remote and mysterious there. It wasn't just that she was drinking an alcoholic drink in a foreign town. She realized that she reminded herself of someone. Who was it? It was almost like the feeling of déjà vu. Snow had started to fall in slow petals on the street outside. Two men in Loden coats and hats walked by. Breath steamed out of their mouths in the cold when they spoke. She sipped Glühwein and catalogued in her mind the books she had recently read and the movies that had lately impressed her. Was it a particular actress? The part would have been something with glamour and possibly espionage. It was almost certainly continental, with sadness and dark portends of betrayal. It was on the tip of her tongue. Oh, what was it? She almost had it. And then, maddeningly, it was gone.

'Oh my God,' Natasha said out loud. Because it was her mother. It wasn't an actress at all. It wasn't a film or a novel. Gifted briefly in a foreign land with the role of the enigmatic stranger, she reminded herself of her mother. And she could not help wondering in that town, at that table, at what secrets endured in her mother's tired heart and troubled soul.

SIX

He had carried her over the mountains because she had never been outside Poland and had no technique for climbing in the snow. He had orchestrated their escape. What partial success it enjoyed was due to his skill. His courage had been important. He was very brave. Perhaps most vital had been the ruthless single-mindedness of his commitment to their flight. He wanted so ardently to save the life of his child. By the end, Julia believed her survival had been just as important to him. He had said it was. He had told her he loved her. He had not been a man to waste the last words spoken as his life departed him on lies and platitudes.

The opportunity for escape was given them by Wilhelm Crupp, the Werhmacht bureaucrat and war profiteer who ran the camp from Poznan. Crupp decided that the camp should become self-sufficient in timber. Hamer knew the wood a few miles away that they would clear first in the drive to self-sufficiency. He went there sometimes. It was said that he liked solitary places.

He saved her life in the camp and then took her, out of loneliness. He was a widower and a soldier and she had never met a lonelier man. The brutality of the camp and its corruption were the mundane realities of day-to-day life to inmates and guards alike. But not to him. Not to Martin Hamer. He was a soldier and had confined his reflections on the conflict to the winning of battles and campaigns. It was in the camp, as his own battle wound healed, that he began to understand something of what the leader of his nation planned to do with the world in victory. It was there he became aware that the Poles had no future in their country other than as a population of slaves.

Later, she could have told herself that she went with him because she didn't have the choice. But the truth was less clear, more contingent. She went with him because they were all afraid of him and if she was his in the camp, she believed no further harm would come to her. She went with him, willingly, because she had become so brutalized by the likes of Rolfe and Buckner that his kindness came as a comfort and a relief. That was the truth. But it still wasn't the whole truth. It suggested hers had been a passive role in the matter. Where, truthfully, it had not.

She had seduced Martin Hamer. That was the truth of it. He would have initiated nothing without her invitation to intimacy. She had seen how he looked at her. She had seen it even in the fury that had compelled her to goad Rolfe as she pegged washing. The instinctive tug of attraction was almost feral in his eyes. He would have done nothing about

156

it, though. His moral code seemed a sort of ironic perversion in the bestial confines of the camp. But he was not of the camp. He was a career soldier. He was an officer, one of a distinguished line from a distinguished family. He would not have put a hand on her without her bidding. Martin Hamer was kind and handsome and she wanted his protection and so she seduced him in the camp. He was of the tribe that had conquered her country and killed her brother in a Poznan barn and confined her in a place of hopelessness surrounded by watchtowers and wire. And he had given her his love and his child and her freedom. He had gifted her this life. With the help of the American who had once been his friend, the brother he had longed for and thought he'd found and then irretrievably lost, he had gifted her this life.

Julia Smollen laughed out loud. She was in the lobby at the Carlyle. Outside, Christmas shoppers in overcoats and hats stepped cautiously on snowy Manhattan Streets, burdened by bags that said Neiman Marcus and Macy's on their sides. Madison Avenue was white and chilly and beautiful in the pale electric light of its windows and the snow falling in heavy drifts from a sky imperious with cloud. There were carol singers on street corners in stoic bands with Christmas lanterns. Here and there a portly, red-cheeked man dressed as Santa Claus would spellbind passing children with his size and shows of booming, hearty laughter. Cops patrolled in pairs in black rain slickers and greatcoats with snow melting in clumps from their shoulders.

They warmed their wet, leather gloves, drying them on their hands over the street braziers used by the peanut and pretzel sellers, cracking cop one-liners, alert and tough and festive with the crowd.

She had watched and enjoyed the tableau of Christmas in New York from behind the window of her yellow cab on the journey to the Carlyle from the airport. She was currently working on two scripts. Both projects were stalled by problems with location and casting. It was something of an impasse but it freed up her time for the work she wanted to do. Her daughter was in Austria, skiing. Julia had never skied but it was something the school said her daughter did boldly and well. She hoped Natasha was enjoying herself in the mountains. She had been very excited to go.

It was the singing of the Christmas carols that delivered her back to the camp. The Germans were a sentimental people and their Christmas celebrations elaborate and heartfelt. During the two Christmases she had endured as their guest she had heard them, often, sing 'Silent Night'. It seemed to be a favourite among their festive hymns. Homesick and lachrymose, they would croon out the pious verses in their huts at night. They lived and worked in abject contravention of everything Christ had preached. But they loved to sing 'Silent Night'. And hearing it sung by the innocents of some New York parish, rattling their collection tins on the streets for charity, had reminded her. She couldn't stand the carol herself. Though it had been one of her own favourites to sing in the village church and to listen to at Christmas as a child.

Crupp put Hamer in charge of clearing the wood. There was logic in the decision. He had helped husband his father's estate as a boy and he understood trees. Rolfe was no longer around to organize these things. Hamer gladly took charge. He hid her in a rolled tarpaulin in the back of one of the two trucks they were using for the job. She hid in darkness wrapped in tarpaulin next to the felling tools and waited for the rain to stop that Hamer said would hamper their saws, causing the teeth to catch and stick against the wet trunks of trees.

He diverted attention during the midday food break by challenging the guard, Landau, to a shooting competition. He had positioned the parked trucks between the contest and the hide he had dug for her. He had marked the hide with a page torn from a book. It was the title page from *Hansel and Gretel*, one of the books he had bought for her, and she saw it fluttering, white, on the ground. So skilfully had he concealed the hide, that she would never have found it otherwise. It was like those his unit used to dig in the steppes in the east to ambush Russian tanks. They would let the tanks roll past them and emerge and attack the tanks from behind.

'It sounds a desperate strategy,' she had said to him.

He had thought about this. 'All battle is desperate,' he had said. And he had held her.

The hides on the steppes had been nothing like as

159

elaborate. They had not been so secure and spacious and safe as he made hers. But he was kind and her comfort was a consideration to him as the felling party completed its work and loaded the trucks and departed the denuded wood and night fell and freedom beckoned.

He had gifted her his love and his child and her freedom.

How did you explain that to your daughter? How did you tell something like that to your daughter, when your daughter still had a crush on Paul Newman from when she saw him play Billy the Kid in *The Left Handed Gun*?

In the lobby of the Carlyle, they were piping seasonal music through concealed speakers. Nat King Cole was encouraging anyone listening to have themselves a merry little Christmas. Porters bustled in leather shoes that clacked across the glossy marble floor. The concierge wrote something with a fountain pen in the massive ruled ledger on the reception desk. People entered the lobby through the revolving door, the men's swagger coats and the women's furs innocent of snow from chauffeured cars and then the sheltering umbrellas held over them in their cosseted transport.

She had cycled across half the country on a stolen bicycle by night to meet him at a rendezvous at a deserted farm by the Odra River. The train ride he planned for them to take through Germany to Austria and the border with Switzerland filled her with appalling fear. She thought seriously about abandoning Hamer and his plan, going to Warsaw alone, or hiding in Poznan, where she knew people.

But Warsaw was a charnel house and in Poznan she would endure a botched abortion and bleed to death. Perhaps also by then she had begun to love him.

The events of the war seemed a world and a lifetime ago here, in America, with its abiding wealth and its young president and its new mood of optimism and hope. But Julia saw Martin Hamer whenever she looked into her daughter's face. She had made him a promise. As the light that had burnt so strongly in him dimmed in his eyes, she had made him a promise. And he had smiled. And the light had died. And the promise had never been kept.

Her struggle with the secret made it seem sometimes, absurdly, as if the war was something that had happened only to her. She had to remind herself that it had touched everyone and many had been damned by it. In Hollywood, the same Sam Fuller made B-movies who had fought from the beach at Normandy to the rubble of Berlin as a grunt with the 1st Infantry Brigade. Jack Kennedy, upstairs in his presidential suite, had lost a brother and almost perished himself fighting in the Pacific. At Cape Canaveral, Werner von Braun ran America's rocket programme, his pedigree the missiles that had come close to destroying London in the years when he put his science at the happy service of his führer.

In a few weeks it would be 1961. Natasha was seventeen and had a crush on Paul Newman and read JD Salinger and Françoise Sagan. She thought Che Guevara a romantic freedom fighter, Byronic in his flowing locks and jungle combat fatigues. There was a picture of Martin Luther King tacked to her wall. She agreed that Kennedy was her country's best hope, but only for the want of a more radical alternative. She believed in the New Frontier and talked about voluntary work in Africa or Israel or a shanty town in Brazil. And Julia was going to sit her down and tell her that her father was one of the iron warriors of the Blitzkrieg who had visited a new dark age on Europe. Worse, that he had been a hero of the thousand-year Reich, decorated in the Reich Chancellery, a moist-eyed Hitler presenting the medal with his own, tremulous hands.

'I'll lose her,' she said out loud. 'I'll tell her and I'll lose her and I'll never, ever get her back.'

Julia looked at the man's wristwatch on her arm. The phosphorescent paint on the hands and numerals had faded over the years in the sunshine of California and the watch no longer glowed in the darkness as once it so luminously had. She needed it less in the night, though. She slept better than she had in the early period of her arrival and Natasha's infancy in San Francisco. Her sleep was still imperfect, but it was better than it had been in those early, difficult, desolate years. And so long as she remembered to wind it, and she always did, the watch still kept perfect time. She looked at it in the lobby of the Carlyle because her meeting with the president had been scheduled for 3 p.m. and now it was almost three-thirty.

Jack Kennedy was not naturally a punctual man. It had taken Bobby to eradicate in him the habit of setting off for an engagement at the time he was scheduled to arrive. He had this blue-blooded insouciance. He almost never carried cash, believing the Kennedy name good for a tab anywhere. It was the same thing as when he would get hot on the quay in the sun at Hyannis Port and pull off his sweater and discard it, expecting someone to pick it up after him because someone always did and always had, all his life. He'd tip the contents of a dresser drawer on a bed, looking for a missing cufflink. The household staff at the Kennedy compound were long-suffering about such habits. But Bobby didn't share Jack's insouciance. Bobby behaved in a much more conventional way. It wasn't that he possessed to any greater degree the instincts of the common man. If anything, Julia thought the opposite to be true. But Bobby was austere and strict in observing social protocols. He reminded her of certain orders of Catholic priest, arrogant in the strength with which they stuck to their vow of poverty.

Jack was arrogant only about his intellect. He thought himself much cleverer than any of those rivals who had sought the nomination. Julia thought he was cleverer than Humphrey, certainly cleverer than Johnson and probably cleverer than Stevenson too. He had written two books and would remind you of the fact. But in other ways he was surprisingly humble. The privileges of upbringing had made him tardy and untidy but he remained astonishingly approachable for a man about to assume the highest office in the land. This was why, looking at her watch again, she

163

knew that something was not right. Even if the president elect was behind schedule, she would generally get the offer of a cup of coffee and the latest on Washington from a gossipy staffer in an ante-room in the presidential suite. But she was here instead, waiting, perhaps forgotten about.

She noticed then a man staring at her from the opposite side of the lobby. He was leaning against the wall under an Audubon painting. He was a slight, shortish man in a trilby and a belted raincoat and the fawn fabric of the raincoat was darkened on the shoulders with patches of melted snow. And snow sat like dew on the trilby and dripped as melt-water from its brim. No chauffeured ride for him, or cosseting umbrella on his journey from wherever to mid-town. He was sallow skinned and his gaze was dark-eyed, even and detached. He looked seedy and out of place in the opulence and polish of the Carlyle lobby. But he looked relaxed. There was a defiant, almost militant justification about his positioning and posture. You don't think I belong, then throw me out, it said. Just come on and try. Seeing that she had become aware of him, the raincoat man smiled slightly, and nodded. The smile was a disconcerting glimpse of narrow yellow teeth.

Julia's arm was squeezed then and she turned to see Bobby settle on his haunches on the chair next to hers. She could tell from his posture that he wasn't staying. And she knew with equal certainty that she was not going up to the presidential suite.

'He's asleep, Julia,' Bobby said. He still had the pin in his suit lapel they'd each worn for the count in Cape Cod on the night of the vote. He looked very handsome and sincere and boyish. It was hard not to think well of him, looking like this. It was a gift the Kennedys shared. 'His back went into spasm and the doctor couldn't pump any more cortisone into him and so he gave him something that'll make him sleep for a couple of hours. We've got a masseur from the New York Athletic Club manipulating his back.'

'Somebody good?'

'Well,' Bobby said, 'he's a democrat.' He smiled at the floor and then looked at his watch. 'Jack's got a big speech tonight.'

'I know. It's why I dropped by.'

'Of course. I'm sorry.' He looked at his watch again. 'Want to go do something for a couple of hours? Buy something?' He smiled again. At her this time. He was at his most charming, on his best behaviour. 'There are worse towns for that.'

She almost laughed out loud. The thought of Bobby Kennedy enjoying a shopping spree was beyond her. 'I'll go and buy Natasha's Christmas present,' she said.

'Perfect,' Bobby said. He rose.

'Do you happen to know that fellow over there?'

Bobby looked across the lobby. 'Know would be an exaggeration,' he said. 'But I know who he is. And what he does. He's a hack reporter. They think there's a cover-up concerning Jack's health. Have you spoken to him?'

'No.'

'Good. Don't. Happy shopping, Julia.' He bent and kissed her on the cheek and walked away.

You need a shave, Bobby, she thought, buttoning her coat against the snow and walking towards the revolving hotel door. A cover-up concerning the health of the president elect, she thought. It was scandalous. She tried not to glance at the man with the raincoat and the yellow smile. Next they would be saying Joe Kennedy paid for votes. They would be claiming Jack Kennedy had been unfaithful to his wife.

It was dusk when she walked onto Madison Avenue. She was glad to escape the lobby of the Carlyle. It always smelled faintly of cigar smoke there. It was one of the affluent, ubiquitous smells of New York's plusher public interiors. But it was more than that to Julia. It took her back even more vividly than did the sound of 'Silent Night' being sung, to circumstances she would rather not be reminded of. So it was good to get out into the chill of the encroaching evening, which only smelled, on smart Madison Avenue, of truck oil and steaming shit, dumped by the horses ridden by the mounted police, and raw cold blown off the East River and stale heat through subway vents and Charles of the Ritz and Shalamar and Chanel No. 5 dabbed behind the ears and on the necks of Madison Avenue's well-wrapped, Christmas women.

She would not buy Natasha a Christmas gift. She had said that for Bobby's benefit. When Bobby was nice, he made you anxious to accommodate him. It was as though the

166

effort of his being nice was so great and so rare that you felt not just privileged, but compelled to do anything you could to sustain his generous mood. You didn't want to be the one to disappoint and disillusion him. She thought that he was probably aware of this effect. Niceness was just one more tool of manipulation for Bobby. He was a brilliant manipulator. He was, let's be honest, a gifted and terrible bully. But he did it all in the service of his brother and if you believed, as Julia did, you forgave him for it. Just as if you believed, you forgave Jack his transgressions. But she would not buy Natasha a Christmas gift. It had been just something convenient, in the circumstances, to say.

She had paid already for 'Tasha's ski trip. The elastic-wrapped roll of hundreds offered by her daughter's smashed godfather had not in the end been required. Julia smiled, as the snow tumbled through the confused winter dusk of Madison Avenue. When did it grow truly dark, when the lights of skyscrapers illuminated the night all the way up to the stars and the weight of falling snow whitened the ground? Oh, Bill, she thought. Bill. Where do I put you in my heart? That was a hard one. It was harder than finding the precise moment of nightfall on a December street in Manhattan. It was easier to think of what to buy as a token Christmas gift for her impossible-to-buy-for daughter.

The money for the trip to Austria was supposed to be 'Tasha's Christmas present. But she had one child and earned more money than she could easily spend. Julia didn't want to spoil her daughter any more than was inevitable, but she did want to bring her pleasure. So she would, of course, buy her a gift for the day itself. She would buy her a saddle. She would buy 'Tasha a splendid western saddle from one of those dude ranch places out in California. She loved to ride as much as she loved to ski. There was little point in buying her trinkets from Bloomingdales or Tiffany's. The girl showed no interest in scent or jewellery. She showed little interest in clothes, beyond an attachment to her black winter coat. Julia smiled and shivered at the same time in the cold. She was slipping on the pavement, but so was everybody else, and she needed to stretch her legs after her wait in the Carlyle lobby. Natasha adored her long black winter coat. Julia thought the coat lent itself to romantic fantasies. Natasha felt exotic and perhaps mysterious in the coat. She certainly looked exotic, with her arctic-blue eyes and heavy, flaxen hair tumbling over its tailored shoulders. Her daughter hadn't the remotest idea of how beautiful she was. It was one of her many impossible charms.

She would go to Greenwich Village and browse in the bookshops there. She would buy a book and smoke a cigarette in a coffee shop and then go back to the Carlyle and maybe, if there was time, talk to the president elect about the tenor of his speech. It was a speech on organized labour and the need to stamp out union corruption. The subject was closer to the heart of Bobby than it was to Jack, she knew. Jack was committed to tackling the corruption. He owed a lot of his electoral support to blue-collar voters and didn't enjoy their exploitation. But it was a tricky area to sound strong on without seeming to side with the bosses. And apart from when he drew his navy pay, Jack was not a man who had ever worked in a regular job. It was a question of pace and emphasis and vocabulary. It was particularly important now that Kennedy's every public utterance could become a banner headline. It was the stuff Julia had been helping with for almost three years.

Lots of people helped. Jack tended to write his own speeches and then have Sorensen and Schlesinger and sometimes Pierre Salinger look over them and make their individual suggestions. Jack was inclusive by nature. He was writing his own inauguration speech and was determined to make it the best and most memorable since that delivered by Thomas Jefferson. But in framing the speech, he was seeking opinions on what informed people thought mattered most to the nation. He would be chief executive but would lead a democracy and he never allowed himself to forget the fact. It was why you could forgive the flaws in him, Julia thought. The flaws were considerable. But the man was so much more considerable than his flaws.

She had first become aware of his name eleven years before she met him. In 1947 he had campaigned for the admission into America of eighteen thousand displaced Polish soldiers, victims of the Yalta Conference, expedient pawns in the merciless hands of Stalin. She had read about it in San Francisco when still a college librarian. His campaign had been a success. What had struck her had not been so much the compassion and the selfless idealism (there were not many exiled Poles registered to vote in Massachusetts), but the fact that he still cared, two years after the end of the war, about what happened in the world beyond American borders. It was a time when not very many politicians in America did.

He had not changed at all, she thought, in the years since she had first spoken to him at the Lawford party under a table umbrella in the dripping rain. He would sit with his tie loosened in a chair cushioned or angled to accommodate the discomfort from his back and he would refrain, in her company, from smoking the little panatelas he habitually liked. This had not been discussed between them. Somehow, he had sensed her discomfort with the smell of cigars. They would go over the pace and cadence and drama of the speech he was to deliver. She would make the suggestions everybody made, she supposed, but she would coach him, too. She had polished film soliloquies delivered by Brando and Clift and by the Welsh actor, Burton. She understood better than most people the relationship between the delivered word and the drama of the moment. On her better professional days, she had seen the first conspire brilliantly to create the latter. She had colluded in that conspiracy. Sometimes, she had orchestrated the conspiracy herself.

It didn't matter where you were in the room with him. Kennedy would sit, it seemed to Julia, in his own privately cast penumbra of shuttered light. He would be at the still centre of something that shimmered with photogenic attraction and impermanence. His presence provided so compelling a visual and auditory moment she couldn't help but think it somehow staged. But she was certain it never was. She heard all the stories about the girls, about the mob money with which Sinatra was supposed to have provided his campaign. None of it took away from the odd, fleeting magic of his presence. He possessed such a strong, transitory spell. It was all very paradoxical and she hoped her instinct was wrong. She was confused by it, in the strength of what he said, in the face of his resolve and certainty, when she shared with him what brief time she was allowed to. She felt a gloomy presentiment that the world would not be privileged to enjoy the gifts of John Fitzgerald Kennedy for very long. She prayed she was wrong. But she looked at the faces among his staff sometimes, and she knew that others shared this odd and baseless anxiety.

Julia slithered, her progress as sedate and inevitable as a liner being launched, across the slope of an icy sidewalk. And she decided that the sane time had come to hail a yellow cab to take her to Greenwich Village.

Perusing the East Village bookshops she found a hand-some, leather-bound edition of *The Pilgrim's Progress*, which she bought for Bill. She did not think Bill would gain greatly in insights or spirituality from reading Bunyan's thumping allegory. But he liked muscular prose and would appreciate the thought. It would look good on his book-shelf, there among the signed volumes by Fitzgerald and

Hemingway, whom he had known in his undiminished days before the war, when Martin Hamer had been his friend. She bought novels in French by Sartre and Colette for Natasha and a translation of the collected verse of Pablo Neruda for herself. She saw a wonderful set of Gibbon's *Decline and Fall* and was tempted, because Jack Kennedy talked a lot about the Roman Republic and its enduring historical lessons. But they were far too heavy to carry. So she went to a store that sold periodicals and bought *Paris Match* and *Vogue* and *Harper's Bazaar* instead. Jack would have understood. Probably, she thought, smiling, he would have approved.

Julia carried her purchases to a coffee shop and took off her coat and hat and scarf and flicked through the magazines. There was a basement in the coffee shop and from the steps leading down she could hear plangent chords and a young, female voice. Curious, she gathered her things. It was properly dark now; she looked at her watch. It was a quarter to seven in the evening. Outside, people were picking a careful path over the frozen pavement, bright with purchases, bright with expectation of the season's joy and the rich colours of their scarves and coats in the falling snowflakes and the yellow pools of light that bathed them from under shop awnings. With her coat and her bags in her arms, Julia descended the stairs and found a table against a wall with a view of a small platform. It wasn't a stage, didn't qualify for so grand a description. It was just a raised dais barely big enough to accommodate the performer, seated on a stool with her guitar under a single spotlight. Julia looked around. There were perhaps thirty people in the basement. Most were self-consciously clothed in the monochromatic style started by Juliette Greco and her clique on the Left Bank a few years earlier. Some of the men wore beards. The women wore their hair flat and brushed with a centre parting.

The singer tuned her guitar with her head bowed over the instrument and her face hidden by a glossy veil of perfectly straight blonde hair. With the tuning accomplished, she lifted her head and smiled without engaging the audience. The smile was for herself. And Julia smiled, reminded of a cocktail bar a few years ago and a world away with Bill, discussing a Bogart movie among cigarette girls in red corsets and berets like the one worn by Veronica Lake. America was so many different places. And it was changing with such accelerating speed.

The girl began to sing. Her voice swooped histrionically between octaves and the lyrics of the song were, to Julia's ears, far too self-indulgently confessional. But she was young and the young were self-indulgent, weren't they? And anyway, her playing was brilliant. Her acoustic guitar filled the space with fresh chords and phrases under the gifted command of her fingers. And sitting there, Julia enjoyed the novelty and sensation of it and the freedom to choose just to be in a place by choice. It was not a freedom she had always enjoyed and it was one she did not believe she would ever take for granted.

173

She did not get to see Jack Kennedy that day. She would not get to see him again until the day of the inauguration speech, sitting among an invited audience on Pennsylvania Avenue in a moment frozen by bitter cold and warm with pride and historic promise with her daughter at her side. Late that night she took a flight back to the West and spent almost the entire duration of it worrying about Bill. She had worried about his drinking and his weekend fishing trips for years. There were far too many desolate places now in Bill's diminishing life. But there was something else to worry about. Something specific and strange and still unexplained.

The wings of the aircraft were heavy with ice and Julia sat in a lounge and smoked and endured the delay while they chipped off the ice in stubborn black chunks and deliberated in the control tower about whether the flight would take place at all. While she waited, she read an article in one of the magazines she had bought on her shopping trip to Greenwich Village. The magazine was *Harper's Bazaar* and the article was about organized crime in Las Vegas. It mentioned two people Julia knew to be clients of Bill's. The article was flattering about neither of them. She ordered a Bloody Mary from a waitress in the lounge and looked out of the window to where the aircraft stood, weighted by its unwanted freight of ice on the wings. It was a four engine plane and stood floodlit, as men in overalls and sheepskins toiled to ready it for flight and snow spilled from the sky in vicious white flurries. Other passengers sat or paced in the lounge and smoked and drank and watched this ritual through the glass.

Someone had followed Bill and had observed him as he picnicked with 'Tasha in an orange grove in the San Fernando Valley. Bill seemed convinced that the man had been armed with a rifle. And Julia was sufficiently know-ledgeable about Bill's instincts and prowess as a hunter himself, that she believed him. But Bill seemed genuinely baffled as to who might want to frighten or kill him. As he said himself, he had made far more influential friends over the years, than he had enemies. He had asked around, though. He had done his own research and he had come up with nothing. And then he had asked Sinatra for help.

'Come on, Bill.'

'You know some people, Frank.'

There was a silence. This was a face-to-face conversation. It took place not over a telephone line but on a golf course, halfway along a fairway to the lush soundtrack of sprinklers. 'It's truer to say I know people who know people who know people,' Sinatra said. He swung his club absently. He looked at the lie of his ball. 'Anyway. I'll ask.'

'I appreciate it.'

'You should.'

But nothing.

So Julia had asked Robert Kennedy. Something very sinister had happened involving the two people she cared about most in the world. And organized crime was Bobby Kennedy's enduring fascination. She had asked him on the beach at Hyannis Port and he had stared at her for a long moment as the wind off the sea tugged at his thick hair where he wore it long, over his forehead. She began to wonder if he had heard her correctly. She began to wonder if he had heard her at all. He drew a curve in the packed sand they stood on with the heel of a shoe. Then he smoothed over the impression he had made with a sweep of the sole.

'We vetted your known associates when we vetted you, Julia,' he said. 'Your friend Bill is clean. He has no gambling debts and no history of narcotic abuse. He does not resort to the services of call girls. I wouldn't vouch for the scruples of any Hollywood lawyer. Anyone in Hollywood, come to that.' This was a dig at her. Maybe also subtly at his brother. Even at his father.

'He plays hardball, your friend Bill. But he plays by the rules. And I'm sure he's right about this. It's a one off. A crank.' Bobby had smiled then. 'Tell me, Julia. Are you still cycling?'

But she couldn't just dismiss it.

The aeroplane bumped on weighted wings through the frozen sky. The cabin grew sour with groans of trepidation and the smell of vomit expelled into sick bags. The cabin crew in their chic pencil skirts and pillbox hats sat strapped in their seats and hugged themselves. It was dark and cold at 6000 feet and the passengers were humble all around her in their helplessness and mortal fear. At least there were no children aboard. At least, that was, none that she had seen.

Maybe I should stop worrying about Bill, she thought, and start to worry about myself. In the seat behind her, a man was weeping into a series of paper tissues. She had recognized him in the lounge as a star of one of those buddy cop series that had suddenly and inexplicably become popular on the television. He was an ex-soldier or an ex-surfer or something in the show. An ex-priest? An ex-something. She didn't watch TV very often. She found it shrill and unengaging.

She could not dismiss in her mind the danger the incident with Bill had presented to 'Tasha. If the man had been intent on murdering Bill, would he have left a bright, seventeen-year-old potential witness to the crime? You went to the electric chair if you were convicted of murder in the state of California. The voltage didn't differ whether that was one murder or two. And would a professional killer really care about a pretty teenage victim? Wasn't it just business to them? 'Tasha had been just as vulnerable as Bill in that sunny October orange grove. She was in Austria. She was skiing in the mountains above Innsbruck, God bless her beautiful, innocent soul. But she had been in danger of her life. Julia knew she had.

The aeroplane pitched and stuttered then and lost height suddenly and she could hear the groan of the wings and the superstructure and the roar of the engines struggling to churn the icy propellers and keep their human load aloft. But she did not think of crashing. She thought of Innsbruck and of Martin Hamer carrying her over the pass to

Switzerland and safety in the partial success of their escape. He had put her down and sat in the meadow and died a short time later convinced that his killer had been Landau, the sharpshooter from the camp.

'Why Landau?'

'Vanity,' Hamer had said, drowning in blood in the meadow.

And she had not understood.

Landau. The aeroplane shook and Julia shivered. The reporter with the yellow smile skulking in the Carlyle lobby had reminded her of him, of Landau, hadn't he? The camp's vigilant killer. The lethal sharpshooter in his watchtower, seeing everything.

She had one more stubborn, uninvited recollection. What a day it had been for memories. And it was not yet quite at an end.

Through her window, on the wing, Julia could see a propeller blur their path through air and snow, powered by an engine with a coughing, reluctant sound. All four engines were coughing, she thought. And three hours into their flight, they sounded as though they all shared the same, frozen reluctance. She remembered a night-shoot in a fog-bound Pacific bay with the English actor, David Niven. Two boats had collided in the mist and Niven and a stuntman had gone into the sea. The stuntman had drowned. Niven had been hooked, semi-conscious, onto the deck of a rescue craft by his pea-coat collar after several hours in the water.

It had not been a happy shoot, even before the accident, which was why Julia was there. The success at the box office of *The Magnificent Seven* had made ensemble pictures suddenly all the rage. But they were a happy illusion, ensemble movies, with their democratic billing on the posters and the idea fostered among their audiences of on-set camaraderie. What they actually involved was much squabbling between six or seven principal players all competing to be the real star. Julia's role, on this occasion, was to make each of the principals believe they shone at least in a crucial scene or two. And then Niven went into the sea.

Julia had shared a drink with him after dinner a few days later. He was quiet and kept looking up at the stars, immense above the bay, above the ocean. The fog, with them for a stubborn, opaque week, had finally lifted. He was playing a commando in the movie. It was a role she remembered he had played successfully in life. She asked him had he feared he might die in the sea.

'Not feared, darling,' he'd said. And he'd smiled. He had this English remoteness, Niven, under the charm. Julia thought him a man of enormous calculation. When you spoke to him he would look at you as though seeing and appraising you for the first time in his life. But on this occasion something shattered the charm, for once breached the remoteness, darkened and troubled his face. And he spoke. 'I should have died in '43, in France, to tell you the truth,' he said. His voice was flat. 'To this day, I don't know how I got out of that.' He sipped his drink. 'Everything since then has rather been icing on the cake. So the answer to your question is no. I don't fear death at all. I feel I've rather lost the right to.'

Ages ago in a forgotten place on the coast of Mexico, Bill had called David Niven a man possessed of qualities that he considered remarkable. He was another, wasn't he, marked by the war and its memories? Julia knew what he meant, too. Life owed her nothing, either. She needed to share a truth still untold with her daughter and she wanted to see her daughter raised to adulthood. What parent didn't wish for that? There was much that she feared. But she did not fear for her own life. Everything since Martin Hamer got her out of the camp had been a life beyond her expectation. Julia Smollen did not fear death in the slightest.

She yawned; she was tired. It had been a day too much occupied with her own irredeemable past. 'Icing on the cake,' she said out loud. She would keep her promise. She would do it after the inauguration. After the inauguration, she would tell her daughter everything. She put her head to one side on her seat. And to the frank astonishment of the passenger seated next to her, she fell at once into a deep and restful sleep.

SEVEN

Bill watched the inauguration on the television as he worked his way through a bottle of vodka taken from the freezer. The freezer had turned the liquor in the bottle viscous and slow. The contents looked almost clumsy departing the neck for his shot glass when he tilted the bottle and poured.

There was nothing clumsy about the broadcast on the television, though. He thought the whole pageant splendidly elegant. The day in Washington was raw with cold. You could see it knife through the troops of majorettes trying their hardest not to shiver on Pennsylvania Avenue. Plumes of breath played and flared in it from the nostrils of the horses drawing the carriage and carrying the mounted police officers. But the sun was bright in the cold and light shone and bristled on the polished stone and on the proud countenances of high office. And Bill was glad the occasion made such a handsome and ornately detailed spectacle. Julia was there with his god-daughter and he wanted it to be memorable for them. Julia had earned her invited seat and

181

Natasha would be thrilled for her mother, seeing it all herself with the crystalline precision of bright young eyes witnessing history being made.

The young president looked as natural as a man ever could in a morning coat and a stiff white collar and tie. Ceremony suited him, even with his clean looks and Florida tan. Johnson, next to him on the podium, managed a lean, altogether Texan dignity. Robert Frost was every bit as patrician as they had no doubt planned him to be, reciting the difficult rhythms of his great poem. But the young president looked born to his trappings and to the moment, so nakedly charismatic it was an effort, watching him, to remember to blink, let alone to tear your eyes away from his composed and compelling performance.

He's playing himself, Bill thought, awed. But of course, he can afford to. What was that line poor old Scott wrote? The very rich are different from you and me. And he was right, Bill thought. They are. They are easy with the world as their audience and do not flinch without a topcoat in the chill January of their destiny. They more resemble John Fitzgerald Kennedy than they do anyone we might be inclined to know.

Bill sighed and raised his vodka glass and toasted the television screen. He had known Scott. And having known him, he thought Scott might have enjoyed this august moment of vindication. On the other hand, he'd probably have been too drunk to appreciate it properly. Irony had been beyond his reach by the end. By the end, everything had been pretty much beyond his reach, except for a bottle. That, and a particular quality of maudlin nostalgia which the terminal drunk accepts and welcomes because of the anaesthetic qualities it happens to possess.

There had come a moment in Scott's work at which the style had overtaken the substance. He had written about those to whom the same thing tended to happen in life. Bill thought there had been much style at one time about his own life. It was certainly true that his life had glittered, at one time, among a glittering fraternity. But there had never been all that much substance. Certainly there had never been enough of it to make the moment when the substance was subsumed by style a tragic one.

Bill drank.

No substance, then. Or not enough substance to count. And not much style, either, these days, to compensate. He had committed too many sordid indiscretions lately to be termed a man of style.

Bill drank.

Take the lie he had been obliged to tell Julia. He had told her that Sinatra had looked into whether the weird business in the valley had any wise-guy implications. For the record, Bill didn't for a moment think it did. But he could not have asked Sinatra to check the matter out for him, one way or the other. Frank had stopped returning his calls months ago, after Bill became abusive towards a favoured guest at one of his house parties. Bill couldn't even remember why he'd been rude or to whom. But Frank surely could. He always could. Frank was an Italian American who feuded with the bitter obstinacy of a bog Irishman. Since their spat, a lot of party invitations had dried up.

Bill drank.

Speeches were being made on the television. Former presidents looked on, statesmanlike and benign. Truman was there. Eisenhower was there, who had won the war in Europe for America. Good old Ike. Plenty of substance there, Bill supposed. You wouldn't even have to search very hard to find it.

When it came to poetry, Bill preferred Eliot to Frost of that now venerable generation of poets he had once in his life taken the time and the trouble to read and even to try to understand. Jesus, he had even met Ezra Pound once, before the war in Italy. What was the line from Eliot? *I've measured out my life in coffee spoons.*

Not quite. Not quite coffee spoons. I've measured out my life in poolside gossip in eternal sunshine. I've measured out my life in worthless bouts of profitable litigation. I've measured it out in incremental grief and self-pity whilst championing the causes of the habitually worthless and the pointlessly corrupt. He pictured oceans of chlorinated water rippling and dappled over mosaic tiles and servile troops of canapé waiters on swishing lawns and he closed his eyes to try to keep from his mind the low murmur and tumult of his years of futile confidences shared.

Bill drank down his vodka and refilled his glass and raised it to the television.

'Here's to you, Scott,' he said. 'Here's to maudlin nostalgia, Old Sport.'

He drank down his drink and refilled the glass. The curtains were drawn against the glare of afternoon sunshine to give the picture on the television screen a greater contrast and clarity.

'Here's to anaesthetic,' Bill said. He raised his glass. On the TV screen the new president was smiling and saying something to Johnson. In his silk muffler and his overcoat, Johnson looked sedate, Bill thought. Like a rattlesnake.

'Where's the patrician guy gone?' Bill said out loud. 'Where's the poet?' Had Robert Frost fallen off the podium? Had that bastard Johnson pushed him? Pretty obvious a Texan rancher and a poet were going to amount to trouble. Maybe Washington had finally adopted the Cold War realpolitik practised on the Russian Politburo and when people were no longer needed they were just erased from the picture and the history rewritten as if they had never been there. Shame, he thought, he had really liked that poem. But Robert Frost had never existed and so nobody could ever have written it, now. Had Pound existed? Course he had. Hemingway had introduced Bill to him once in Rimini. Hemingway, who had only existed because he had made himself up.

Bill was drunk. It was an auspicious moment in his country's history and he was very drunk, celebrating it. Light in chinks and motes made dust sparkle like blind movie projections all around the den where he hadn't drawn the curtains well enough to block it out. He filled his empty glass again. The new president had just said something possibly palindromic about what your country should do for you and you for your country. Beside the television, the bureau in which he kept the remnants of his life blurred and rippled in Bill's tearful vision.

What have I become?

'Here's to the maudlin nostalgia,' Bill said. He raised his glass. Here's to the man I can no longer remember ever having been. He drained his glass and threw it at the wall. The bottle, empty now, followed. Through the tinted glass and concrete of his domestic shrine to modernism, these small explosions failed to carry any noise. On the television set, the camera was panning across the seated guests, cold and shining with privilege in their coats and their hats. Julia was among them. He didn't see her there.

Bill was weeping. He curled up on his big leather sofa like a child and hid his head under a cushion and cried. Make the bogeyman go away, Daddy. Make the bogeyman go away. But the bogeyman would not go away. His daddy had died long ago. And he was the bogeyman.

There was nothing different from usual about the remorseful hangover that followed for Bill except for the finding and the reading of the note. And the finding and the reading of the note eventually changed everything. But he only realized that much later, in retrospect, like everyone always does.

Natasha had hidden the note in the coat pocket of his

most sober suit. It was his mea culpa suit, the suit he always wore hungover, so he supposed there was an element of calculation to the choice of hiding place. A further element of calculation that was, beyond its being written and left for him there. She'd had to enter his bedroom and open his closet to place the note.

'You're in pretty deep, girl,' he said to himself, making his hangover breakfast of dry toast and a pot of coffee. 'The evidence is stacked high,' he said, resolving as he sipped his coffee that he would have to curtail this new habit of talking to himself. If he didn't, men in white coats would come before long to curtail it on his behalf.

The note comprised four sheets of plain paper crammed into an envelope too small for what it contained. Maybe she had written more than she had originally planned. The young tended to be opinionated. And Natasha had never been short of something to say. He took the sheets out and unfolded and counted them and put the note beside the rack of dry toast on his breakfast table. But he didn't read them. Seeing his god-daughter's handwriting was a poignant enough reminder of just how tender he felt in his sorry, self-pitying state, without enduring yet what it was she had to say to him.

He had no intention of going into his office. Despite the hangover, he had not intended to wear the suit today. He had emptied the pockets of all his suits because today was the day the woman who did his laundry came in and gathered them up and took them away to be dry-cleaned for him. Bill was far from being a frugal man. He had the divorce settlement to prove it. He did not empty the pockets of his suit coats looking for bills and cheques un-cashed and change. He did it looking for phone numbers and written notes and cards and matchbooks, the odd, indiscreet clues and scraps of confidential business dealings. He was very private on behalf of other people. He thought the phrase 'harmless gossip' probably an oxymoron. He vastly preferred harmful gossip, given any kind of conver-sational choice. But his clients paid him very well not to have themselves become its subject. The more deserving they were of this dubious Hollywood accolade, the better it was they paid.

Bill maintained an office, because it was good business practice to do so and also because it gained him tax relief. It occupied a suite in a smart building designed by a fashionable architect and it enjoyed the requisite panoramic view. A decorator had filled it with onyx and hide and chrome and good post-impressionist prints in understated frames made from pale, lacquered wood. Staff these days comprised only a bilingual secretary Bill had employed almost entirely for her looks. He paid her a salary and a clothing allowance. She favoured cashmere sweaters to enhance her creamy complexion and to combat the effect of the fierce office air conditioning the building always ran. But the fact was, Bill did not need to go to work. Business came in anyway. His area of legal expertise was damage control. Hollywood was full of damaged people seemingly intent on damaging themselves further. Not even the divorce settlement paid to his expensive second wife had dented what he accrued from shrewd investments made years ago and the fat retainers the studios still paid for him to keep their talent breathing, walking unaided and out of the newspapers. Frank could turn the whole town against him tomorrow and he would still never need worry about money again in his life. But Frank wouldn't do that, Bill didn't think. In feuds, as in all things, Frank enjoyed a measure of exclusivity.

Bill considered the lie he'd told Julia one he could forgive himself. He'd done some exhaustive checking on his own account and paid a talented police lieutenant working out of Santa Monica to do some more. Scoping, lanolin secretion and wearing Old Spice were not a lot to go on. But this was someone adept at covering his tracks. Bill went through every case file to see if there was someone (apart from Frank and Frank's stuck-up, English party guest) he could have offended. Meanwhile, the LAPD lieutenant concentrated on gun clubs and reported gun crime involving a rifle. The cop was scrupulous and smart, but he came up with nothing. After three weeks of independent checking they met for a beer at a tavern on the outskirts of Santa Monica and compared notes. And their conclusion was the same. The guy had been some random nut.

'You couldn't even call him a perp,' the cop pointed out to Bill. 'He may have spooked you and your god-daughter, but he didn't commit any crime.'

Bill handed the lieutenant a thousand dollars in cash and thanked him.

'If I think of anything else.'

'Sure. Thanks.'

They shook hands.

Driving home, Bill knew that the money hadn't exactly bought peace of mind. But he was as satisfied with the explanation as he could have been.

After his coffee and his dry toast, Bill showered lengthily and then brushed his teeth until his gums bled and dressed in blue jeans and boat shoes and a polo shirt. Dressing, he appraised himself in the mirror. He was taut and tanned, the big muscles of his upper arms and chest smooth and hard, very little sagging skin to betray his years or advertise his persistent fondness for the bottle. For years now he had traded on the genes he'd been so blessed with. Probably his liver wasn't in great shape. But the whites of his eyes were surprisingly white still and he had a healthy enough pallor, even today. He stood every chance of achieving his three-score-years-and-ten. Unless the phantom scoper got him, that was. If he cleaned up some of his personal habits, the decade Biblical prophecy owed him might not even be that much of a chore to live through. He took some pieces of ripe fruit from a bowl and put them in a paper sack and put on his wristwatch. It was eleven o'clock on a tautologically perfect Californian morning. He had showered and dressed to the sound of a rip-roaring Count Basie soundtrack, pondering on the contents of his god-daughter's note. He would drive the Jeep to a deli he liked near Newport Beach and drink more coffee and read what it had to say. Then he would drive to a boxing gym he went to sometimes in Anaheim.

There were two ways, to Bill's mind, you could deal with a hangover. You could tiptoe apologetically around it. Or you could confront the thing head-on and beat the crap out of it. Though he despised the bombastic side of his nature, Bill invariably favoured the latter approach. He would eat the fruit in the paper sack after his coffee and the note and go to the gym in Anaheim and skip rope and work the heavy bag for six or seven rounds. Then he'd wrap himself in a clean sweatsuit and pedal the stationary bike for an hour.

Bill co-owned the gym in Anaheim with a trainer-promoter convinced they'd one day discover a world boxing champion in the murky pugilistic talent pool of East LA. This trainer knew his fighters and the two men got on well as business partners. But he had confessed himself mystified by Bill's insistence on the introduction to the gym of a stationary bike. It was true that you didn't really see stationary bikes around fighters. This one sat behind the hanging bags and the speedballs and the rack of hand-weights. It was poised like some curious boxing non-sequitur, bolted to the concrete floor between the steam room and the practice ring. Frequently goaded about it, Bill would never discuss the inspiration that had led to his buying and installing his controversial piece of gym hardware. This was because the inspiration was Julia Smollen. Bill was pretty confident that Julia had never laced on a pair of gloves in her life. But he had studied her limbs and what they were attached to often enough to appreciate that cycling must be awfully good for the body.

Bill sat at a pavement table outside the deli in Newport Beach and thought about age and its corollary: decline. The interesting thing about decline was that as the years passed and you grew older, you didn't grow any less indignant about it. You just possessed less mental energy and so the indignation you felt at your decline dissipated more swiftly. The same was true of failure. With age, you felt just as bad about failure. It just didn't hurt for the same length of time as once it would have because an aging mind wouldn't let it. It was like with an athlete. The first thing that went was the focus. The focus went even before the reflexes started to slow. Concentration was the first casualty of advancing years. Maybe it was nature's blessing. As you grew older and the calendar insisted your failure grew more acute, age prevented you from dwelling on the fact. He sat there, a big, disgruntled man in jeans and a polo shirt and watched traffic. Who was he kidding? As you got older, failure just felt worse and worse and worse. Because age extinguished hope. He took the note from his jeans pocket and unfolded the pages on the table top. Be thankful for small mercies, Billy Boy. At least he didn't need eye glasses to read what 'Tasha had written. He could bench press more than he weighed. When he threw a hook, with either hand, the heavy-bag still shuddered under the meat of his fist. He wasn't having to get up twenty times every night to coax pee from an empty bladder. His memory might be wilfully selective, but it still functioned when required. Small mercies, my elderly, crotchety friend. Small mercies.

Dear Bill,

I hope you watched out for us on the television. I plan to wear my black coat and to look as elegant and mysterious as possible. If you did see me you are welcome to review my performance. I picked up some tips on elegance and mystery on my recent trip to Europe and think the key to achieving these attributes is to be emotionally detached from whatever is going on around you.

Of course, it is very easy to be emotionally detached about snow flurries and conifers, sipping Glühwein and watching an essentially alien world through a café window in a pretty Austrian town. It is quite another when you are seated at the presidential inauguration next to your mom, thrilling with pride in what she has accomplished and how poised and beautiful she is. It is her moment and I am prouder of her than I can say. Did you see her, Bill, on the television?

Anyway, the real purpose of this note is not to wallow in the Smollen family's Brief Moment of Reflected Glory. The real purpose is quite serious and concerns you. The thing is, Bill, I know you will be reading this with a hangover. And believe me, the temptation is to be jocular and rerun one of the old jokes. You know: there are states in the southern part of this august republic in which the sale of vodka is a crime against God, punishable by lethal injection. Furthermore, southern California is renouncing state rights and ceding full judicial authority to Georgia.

Hallelujah for the Confederacy.

Is that a sea-breeze in your hand, Suh?

You know. That kind of thing.

Except that it isn't really all that funny. And if you don't do something about it, it really will become a death sentence.

You have always taken your job with me very seriously, Bill. You and Mom have always joked around about you being responsible for my 'spiritual welfare', but I know in my heart that you've always treated it with absolute seriousness. You have been as generous and kind and loving as any father I could have wished for. And when I've needed you to be, you've been wise.

But now it's my turn to talk about your spiritual welfare.

In an ideal world I'd have you and Mom grow old together. To accommodate Mom's more ethnic domestic urges you would need to share the occasional period of dark brooding and from time to time there'd be mandatory plate throwing. But you are skilled at conciliation and agile enough to dodge and, on the whole, I believe you would be fantastically happy together.

Sadly, we don't live in an ideal world (a fact likely to remain unchanged even under the full presidential force of JFK rhetoric). We have to work with what we've got. And I honesty think that your world would be much more to your own liking if you were more often sober experiencing it.

You use booze the way a dope addict uses morphine, Bill. If things are that painful, shouldn't you be trying to change them rather than trying just to deaden the pain?

Please forgive me for speaking so out of turn. But if you can't turn on your family . . .

And I only write these things because I love you and I believe them to be true.

I'll end on a piece of news to try and distract you from being mad or disappointed at me for what I've said in this letter up to now.

I'm going to join the Peace Corps.

There's nothing political in this decision. And there's certainly nothing elegant or mysterious about the Peace Corps. I just feel I've had a very fortunate life and want to do something for those born into circumstances less blessed. God knows, there are enough of them in the world. Having emerged (relatively) unscathed from my revolutionary phase, it's going to be the Peace Corps and then med school. All I have to do now is break the news to Mom.

Wish me luck!

Take care, Bill. And please think about what I've said.

Love always,

Natasha

PS The Glühwein, for reasons too obvious to mention, must remain our secret.

PPS One obvious reason is that Mom and I do need at least some unbroken crockery at home.

Bill took off his sunglasses and rubbed sweat from his eyes in the bright reflection of sunlight from the white deli tablecloth. He folded the note into four and put it back into his jeans pocket. 'I didn't know you threw plates, Julia,' he said out loud. 'The Peace Corps,' he said. 'Jesus.' He shook his head and looked down at the cradle of his linked, empty hands. 'Go, Coppi.'

Natasha had inherited her father's handwriting and on the drive to Anaheim and the gym in the jeep, Bill thought about her father and, in particular, the last occasion on which he had ever seen his friend. It could have been the handwriting that reminded him, but he thought it was more likely that phrase she had used, 'an essentially alien world', in describing her endearing bid at teenaged existentialism in the café in the snow in Austria. That had been how it was for Bill when he attended Lillian Hamer's funeral. He walked straight into an alien world, one that announced itself everywhere in hateful iconography and a subdued atmosphere of ever-prevalent foreboding.

Martin Hamer had never been a Nazi. He had watched as a boy as a pair of carpet-bagging Americans came to enforce the vindictive peace that followed the Great War. They inventoried his father's possessions and then parcelled off his land as reparation. It was the Hamer family's misfortune to own an estate on the border with France. They would pay the heavy price agreed at Versailles by Wilson and Clemenceau and charged those who had lost the war by its winners. Martin found his father's body next to his shotgun the morning after the Americans had proffered their bill and departed. Fighting Germany's war had worn his father out. But it was the peace exacted by her defeat that had killed him. When Martin went back there years later, at Lillian's insistence—'to try to lay the ghost'—an open-cast mine scarred the land he would have inherited, exhausted now, worn out and derelict.

No ghost was laid. But Martin Hamer made himself a promise. And his own military career was his chosen way of keeping it.

No Nazi, then. No anti-Semite or believer in Aryan destiny or euthanasia or eugenics or any of the other grotesqueries of the creed. But without men like Hamer to fight their wars, how far would the true believers of the blood banner and the bier keller putsch have got? How far would men like Joseph Goebbels and Heinrich Himmler have got, marching with a rifle at the head of a column through the steppes of Russia or patrolling the Atlantic, captaining a U-boat crew?

In 1937, no one outside Hitler's ghastly inner circle could have predicted the way that Germany would prosecute its war. But it was obvious that war was coming and when wars were declared, it was soldiers who fought them. It was soldiers and airmen such as those Germany had sent to Spain to aid Franco in a callous rehearsal the previous year.

In the spring of 1937, Bill deliberately severed his friendship with Martin and his wife. Then, in the autumn, he heard that Lillian Hamer had died at the wheel of her car in an accident. And he went to the funeral. He went because Martin had been the best friend he had ever known. He went because he knew it was the right and proper thing to do. He went because he had felt very fond of Lillian. He went mostly because he knew that his friend was in need of him.

He was incredulous that someone so full of life as Lillian Hamer could have died so young and carelessly. When he and Lucy had first met them on the Côte, he had thought them the most beautiful couple he had ever seen. Lillian was tall and slender and colt-like then in the clumsy way of the young, but she was growing into grace. She covered her mouth shyly when Lucy made them laugh with line after line of imperious sarcasm delivered from her canvas throne aboard the boat. Lillian had skin that turned gold in the sun and eyes the dusty blue of mountain snow and hair that fell

198

around her shoulders in ringlets when it dried on the boat in the wind off the sea after swimming. And she carried that beauty into her maturity. And so it was very difficult to imagine Lillian dead in a bloody car wreck in a ravine in a forest in the rain.

Bill almost missed the funeral. He only had the time to travel the distance at all because an investigation surrounding the death delayed Lillian's burial. There was much sneering anti-Americanism in those years in Germany. He had travelled by rented car from France and kept being stopped by petty officials manning arbitrary checkpoints on the autobahn to Berlin. There was an angry stand-off at one of these when, weary and grieving, he was ordered out of the car and told to deliver a Hitler salute. Acknowledging the führer, a functionary explained, was the key to further progress.

'I honour only one flag, sir,' Bill said. 'And it isn't yours.'

A rifle was trained on him then. He spread his feet and crossed his arms and hawked and spat on the macadam and, he believed, came very close to being shot. 'Fetch your superior,' he said, in German.

The superior was duly fetched. Bill's passport and travel documents were examined. The salute was never given. But the delay amounted to ninety minutes and made him very late for the burial.

When he got there, it was raining hard in the cemetery. Almost everybody in attendance seemed to be in some kind of uniform. The graveside smelled heavily of freshly turned earth and wet wool from sodden greatcoats. Cap badges and flashes of rank were dull in the leaden, rainy light and most of the men wore boots which had grass and mud stains now on their polished leather. Lillian's father, Dr Stresemann, wept over the grave. One of the few mourners dressed as a civilian, Bill remembered he wore dark spats buttoned over his shoes. A Homburg hat covered his head and rain gathered like dew on the fur collar of his overcoat. There were women in cloche hats and League of German Maidens' pins, and children like malevolent scouts and girl guides in their martial khaki drab, their swastika belt buckles and ornamental daggers.

Martin was grey, ragged and bereft. His eyes were raw with weeping and focused only on the ground. Bill walked across to him and put a hand on his shoulder and Martin must have recognized the familiar shape and weight of it. He covered it with his own. Martin's hand felt gritty, Bill supposed from earth thrown onto the coffin containing his wife. And he could feel the hard insistence, pressing on a knuckle, of Martin's wedding band. There was a commotion at the graveside then as Stresemann slithered into the slit in the ground and tugged at the coffin, unmanned by the loss of his daughter, unable to accept its rainy magnitude and muddy finality. Bill saw strong young men in uniform pull the doctor free with disdainful looks on their faces. There was a protocol, after all. There were standards and disciplines to observe.

He realized that Martin was saying something to him,

asking him a question, repeating it. He could hear rain dapple on the leaves of trees and drip from them and the sound of Stresemann's boundless grief at the side of the grave and the coughing and firing of engines from the nearby convoy of black saloons that would take them to whatever gruesome ceremony passed for a wake in a suburb of Berlin these days in the new Germany.

'I said do you think it is true?' Martin said.

The skin was tight over his face and his eyes were blood-shot and his lips were pale and bitten. He was bareheaded and blond hair tumbled over his forehead in the rain giving him the oddly youthful look of a broken boy.

'Do I think what is true, Martin?'

Hamer patiently repeated what he must already have said. 'I met a man recently. High ranking. Shrewd. He told me that no one knows anyone really, really well. Do you think it is true, Bill?' He waited for his reply, blinking, innocent. He was a boy. He was not yet thirty and his wife had died and he was lost. Rain trickled from his hair down his face. This was very important to him. 'He said it was a seductive theory.'

Bill breathed, deeply. 'And what did you say?'

'That it was a vision of hell.'

Bill looked around him, at the uniforms and the sleek black cars. At the sodden, khaki children. At the gravediggers leaning patiently on shovels with wet blades gleaming at their edges. At the grey ghost of Dr Stresemann. At the cemetery in the unrelenting rain.

201

'You were right, Martin. You were right. And he was worse than wrong.'

Bill drove back from the gym in Anaheim with his hands tender on the wheel of the Jeep, both of them bruised from the sustained beating he had given the heavy bag over six brutal rounds. He felt good. Or he felt good by his standards. Everything was relative. Just ask Albert Einstein, ho ho. But bad jokes apart, he did feel good. And his mood bettered when he got home and called his cashmere-clad secretary to see if there were any important messages he needed to hear.

'Miss Smollen called.'

'Miss Smollen Junior, or Miss Smollen Senior?'

'Miss Julia Smollen. She didn't leave a message.'

'Anyone else?'

'Mr Sinatra.'

Bill chuckled to himself. Miss Cashmere had given Frank second billing. He'd have been furious. 'Any message?'

'Mr Sinatra dictated it in the manner of a telegraph. Should I recite it likewise?'

Bill thought it was true what they said about a little education. 'Go ahead.'

She cleared her throat.

'Your original supposition correct. Stop. English guy proved total asshole. Stop. To err human, to forgive divine. Stop. Drinks Thursday? Stop by. Stop.'

Bill thanked his secretary and hung up. He put a Sam

Cooke record on the turntable and sat in a chair and started to look through the newspapers, laid out for him where he liked them by the woman who had come in the morning to clean for him and, today, to take away his suits. He took the *Los Angeles Times* and the *Washington Post*. He looked through the Hollywood trades, but didn't scour every line of print on their pages like some people did. It was easy to become obsessed by the movie industry. He lived and worked on its periphery, and wasn't.

The real papers were full of the inauguration. A *Post* editorial opined that Kennedy's was the most graceful and intelligent speech since the one delivered by that renaissance man of the republic, Thomas Jefferson. So JFK had won the comparison he had wanted so dearly. Bill thought it was the style of Jack Kennedy to set high goals and achieve them with an apparently effortless grace. He was a war hero. He was a Pulitzer Prize winner. He had achieved the highest office in the land at the age of forty-three and as a Catholic. Bill knew there was some manipulation in the image, a certain guile and craft to its construction and its maintenance. But he thought, too, that the new president had in him the promise to be authentically great.

'The promise or the threat,' he said, riffling through newspaper pages. Nuclear war was never further than a failed bluff away from destroying the world. And Bill did not think Kennedy would be the sort of man to blink first.

He figured that JFK quite probably, if unwittingly, supplied the real reason for Frank's olive branch, itself graciously offered. There were plenty of people Frank preferred than Bill to drink with. What he probably wanted come Thursday night was a little confidential legal advice. His close association with the Kennedys had brought the affairs of Frank Sinatra under very close press scrutiny. Most of the rumours were ridiculous. Some of the more damaging Bill regarded as practically invited by Sinatra himself. He was a paradoxical, impulsive man and no stranger, in his rages, to the self-inflicted wound. He was the peerless performer and tireless lothario who could appear almost shy with Julia Smollen and goof around like a kid with 'Tasha, buying her ice-cream, taking her to a funfair for the afternoon. But he was useful as well as colourful to know. There was a pragmatic, even ruthless side to Bill's nature where business was concerned. And Frank had proved over the years to be a profitable friend to have.

Like almost all of Sinatra's friends, Bill was also an unashamed fan, and he put *Come Fly With Me* on the turntable now, looking forward to hearing it again after deleting it from his domestic play-list for the duration of their silly feud. He laughed to himself at his pettiness in doing that, anticipating the look on his host's face come Thursday when he refused the offer of a Martini in favour of fruit juice or iced tea. But that was what Bill sincerely intended to do. For the foreseeable future, he had taken his last drink. In a minute he'd make some tea, he thought, enjoying the record, listening to the rhythm swing through Nelson Riddle's punchy, skilled arrangement. He'd drink it with his pinkie raised like the English playwright Noel Coward did. Bill practised raising his little finger and winced with the pain his bag-work of the morning had inflicted on his hands.

There was a knock at the door then, and Bill got out of his chair thinking it probably a lost tourist looking for directions. His house was isolated. He would not hear the approach of a car through the concrete and glass of his walls, with the windows closed. His cleaning woman always closed and locked those of his windows that she opened after polishing their panes. And it was January and chilly after the Jeep ride back from the heat of the gym in Anaheim, so Bill had left the windows shut on getting home. He was relaxed, happy about the Sinatra resolution, in the grip of the album he was playing, totally off-guard. He opened his door with no trepidation at all, picturing a clueless, star-struck couple from somewhere in the mid-west to be standing on the step outside. They would be looking for a real-estate bargain. They would be hoping to locate the property of a movie star to rubberneck. But instead it was Julia Smollen.

She was wearing a grey coat with a sable collar and the coat was crumpled and a wilted bloom was still pinned, in celebratory style, from the inauguration ceremony of the previous day, to the fur on one of its lapels. She was bare headed and her hair hung uncombed down her cheeks. She was very pale. The knuckles were white on her hands, clasping a small dress bag in front of her and Bill could smell a sour, feral odour on her breath and her skin. She was shaking in the coat. Her legs were unsteady and one of her stockings was laddered, Bill saw, shocked, over a gashed shin. She stood there racked, shuddering in the bright, January sunlight, framed by his doorway. She was like an apparition, like a painting of despair. He stepped forward and put his arms around her.

'He's got 'Tasha, Bill. He's taken my daughter,' Julia said.

'Julia. Julia. Come here.' She shivered in his arms, against his chest. He could smell the feral odour strong in her hair, the secretion of fear.

'He's taken 'Tasha.' Her voice trembled, her breathing reduced to gasps and sobs beyond her control. 'Oh, God. Oh, God. I don't know what to do.'

He brought her into his house and took off her coat and found brandy in the drinks cabinet and forced some of it into her. He lit the kindling under the pine logs in his fireplace and switched the music off. She sat on the edge of her chair still gripping the clutch bag, absurdly chic and inappropriate, between both hands on her knees. Somewhere, she had lost her little pillbox hat. They all wore them now, those little hats made fashionable by the new first lady. Her hair was lank and her leg gashed and the bloom wilted on her best outfit. She'd got here like this, he thought, in this condition, flown from Washington and presumably come from the airport in a cab. She was the strongest woman he had ever known, easily the most self-possessed, doing everything she could to prevent herself from being overwhelmed by the shock and panic assaulting her. The love and the pity in him for her fought the concern. Julia was at least safe. What had happened to 'Tasha?

'When?'

Her head snapped around on her neck and her eyes were vacant with adrenaline. 'Last night. She went shopping on the same block as the hotel. After an hour I was worried and went looking for her. I didn't find her. When I returned to our suite I found this.'

Julia fumbled with the clasp on her clutch bag. In her absence of composure, her accent had returned. She was speaking in a voice Bill had not heard Julia use since her time in San Francisco. And her fingers would not obey her and open the bag. Bill took it from her and snapped the clasp and emptied out its contents onto the table beside Julia's chair where his newspapers still lay. Tissues and a Cartier lighter and a scent bottle spilled out. A little appointments diary with a tiny pencil in its spine. A pack of Gauloise. Woman's stuff. And a long narrow brass cylinder flattened into a neat ridge at one end. For a moment, absurdly, he thought it a lipstick container.

'You know what that is?'

'A bullet casing.' He picked it up. He coughed to disguise the growing dread he felt in his voice. His skin had gone cold and prickly though the fire had caught and the room was warm now with the scent of burning pine logs. 'A high velocity round. I don't know what calibre it is. And there are no case markings so I can't tell you who manufactured it.'

He switched on a desk lamp and examined the casing. 'It's machine made, but it doesn't look mass produced. There's usually a stamp or serial number. I think the user may have made it. It looks like the sort of ammunition a sniper might use.' The chill spread through him. He could feel goose bumps on his arms. He thought of lanolin and Old Spice. Sweet Jesus.

'It's the casing from the bullet that killed her father,' Julia said. Her voice was inflected and flat. 'Before he died Martin told me it was Landau who had killed him.'

Bill nodded. Of course he knew the story. He smelled the casing, but it smelled of brass, of nothing. No powder residue. It had been fired a long time ago. Used lethally eighteen years ago, in the snow? Aimed at Martin Hamer, with Julia in his arms and Natasha carried in her belly?

'You should not have picked it up. There might have been prints.' He put the bullet casing into his pocket so she would not have to look at it. 'Here, drink your brandy.' He handed her the glass and she took it in both hands and it still wobbled as she gulped a mouthful down. Her leg was bleeding under the ladder in her stockings and fear came off her skin in sour waves. He saw that her shoes were new and scuffed, the patent leather worn with stumbling, the tip gone from one of their heels. In their moment of shining privilege. On their proudest day. Bill felt fury rising from his gut.

'Have you called the police?'

'No.' Julia laughed. There was no mirth in the sound. 'I read a book about the Lindbergh kidnapping.'

'You have to call the police.' Everyone knew about the blunders in the Lindbergh case. Bill knew that most kidnapped children were dead within hours of being abducted. But he had also encountered some very good cops in his life.

The phone began to ring. Bill looked at it and Julia dropped her glass onto the rug and ran across the room and snatched the receiver from its cradle.

'Yes?' She listened. It was for her.

Bill picked her glass off the rug and smelled brandy as he took it into the kitchen and put it into the sink. His brandy was five-star Hennessey and the smell was rich and powerful and Bill realized almost vaguely that the last thing on earth he wanted right now was a drink of anything at all.

'Who was that?'

She was off the phone, pacing the room and wringing her hands, when he returned.

'Who was that?' He tried to make his tone casual.

'It was the Attorney General's office. I asked Bobby Kennedy would he find something out for me and gave him this number as one I might be reached at.'

'Did you tell him why you wanted the information?'

'Not precisely. I told him about the orange grove. And he agreed to ask Hoover to see if the FBI had anything on Landau.'

Bill remembered Lyndon Johnson's remark when the Kennedy brothers had wanted to sack J. Edgar Hoover. About it being better to have the FBI chief inside the tent pissing out. Thank God for Texan logic. 'And they did? They do?'

'A man called Peter Landau worked at a hunting lodge in Colorado until three months ago. He sold Remington rifles and ammunition. He was an expert marksman.'

'And he committed a felony offence?'

Julia looked terrible, terrified, visited by a vengeful ghost. 'He climbed to raid eagles' nests and sold the eggs. He sold them to foreign collectors. There's a black–market trade, apparently. He had no export licence.' She smiled. Bill thought the smile very brave. 'He did not declare the income in his tax returns. The lodge owner found out about the trading and he was reported. And he was fired.'

'He won't kill her, Julia.' Bill knew he had to say this. He had to confront the possibility out loud or risk Julia's breakdown and derangement. However facile the hope turned out to be, he needed to give it to her now. 'He could have killed her, killed both of us, in the orange grove. He wants money.'

'He wants revenge,' she said.

'For what?'

'Martin took his life away,' she said. 'Martin took Landau's world. Now Landau's taking what's left of his.'

Bill looked at his watch. It was four o'clock. 'I'm leaving for Colorado tonight,' he said. 'It's where he'll take her because it's where he knows.'

'Oh, Bill,' Julia said. She started to cry. Her shoulders shook with grief and her eyes filled with tears and despair.

'This isn't strapping fishing rods to the sides of your Jeep and provoking fights in cowboy bars. This is not some silly trial of strength and manhood. What use will you be? A sixty-year-old man, wading through winter snowdrifts. This is my daughter.' She sobbed. 'He has 'Tasha.'

'Do you know the name and location of the lodge?'

She shook her head. 'The name only.'

'That's enough. I've fished and hunted and skied in Colorado since I was eleven years old, Julia. I used to hunt there twenty-odd years ago with 'Tasha's father. I know the ground. I know all of it. And I won't be stopped from going.'

Julia nodded. She looked defeated.

'I'm going for the two people I love most on earth. Not to prove anything,' Bill said.

'He'll kill you.' She said it flatly, resignedly.

'No doubt he'll try.'

Bill went over to her. He stroked her face and kissed her cheeks and the top of her head and his heart cleaved for her. But his voice was calm. 'Call the police. Call them now. I'll stay with you until the police arrive. And then I have to go.'

211

EIGHT

He had drilled holes in the trunk of his car so that she would not suffocate despite the ropes and gag that restricted her breathing and terrified her and inflicted the cramp she endured. During the short January days on the road she could see pinpoints of light and sometimes, thin shafts of sunlight pencilled through the small prison of her space. Mostly, though, they travelled in darkness and cold. Her hurt leg ached with cold and confinement. Hungry and, worse, very thirsty, she would remind herself of how uncomfortable she had thought the bus journey to New York Harbour for the boat to Europe and her ski holiday. Reminiscing about anything before her kidnap was, she knew, a dangerous thing to do. The nostalgia for freedom it invoked seemed almost overwhelming considering just how recently she had been free. And reminiscing brought with it a sort of despondent self-pity that threatened to rob her of her alertness and paralyse her mind. On the other hand, only reminiscing could keep her sane. She would think about how grumpy the chilly tedium of the bus journey had made her and would be almost able to laugh, picturing her own pompous disgruntlement. If only I'd had a crystal ball, Natasha thought. I'd never have complained. But then if I'd had a crystal ball, I'd never have been caught.

Her kindness had allowed her to be taken. The road shuddered under her and she gritted her teeth against cramp and thought of that line from Tennessee Williams. What was it? *I have always depended on the kindness of strangers.* She hadn't really known what it meant when she'd seen Claire Bloom in the play on Broadway and she didn't know what it meant now. But she had tried to give comfort to a stranger, seeing a slight, bedraggled man apparently taken ill in a dark doorway on a Washington Street. And she had awoken here, with her tongue swollen and dry and her head pounding worse than it had after an evening of Glühwein with that cabal of school reefer-smokers in Austria. Much worse, actually. It was Bill, she remembered, who had told her that nobody under thirty really gets a hangover.

'Then from thirty to forty, you learn to deal with a hangover. After forty, life itself seems to take on many permanent hangover characteristics. My advice, kid, is to make hay while the sun shines.' And he had smiled. But the humour had not touched his eyes. And she had resolved then to confront him on the unhappy and persistent subject of the hangover that had become Bill's self-imposed life sentence.

The car went over another bump and she winced behind the tightness of the gag. The gag was a real pain because it

213

was full of the dribble and snot that she had cried into it before she had got a grip on herself. It was crusty and it stank, to tell the truth. Did it mean she had bad breath? She hoped not. But halitosis, though a pretty disastrous affliction, was not at this moment the most compelling of her problems. Escape was the most compelling of her problems. She planned to escape. But that was not the same thing at all as having an escape plan. Formulating one of those had so far defeated her. It wasn't like being abducted in the movies. Should she ever get out of this, she would have to confront her mom on that score, tell her mom that life wasn't at all like the movies.

Thinking about her mom threatened to bring more tears and panic and Natasha reminded herself fiercely that the gag in her mouth was disgusting enough without a fresh onslaught of tears and mucus. She blinked and counted the breaths until composure returned to her. He didn't intend to kill her. Not straight away, he didn't, or he would have already. He was feeding her, after a fashion, at deserted stops on the route at night, when he would untie the gag and give her candy and cola with his left hand while his right gripped a large hunting knife. Afterwards he would let her squat and pee at the roadside. He did all this with a light, she thought a bicycle lamp, hanging from one of his shirt pockets and shining in her eyes. It made him a silhouette, and so far, she had not clearly seen his face. The breathing holes punched in the trunk lid and the feeding stops told her he didn't intend to kill her yet. But she needed a plan of escape. Because he would kill her, wouldn't he? He would kill her because in real life, they almost always did.

She thought the guy might be an ex-cop or maybe a prison guard. He followed strict procedures and seemed to possess some weird kind of expertise in dealing with a prisoner. It was what made the possibility of escape so damn difficult. So far, she didn't think the guy had made any mistakes. And there were no flaws in his method. That would have to change, though. They would have to arrive somewhere eventually, wouldn't they, and the situation would be obliged to change. He had not hit her. He had not molested or raped her. There was a temptation to feel almost grateful for that, but Natasha knew this was a seductive trap. Hating him was dangerous, but it was her best chance of survival. Feeling gratitude for what he hadn't done to her was just foolish weakness. She thought about her bonds and the way her kindness had been abused and her freedom violated. She thought about her short life and her poor bereft mother. And she knew that if she were given any kind of chance, she would kill her abductor. She would kill rather than die. If necessary, she would kill him with her bare hands.

What the girls at school called her jock instinct had kind of embarrassed her in recent years. It was hard to think of yourself as Holly Golightly (in the film, not the book); or Juliette Greco, when the athletics coach was always on your case to run track or throw a discus. Skiing was different because it was basically European and the clothing was

215

incredibly cool. Riding was riding. Jodhpurs and boots could look pretty good. Riding was okay. But the other stuff? The problem was that she was naturally good at it. She was quick and she was very strong. Once, for a bet, she had been challenged to see how many pull-ups she could do in the gym on the chinning bar. She'd given up at ten, when Alice Dorne had emerged from her Rod McKuen dope stupor and begun ironically clapping.

'Easy, Alice,' Natasha had said, dropping from the bar. 'You'll wear yourself out.'

She could have done a lot more than ten pull-ups. She could have done twice that number.

She was slender, disproportionately strong, the coaches always said; surprisingly strong. She thought her strength might come in useful now.

On the third evening of her abduction he cut off all her hair. She had been proud of her hair and began to cry. He told her to shut up, the first thing he had said to her. Everything prior to that had been gestures and shakes of his head. 'Shut up,' he said. 'If I had pliers, I'd take a tooth. So shut up.'

His voice was guttural and his accent harsh. Italian? The Bronx? He cut her hair off, cutting her head, twice, in his hurry, with the shears he used. She thought that the cuts to her scalp probably felt worse than they actually were. When had she last had a tetanus jab? She did not cry out and she tried very hard not to provoke him further by wincing as he carried out his wretched task. She could see no lights, but the air was colder and thinner than it had been, she was sure of it. It was almost mountain air. He had forgotten to bring pliers. It was a mistake, wasn't it? He had meant to bring pliers to pull one of her teeth. It wouldn't do to dwell on what would be happening, now, on this dark roadside, had he remembered them. The fact was, he'd fouled up. As she watched her hair spill down the face of her ruined coat in cloudy moonlight, as he gathered dead, flaxen tresses from her shoulders and put her hair into a bag, she did what she could in her mind to take encouragement from that small fact.

He'd fouled up.

When he fucked up, she would be ready and she would kill him.

Sorry, Mom. About the swearing, I mean. I don't mean about the intent.

He pushed her back into the trunk of the car and her head felt cold and small, her scalp naked now to the cold of the night air. She sniffed and bit on the gag. She still had all her teeth. And her hair would grow out and she would have it styled short, the way Jean Seberg had worn hers in the movie *Breathless*.

She played games in her mind. She played the fame and the fortune game but mostly she played the dating game. In an ideal world she would find someone who looked like Alain Delon had in *Plein Soliel*. But he'd have to be taller. According to Alice Dorne, dope fiend, failed ballerina and oracle of all knowledge, Alain Delon was only five-eight.

One of the many privileges of being her mother's daughter was that she got to see final cuts in preview theatres sometimes before movies were actually released. So she had seen *Breakfast at Tiffany's* already, even though none of her friends had. And she had seen *The Hustler*. Playing pool wasn't really an accomplishment she admired, though, and Paul Newman's Eddie Felson character was about as dumb and self-destructive as you could get. But God, he looked beautiful. Writing was a much more beguiling talent than hitting pool balls, but George Peppard was much too preppy in *Breakfast* for her taste. Given that raising Alain Delon to six feet defied the laws of physics, what she'd like to do was date someone with the soulful nature of Peppard's writer and the looks of Paul Newman. It would be a good start.

She had asked her mother could she meet Paul Newman, before *The Hustler* was finished, on the set.

'Absolutely not,' her mother had said. 'He works on a closed set. Also he's a method actor and therefore very aloof. Also he's thirty-five years old and you're a schoolgirl. It's a ridiculous idea.'

She smiled to herself at that. Her mother dismissed lots of ideas as ridiculous. She didn't understand the fun of just being a fan. Her mother admired some men. She certainly admired Jack Kennedy. But she had probably never had a crush on anyone in her life. It would be much too undignified. Natasha wondered had her mother ever loved a man. No, she decided. It would be much too undignified.

She wondered would she get the chance, the time now, to have a non-celluloid romance of her own. There was a lot she wanted to do, to experience. Her love life had been limited to a few flirtations. She was seventeen and she didn't want to die at the hands of the guttural stranger who had stolen her.

She knew it was the guy in the creepy pickup with the blind windshield who had followed her and Bill from the airport. She had smelled the lanolin and Old Spice smell on him. She thought it was probably something to do with her mother and the Kennedy connection. It was some creep with a grudge against the government or the Kennedy family or maybe the new president himself. But no matter how hard she tried, she couldn't make the connection. And the alternative, that it was actually about her, was too terrifying for her yet to consider. She closed her eyes and her naked head prickled in the raw cold and she imagined another version of events. In this one, Bill had run the creep off the road and dragged him out of the pickup and brained him with that bike lamp thing he wore clipped to his breast pocket. Or Bill had surprised him spying on them and sent the creep tumbling and cartwheeling down the hill, knocked cold by a mighty blow. If only. If only. If only that had been how it had happened instead of this.

They were definitely getting higher. The air was thinning and she recognized the frigid cold she had felt in the Alps in Austria. They were at altitude, among mountains. The car climbed an almost constant gradient that forced her weight

219

towards where the trunk locked. The gears ground and the engine complained as the car took a series of narrow turns that reminded her body of how bruised it had become, trussed up and confined.

He'd said something really odd when he'd cut her hair. She wondered had she heard him right. His accent was heavy and his words indistinct and she hadn't exactly been concentrating on what he was saying. Forced to avert her eyes by the power of the torch beam, she had seen the car interior briefly bathed in light and noticed a long canvas bag on the rear seat. It was dun coloured in the torch beam and had a thin leather strap. Bags like that carried rifles or they carried fencing foils. She did not think this was the sort of guy who would fence for recreation. He had pulled her shorn head around, then, back to face him and the blinding whiteness, and he had turned her head this way and that, her jaw held hurtfully in the grip of his finger and thumb. She had smelled burnt tobacco strong on his fingers. '*Gott*,' the silhouette had said to her, and it had barked laughter. 'It's like looking at a ghost.'

Maybe Bill had been right. Maybe it was just some random lunatic with a grudge against the world in general. He'd hit on her at the airport when they dropped her mom and followed them and then done that scoping thing from behind his rock above the orange grove. He must have known Bill had spotted him, but that hadn't put him off. Bill was a big, fierce guy, big enough to put most people off. But this guy hadn't been put off at all. He had been clever and persistent enough to follow her to Washington. And he'd been cunning enough to trap and abduct her too.

It was about her, wasn't it? It wasn't about the Kennedys or politics or anything like that. It was about her, no matter how random his fixation or weird his motives. The ghost remark was personal. Whatever it meant to him, it was personal and it was the proof. Natasha shivered with this realization in the darkness of the trunk. Suddenly she felt very tired, overwhelmed by a narcotic, smothering blanket of fatigue. It was the onset of shock, she imagined, or her body's response to the onset of shock. But sleep was a blessing. It would block out the pain and it would make her stronger and she needed her strength as never before. And so when sleep engulfed her she was glad and grateful and she surrendered entirely to it.

He must have chloroformed her again or used ether on her while she slept in the trunk. She awoke strapped to something rigid with the sun shining directly into her eyes. Her head ached terribly in pulsing thumps and she was moving and the motion made her nauseous. Her tongue was swollen again and felt blistered. She turned her head to one side and puked and choked behind the gag. She heard him swear from somewhere in front of her and he knelt down and pulled out his hunting knife and pressed the blade against her throat. The meaning was clear. She nodded and he cut the gag and she coughed out vomit. There was blood in the vomit. She must have bitten her tongue. He was wearing snow goggles and a hooded smock and a harness to pull the sled he had bound her to. She groaned and he stood and kicked her. The knife had a handle carved from bone and a brass pommel and had felt very sharp. It was a bowie knife with a groove along the blade to channel blood. It was the biggest knife she had ever seen.

She was in the mountains. The snow was too white to look at and the sky too blue in the sunlight. She blinked and tried to accommodate the brightness. He had the rifle strapped across his back. He was a slightly built man, not tall. Maybe she had been kidnapped by Alain Delon. She coughed again and winced from the pain in her ribs.

'You laugh at me? You think this is funny?'

She shook her head. German. The accent was German. He looked like a mountain soldier in the get-up he wore. With the accent and all, he looked like one of the bad guys in a war movie. Now if only Kirk Douglas or Burt Lancaster would come round a bluff and kill him. Wouldn't that be great? She was giddy from the chloroform. Should she survive this, she would have to tell Alice Dorne about chloroform. This stuff beat reefer hands down.

'You think this is funny?'

She shook her head. No, she didn't think it was funny at all. She didn't want to get kicked in her ribs again. If she kept her eyes open she would give herself snow blindness. Her feet felt numb with cold but her toes were hurting her through the numbness. And black clouds like frozen thunderheads loomed above the peaks that seemed to be where they were headed. It was going to dump snow. The snow would cover their tracks. They would likely get caught in a blizzard and die of exposure or be torn off a slope and hurled into the void by the force of the wind. A month before, she had narrowly avoided death in an avalanche in Austria and thought then it must be her fate to live a long life. What a joke that assumption seemed now. But it wasn't funny, was it? It wasn't funny at all. The creep was right. Nothing was funny.

She was in Colorado. The landscape was silent and mountainous and they were high up. She had skied in the Rockies in Canada but the air felt different there. She knew from the dry texture of the air and the snow that she was in Colorado. And her heart seemed to fold up inside her at the sight, through her wincing vision, of this white, craggy wilderness. She would never be found here in all this vaunting, empty space. In front of her, her abductor trudged ever upward and her harnessed sled followed. She was truly lost. Above the peaks, the clouds roiled now in a vast black and purplish spill. The air had the compressed feel you felt in your ears before a storm. It didn't matter, did it, that it was going to snow? No one knew where she was. No one was coming to try to rescue her. She was in real life, not in a movie, and there was no Burt Lancaster poised to emerge on spiked boots from a crevasse and save her with a burst of machine-gun fire and a trademark Lancaster grin.

He had not yet made a mistake. Two days and two nights and he had not put a foot wrong in his procedure. He had forgotten the pliers with which to wrench out one of her teeth. But that was all. Probably he would have a tool kit wherever it was he was taking them. And there he would do with her whatever he wanted. He was a methodical man. She knew that much about him. And he was short, like Alain Delon was short. Natasha could feel her eyes brim with tears. But she would not give in to self-pity. She would nurse her precious flame of anger, let it flicker until it got the chance to roar. That's what she would do. She would ignore the pain from her freezing toes and her blistered tongue and contain the fear and waste no energy on grim and ghoulish speculation. It was what it was until it changed, her situation. It might get worse. But it would certainly change and she took hope at that prospect and kindled and nourished the flame of the anger burning fiercely now inside her.

He must have read her thoughts. He turned and looked at her and then looked at the sky. The sun was covered now by cloud and the light looked as compressed in the absence of the sun as the air felt. The bird was maybe a peregrine falcon and it was the first living thing apart from the creep Natasha had seen from her sled in the mountains. It was flying away from them in fast, muscular swoops. The rifle was off his back and in his hands and then at his shoulder in a single movement so swift and fluid it looked predetermined, choreographed by fate. Then there was the tiniest hesitation and he squeezed the trigger and the bird was jerked out of life and plunged towards the snow in a last, ungainly dive. There was a telescopic sight mounted on the barrel of the rifle and she knew that he had seen her through it, once. He had sighted her through its cross hairs during a sunny October picnic. He turned and smiled at her and ejected the spent bullet casing and caught it before it hit the snow, with the rifle held easily in one hand.

'My name is Peter Landau,' he said. He took off his snow goggles. And she knew for certain that he would kill her having told her his name now and shown her his face.

'You can shoot.'

'Oh, you've no idea,' he said.

She was silent. She did not want a conversation with Peter Landau. Her mouth hurt and anyway it seemed a dangerous thing to have.

'That name means nothing to you, does it.'

It was a statement rather than a question. Landau looked around. But the rifle report had been a tiny sound and there was no one there to hear it.

'You have not the remotest idea of who you are, have you.'

She looked at him. I know who you are, she thought. I know what you are, too.

He sniffed the bullet casing in his hand and put it in his pocket. He looked around them at the encroaching weather, at the peaks. 'I was right,' he said. 'You see, you really are a ghost.'

'I'm very cold,' Natasha said. 'I'm not dead yet, but if you don't do something about it soon I will die on this sled and be of no use to you.'

'Americans know nothing of the cold,' he said. But he said this absently, as though to himself. 'You've already been of use to me,' he said. 'And we are almost at our destination.'

The blizzard hit just after they arrived. His shelter was a hut built from pine logs under a granite overhang that protected it from the worst of the wind and any risk of avalanche. He had chosen the spot well. Or he had if solitude and seclusion were what he had built it for. It wouldn't get much light, under its high awning of ancient rock. But he had packed snow all around the hut to insulate it from the chill of granite. She could see where he had tamped the snow down with a spade. And from the single window beside his door he could cover the one approach. He's built this place with the instinct of a sniper, Natasha thought, pulled up the merciless field of fire that formed the single route to his door. She saw that the snow flurries were thickening around her. He's built himself a home in the mountains with a killing ground for a front yard.

'Why am I here?'

'To punish your mother.'

'To punish her for what?'

'Once, your father built a hide for your mother.' Landau smiled. 'It was a skilled construction. Cunning. But it was not so well built as this one is.'

Her stomach pitched and rolled with revulsion. 'Are you saying that you are my father?'

He chuckled at that. 'I knew your father, Natasha Smollen. I killed him.'

He had lit an oil lamp when they arrived. A white-out was descending as they got to the hut and the snow was pouring in big flakes out of the blankness as the wind rose and made the flakes spill in frantic gusts on the hide roof and on the descending slope outside. She had studied what she could of that slope on the ascent, but, bound to the sled, it had been hard to keep her bearings. He used the bowie knife to cut her bonds and blood returned agonizingly to her feet and her hands. It was a blind, the slope, she knew. It was a trap. It ended abruptly, sheared by an abyss of black granite. That was what her skier's instinct told her. You would snow-plough down a slope like that, cautiously, sensing the sudden drop-off with a curious sort of dread in your stomach. The route down the mountain, she was pretty sure, was to the left of it. But their tracks were being obliterated now and Landau would have utilized many of the mountain's defences.

He had shut and bolted the door. The four panes of the small single window were covered in some kind of film. It was probably the same stuff he had used on the windshield of the pickup he had first followed her and Bill in. It didn't reflect sunlight. It absorbed light, but you could see out of it, if there was anything to see. The hut was just high enough to stand in and about eight feet long and six feet wide. The roof sloped from the rear, Natasha supposed to ease the shifting of drift snow when the weight of it got to be too great a burden. Cured meat in various stages of maturity hung in strips and bunches on wires stretched across the

227

width of one wall. There was a cot and a chair and a metal ring had been screwed into the wall above the head of the cot and a pair of handcuffs hung from the ring. Soot spread in a stain on the roof above the lamp. And there was a patch of charred wood and grease rising from a camp stove against the wall opposite the single chair. There was a trapdoor cut into the floor, but she didn't really want to think about that. She looked at the handcuffs. Oh well. It was better than the sled. And the sled had been better than the trunk of the car. And nobody bothered handcuffing a corpse. Not even this creep, not even Landau, would bother to take that precaution. Natasha lay on the rough planked floor and massaged her wrists and then her ankles with numb hands. The hut smelled of drying animal flesh and stove oil and paraffin and smoked cigarettes. It was cold, but warming with their body heat in the insulation of the packed snow outside. The wind out there screamed now. It sounded as though some tattered banshee railed and furied on the roof. Listening to the wind, Natasha wondered what would be her best strategy for staying alive.

'Have you any coffee, Mr Landau?'

'Make some,' he said. He sat in the chair and cradled his rifle in his hands. 'Use melt-water. There are matches next to the stove. Palm matches and I will kill you. Think about scalding me and it will be the last thought you enjoy.'

She brewed the coffee, moving on her knees, her body perhaps two feet away from the end of his rifle barrel, amazed that she could perform tasks such as spooning coffee and adding powdered milk to a tin mug without spilling everything in fumbling panic. When it was made, she poured the coffee and then slid his to his feet along the floor. The floor was rough, but she was careful not to spill any of his coffee. He picked it up and sipped at it without comment, his right hand still holding his rifle near the trigger guard.

'Go and drink yours on the bed over there,' he said. 'When you've drunk it, cuff yourself. Cuff yourself firmly, or I will punish you.'

She nodded. She sat on the bed and sipped her coffee. It was without doubt the most wonderful drink she had ever tasted. She had promised herself, being force-fed the previous night, that if she lived to survive this ordeal, she would never in her life again drink Coca Cola or eat Reece's Cup Cakes.

There seemed to be some kind of lull in whatever plan Landau was carrying out. Natasha figured it had been caused by the storm that raged and billowed now in full force outside the hut.

To punish your mother.

That meant her mother had to know. And the longer he strung the thing out, the more her mother would be punished. He had only allowed her to make the coffee to enjoy the small sideshow of her awkwardness and sub-jugation. Allowing her to make the coffee had been killing time for him. He could have cuffed her straight away and made a pot for himself. It would have been quicker to do that. They were waiting for something. And that would be the worst ordeal yet for her; awaiting an uncertain fate while knowing her mom tortured herself with a mother's frantic worry at home.

Oh, you bastard, Landau. You sadistic piece of shit. Natasha closed her eyes and regulated her breathing. I'll kill you. I swear to God I'll kill you for this. The coffee had made her mind alert. She was his prisoner. She was not his slave. She would never be that. She would take her mind away to where it would rather be in the wait forced upon her. She would not sit worrying to interpret the creep's every tick and gesture. A few days ago she had witnessed history. She had. She had witnessed history. In Landau's stinking cabin, in his vile company, she would travel in her mind to visit that shimmering moment once again.

When she had first been to Hyannis Port at the age of fifteen the Kennedys had seemed to her like characters from a Scott Fitzgerald story. They personified that combination of effortless grace and incalculable wealth that seemed so romantic on the pages of his fiction. Their lives in Cape Cod seemed to the adolescent Natasha a pageant of tennis games and sea bathing and voyages on the ocean aboard sailing boats with crisp, white sails. There were Labrador dogs and ancient, unfunny family jokes and cocktails to sip watching idle sunsets while somnolent waves lapped the shore. She was fifteen and liked to think of herself as a radical and she thought them all very pampered and self-indulgent.

But that was how they played rather than how they lived.

Over time she realized there was a seriousness to them and their ambitions, most particularly to those surrounding Jack. The Fitzgerald comparison was seductive, but it was misleading. Jay Gatsby's fictional life was a failed striving after a certain style. Jack Kennedy's factual life was a successful striving after substance, marked all the way by a characteristic certainty.

People had laughed when he first revealed to them he wanted to become president. He'd told her so himself. She had been in the family library, which she used with old Joe Kennedy's grumpily granted permission. The library had a big carved pendulum clock and some horrible deco bronze figures her mother referred to as Old Joe's Xanadu Collection. There were pictures, too, of Jack in his PT Boat and Joe Junior at the controls of the navy bomber he died in. But it was a working library. Among the morocco-bound collections and first editions of Gibbon and Macaulay and Dickens and Thoreau were thousands of proper, well-thumbed books. Jack came in with that taciturn brother of his to look up some congressional fact or senatorial statistic. She knew them well enough by then to know the motive for the search could equally be the plotting of a strategy or the winning of a bet. Politics absorbed them.

She had been crying. Jack came over to her straight away, left Bobby searching the shelves, pulled up a chair next to hers and put a hand on her shoulder and squeezed. It was summer and he had a tan and freckles and the concern in his pale blue eyes was genuine.

231

'What's the matter, kid?'

It was silly, really. She had been talking about poetry to her mother. Her mother took her poetry straight. She loved Thomas Hardy. Natasha said she thought Thomas Hardy should maybe have lightened up, gone to the village tavern, had a few brews with the farm boys. Drunk a glass of cider or something with the milkmaids. Might have given him a whole new outlook.

Her mother had smiled. 'And which poets do you read, darling?'

Allen Ginsberg, she'd said. And her mother had quoted the first couplet from *Howl*, the famous lines where Ginsberg said he'd seen the best minds of his generation basically beaten and disillusioned and abused.

'Which best minds do you think he meant?' her mother asked. 'The intellectual giants he consorted with flunking his course at Columbia University? Or the Benzedrine and heroin junkies he mixed with in Times Square?'

Kennedy laughed, when Natasha told him this, but the laugh was kindly. 'Your mother has a point. But so do you. It's a rare poem that brings its author to the attention of the FBI.'

She wished she'd thought of saying that.

Jack Kennedy enjoyed her mother's sometimes caustic wit, she knew. With her adolescent sensitivity in full quiver, a fifteen-year-old Natasha was less of a fan.

He squeezed her shoulder. 'You need to have the courage of your convictions, 'Tasha. You must learn to come out of your corner fighting.' (Only Kennedy said it 'kornah'.) He winked. 'To extend my absurdly inapt metaphor, you need to come back off those ropes punching hard.'

'Always aim for the knock-out, Natasha,' Bobby said from over the other side of the room. 'Fight dirty. There's no referee in the boxing bout of life. Hit low and hit late.'

And Jack laughed, this time at his brother's making fun of him. That was the thing about him. At fifteen she thought his politics conservative and cautious and lacking altogether in glamour. But he was funny and kind and wise and humble and had time for everyone and he never, ever patronized her.

And he had the courage of his convictions, too. When Humphrey and Stevenson and Johnson among the Democrat heavyweights referred to him contemptuously as 'that boy', mocking his youth, calling him callow and inexperienced, he came out fighting. And he out-punched all of them.

Much about him was more mythic than real. His athleticism was far more of the heart than the body. He was a jock in his mind. But Natasha was in Hyannis Port often enough to know that he suffered terribly with his back. He wanted to swim and sail his boat and to play tennis and sometimes he scorned his doctors and did so. But he always paid a dreadful price afterwards in pain. Doctors attended to him in relays, sometimes it seemed to her in teams. They were a grim-faced, squabbling lot. But they didn't cure the ailments. She asked her mother about it once, back at the beach house they were lent, after seeing him hobble between two outbuildings at the compound on crutches. The shock was that he seemed so practised using them.

Her mother had been combing her hair for a reception and she stopped, the comb still poised in her hair. And Natasha knew she had blundered into an area kept secret among the loyal.

'People say Jack is young to want to be president,' her mother said. 'What they don't realize is that in four years, it might already be too late for him.'

He looked wonderful at his inauguration, though. There seemed something so fundamentally right about the ceremony taking place on that chilly, lucid day. Natasha was no longer fifteen and her opinions had matured. She put this down to the bomb, which sobered your thinking quickly if you were an American. In the biting cold and sunshine of Pennsylvania Avenue that day, it seemed like America had got the president the country needed and deserved. Her mother sat beside her in her coat with the ermine collar and a perfect bloom pinned to the fur. She had a pillbox hat with a short veil and her hair tied in a chignon. She looked impossibly sophisticated and glamorous, her mom. She smelled of Joy perfume. And she cried when Robert Frost read his poem, tears splashing down the cheekbones that usually gave her face its look of frosty hauteur. And Natasha realized all at once what the words of the poem must mean to someone like her mother, an immigrant, a refugee, making her brave, lonely way in the new world Frost spoke so eloquently about earning the right to be worthy of. Her mother fumbled Kleenex out of her bag, but the tears didn't stop. And Natasha didn't comfort her. The dignity of the moment, its august and martial formality, prevented her from doing so.

She was shocked out of her happy reverie by the pain and suddenness of a hard slap across the face. And Peter Landau stood in front of her where Robert Frost had been, an angry face looming out of the backdrop of his homemade mountain hovel. She lowered her mouth to her cuffed hands and saw blood from her lip on her fingers.

'You are such a jerk,' she said. 'You are a total creep.'

He hit her again, harder, and her jaw was numbed by the force of the blow and black lights flared briefly before her eyes. She swallowed, swallowing blood and pride and rage. She would have to stop. His anger was rabid. She did not want to be beaten to death. She did not want him to remember the gag. She did not want him to remember in his anger what pliers could do to a healthy young mouth.

And she had a plan. It was true that her plan would require a degree of compliance on his part. But ju jitsu was said to need some compliance in its victims. And Natasha had heard what that could do, when Elvis Presley demonstrated his ju jitsu skills on one of Frank Sinatra's bodyguards at one of Sinatra's parties. She had overheard Bill laughing about the occasion with her mom. Bill said Frank went into a terrible sulk and started mumbling about Presley's Cadillac and a sledgehammer he claimed to own.

The King didn't get invited back after that. But he made a terrible mess of the bodyguard. The poor guy was in traction for weeks. Her plan needed Landau's compliance to work, but that could be arranged, was part of the preparation and the skill. She would go over her plan in her mind a thousand times if necessary before timing the moment of its execution. And it would be necessary. Landau was a disgusting excuse for a human being but he was methodical and careful and clever, too. She would need to be better than him. She would need to be far quicker and stronger. Her plan would only get one chance to work and she would certainly be dead if it didn't.

'Time for a history lesson,' he said, sitting back in his chair with his rifle across his skinny lap. Blood dripped from her chin onto the coarse blanket underneath her on the cot. The wind howled and snow hit the walls of the hut in frenzied clumps that seemed to make its pine walls shudder. He wanted to give her a history lesson. He was mad. He was barking mad, as one of the two very posh English girls at her school might have said. He was absolutely barking, dear. She was buoyant, now, because she finally had a plan.

'Let me tell you about your father,' Landau said.

'I'd prefer another story if that's okay with you, Mr Landau.'

There was a silence.

'You don't want to know about the man who sired you?'

Sired. She had thought that only horses were sired. He had neglected to trim the wick of his lamp and in the fug of lamp smoke and the bleary paraffin fumes, the corners of the hut were blurred and diminished and the burr on his rifle stock seemed to glimmer and pattern with life. She very much wanted the opportunity to put her plan into effect. But in that moment, in her unhappy refuge from the blizzard with Landau, she very much doubted that she would now be given the chance.

She coughed blood out of her throat. 'My mother was raped. My father could have been anyone.'

He chuckled. Whether through fatigue or diminishing light, or the concussive effect of his blows to her face, she could barely make him out at all, now.

'You are not the progeny of rape, Natasha Smollen. On the contrary. It was romance and treason that made you. So let me tell you.'

'Tell me?'

'About the Polish whore, your mother. And about your father, who I was proud and delighted eventually to kill.'

It was more than an hour before he finished his story and his voice had become, with unaccustomed use, a harsh rasp in the thick air of the hut.

'Can I make you coffee, Mr Landau?'

He nodded and tossed the keys across to her and she caught them nimbly and unlocked the cuffs.

'You have your father's reflexes.'

She lit the stove under the pan of melt-water and watched the flame, bluish, as it steadily burnt. She did not honestly know how she had managed to grip and strike the match. She did not know how she had caught the keys he had flung to free her unfeeling hands. She needed to make the coffee. She needed to perform this most mundane of tasks in order to compose herself in the aftermath of what she had been told. She glanced up at the strips of flesh torn from the carcasses of what he'd slaughtered and hung in his hovel to cure and stink until he considered them edible meat. She heard the wind shudder and wrack against wooden walls. She inhaled the paraffin stink that provided his fuel and the flame for his lamp and under it caught the sweetish odour of Old Spice cologne splashed on unwashed skin. She closed her eyes. She had to remember to breathe, to count and measure the individual breaths, or she would suffocate and faint. She prised off the lid of the coffee tin. She extended her fingers until the tips touched the blue flame under the melt-water pan and pain bristled through her and she recoiled, having regained herself.

'What are you doing?'

'Making your coffee, sir.' Her back shielded her hands from him, the self-infliction of her burns. She could feel her fingertips blistering. She felt sobered, restored a little by pain.

She had listened with incredulity at first, sure that he was in the grip of some dismal fantasy inspired by his obsession with her mother. But as the detail accrued, she realized that he was not a man capable of inventing such stuff. There was a hateful conviction to Landau's testimony. He told his tale with such evident loathing for its subjects it was obviously an ordeal for him to recall it all so vividly. He recounted its dogged chronology in what was still for him an awkward, alien tongue. And as he did so, the story started to tingle through her with the hot compulsion of truth. She was seeing her mother's stubborn secrecy revealed. She was hearing her own history. And so she listened, dismayed that she should find herself so ardent an audience, so desperate to learn her truth from so grotesque a witness to it. A witness, at least, until the moment he became such a willing participant in the events he described. Disbelief and scepticism gave way in her to shock and a sweep of revulsion that had her shivering and sweating at once as she listened to Landau's story, handcuffed, on the cot. Her skin pricked and blotched and a furious itch spread under her scalp. Her skin sang with tension and her lips trembled and her mind would not be still as her heart hammered under her ribcage as he spoke.

She stared into the flame and waited for the water above it to boil. She knelt feeling angry and indignant until an overwhelming disappointment engulfed those lesser emotions, drowning them, leaving her feeling drenched in sudden futility, more lost suddenly than she had ever known it was possible to be. Oh, God. God help me. She wanted to put her arms about herself, to cradle her body and rock in her abandonment and desolation. It would deliver her some comfort just to hold herself, in the absence of anyone else to comfort her with their sheltering arms, with the warmth of an honest embrace. But she couldn't. Such extravagant movement would be rewarded by her captor with a bullet. She was in Landau's prison. Landau was her vigilant, merciless guard.

As he had been her mother's, once. As he had been when her mother's only offence had been the crime Nazism decreed was committed by her mother's Slavic blood, by the geographic proximity of her mother's homeland to its predatory neighbour. Natasha was reminded of something her mother had said, years earlier, on a weekend trip with Bill here in Colorado, as the two of them argued over politics, Bill over on the other side of their tent, building a fire to keep away the wolves.

When you live without freedom, hope becomes difficult to sustain, her mother had said, who had discovered much during the war about living without freedom.

You kept the wolves away, Bill, she thought. But one of my mother's wolves came back for me.

Landau approached her then and knelt behind her and held the flat blade of his bowie knife in front of her face. And she saw herself, saw her face in its bright reflection in the cabin gloom. And she thought, as she always thought, how little she resembled her mother in looks. And she saw, as she had never before seen, her father's pale eyes carefully watching her under his shorn, flaxen hair. And she felt some of his strength returning to her. She felt it in his blood, beating through her. She felt it in his kindness, in the courage and resolution that had saved her mother's life and allowed her to be born. It was a fundamental feeling, this, an obdurate determination in the marrow of her bones. It coursed and crackled in her, her father's life and will for her to live.

'What do you think of your mother, now?'

'The Polish whore,' Natasha said.

'Your father?'

'A man without honour. A traitor, as you rightly said.'

'Good,' Landau said.

And she could have sworn she saw her father smiling back at her as she stared at her reflection in the polished blade of Landau's bowie knife.

He rose and kicked her. 'The water is boiling,' he said.

Later, after the coffee and secured again, Natasha wished with all her heart that she had dried her mother's tears when the Robert Frost poem made her mother cry in the cold at the inauguration. She wished she had lifted the veil away from her mother's face and kissed away her mother's tears. But she had not. And it would always be too late to do so now. She would never forgive her mother for the harbouring of her shameful secret. She was to be denied that opportunity. She would never get the chance to tell her mother that her secret bore no shame. That was her fear, at least. That was her fear.

Hope becomes difficult to sustain.

But not impossible, her father's voice insisted. Not impossible, Natasha.

She closed her eyes and heard Peter Landau loading and reloading the rifle across his lap with practised hands.

241

NINE

Bill was asked to wait in the bar for the manager of the lodge. It was one of the lesser ironies in a life that had inflicted on him many much greater ones. They had told him to help himself to anything he might want to drink. Days earlier he might have wanted to drink everything. He looked at the bottles ranked on the wooden shelves behind the waxed and burnished bar. There were rare single malts from Scotland and bottles of Kentucky bourbon and Irish whiskey in tall, high shouldered bottles from Dublin and Limerick and Cork. Their labels were arcane with detail against glass that was amber and tobacco coloured and caressed by dabs of yellow light. He saw a bottle of Oban and seeing it made him smile. Martin Hamer had drunk Oban whisky, developed a taste for its peaty subtlety on a trip to Scotland a few years before the war. He'd been very rude, subsequently, about the relative merits of whisky and schnapps.

'Maybe you're a Scotsman in your soul,' Bill had said.

'I like almost everything about the place and its people, Bill,' he said, forlornly. 'But in the end, I don't think so.'

'What's the catch?'

He hesitated. 'It's the kilt, Bill. When all is said and done, it's the kilt.'

'You're absolutely right, kid. You'd be more than wise to stick to lederhosen.'

Bill smiled further. Martin had detested lederhosen.

A few days ago he would have seen this recollection as the poignant justification for a drink. He'd have poured a glass of Oban and told himself he was drinking it in fitting tribute to his dead friend. It was what drunks did. It was how drunks lived their lives, how they functioned. They came up all the time with compelling reasons for raising the glass in their hand. He should know. He'd seen and done enough of it to be a real authority.

Bill poured coffee into a mug from a percolator behind the bar and took it over to the large window that made up one wall of the room. He imagined the view through it was usually magnificent. He also imagined the glass to be inches thick. It was blind now, this glass wall, with snow that billowed and pushed against the great pane in dense and ceaseless patterns of white. The storm was uncannily silent, in the calm of the bar, robbed of its violence once deprived of its withering screech. He looked around. There were hunting trophies on the walls, of course. He saw moose heads and spreads of antelope horns that looked almost prehistoric in their runic grain and span. There was a snarling timber wolf. There were stuffed cougars and bobcats and a bald eagle spread its wings, haughty forever in death, above the big double door. All they lacked was a grizzly bear, Bill thought, sipping coffee. There was probably one in the basement, hauled up for sorority parties and corporate get-togethers. The floor under his feet was an intricate parquet and there was much rosewood and oak in the room. It smelled of teak oil and money and tradition. Bill wondered how a man like Landau could have survived here for so long.

The double door opened and a man came in and Bill introduced himself. The manager of the hunting lodge wore a well-cut plaid suit and a cravat and his leather shoes clacked on the parquet. They sat on upholstered leather stools at the bar. His name was Charles Dupre and he invited Bill to call him Chuck. With his slicked-back hair and his English suit, Bill thought he had never met any Charles less Chuck-like in his entire life. The lodge manager looked more like John Cheever than he did any sort of hunter after game. It was all wrong, out of kilter, the atmosphere of the place, its charged off-season emptiness. Bill looked at the Oban bottle and suddenly knew that the liquor inside it was something cheap and fraudulent, distilled unlicensed somewhere like Boston maybe, or Chicago.

'It's good of you to talk to me, Chuck.'

Dupre nodded towards the window. 'I'd talk to anyone who took the trouble to come up here and see me in this. Frankly, I don't know how you did it. And I think you have wasted your time, because I've told the police in Denver everything.'

'I have a personal involvement.'

He nodded. 'The police told me that when I called them back and mentioned you were coming. They said to assure you they'll get a helicopter and dogs up as soon as this storm clears.'

And Landau will see the helicopter or hear the dogs and he will kill her, Bill thought. He was trying not to dislike Dupre. But his instinct wasn't letting him. There was something bogus about Chuck, something counterfeit in the clothing and the way he forced his vowels. And his hunting lodge had the dead opulence about it of mob money. It was a mob investment and the mob weren't too fussy about employing the likes of Landau because they didn't possess an instinct for what was wrong and what was right. They were too dumb and amoral to differentiate.

'Who owns this place?'

'Is that relevant?'

'It's a harmless question.'

'A conglomerate of business people from New Orleans.'

Ah, Bill thought. Chuck, who didn't look so much like John Cheever anymore, examined his nails.

'How long did Landau work here?'

'We inherited him. I guess eight or nine years.'

'Enough time to get to know the terrain.'

'Plenty,' Dupre said. 'But he always had too much sense to go out there in weather like this.'

'He was fortunate to have the choice.'

'I'm sorry. That was a joke in bad taste. How did you, by

245

the way? Get up here?' The road had been obliterated by drifting snow. He had done it with bloody-mindedness and a compass, feeling for crevasses with a ski pole, virtually blind behind his ski glasses and all the while thanking Christ he was still in some sort of shape. For once, weighing a solid two hundred and forty pounds hadn't hurt. His weight anchored him in his boots on the screaming slopes in the wind. The compass was German, military issue, taken by Julia Smollen from Martin's corpse as he lay in a Swiss meadow eighteen years earlier. Julia had also insisted he strap on his friend's old waterproof watch. It was as though she believed these items had some talismanic quality, as though they would protect him or bring him luck in his search for the daughter of the man to whom they had belonged.

'He was a good man in the mountains,' Bill said, fiddling with the lugs to put his own watchstrap on the watch, thinking of a truth he'd teased her with once: *you can take the peasant out of Poland*.

Julia put a hand on his arm. 'I'm sorry, Bill. I'm so sorry for the unkind things I said about you going.'

'Forget it, kid. I never take any notice anyway.' And she reached up and kissed him and he held her hard in his arms for a moment before turning away to go.

He'd called her from Englewood before first light and setting out for the lodge.

'Any word?'

'Nothing. Frank sent a bouquet and a basket of fruit and a card.'

'How did he find out?'

'Someone in the police department, I suppose. There was a blank cheque with the card. He'd signed it.'

'That's thoughtful, I suppose.'

'I don't want show-business gestures, Bill,' her voice broke. 'I want my baby home.'

Bill looked at Chuck Dupre in the mob lodge in Colorado and wondered, even after the battle to get there, how he could have missed the Cajun flamboyance of the cravat and the hint of the Delta in the accent the man struggled to conceal.

'I'm not going to waste your time, po' boy, and I'm sure as hell not going to let you waste another minute of mine.'

'I've told the police as much as I know. As soon as we knew he was breaking the law we informed the authorities and Landau was fired.'

'Except that's not true. An indignant guest with an interest in wildlife conservation was birdwatching through his binoculars when he saw Landau raid a nest. That's what actually happened. The guest reported what he saw and you were left with no choice but to fire Landau.'

Dupre lit a cigarette and blew out smoke. His eyes were on the white wall of blizzard and his face took on a stubborn cast.

'You had me checked out immediately after I called you,' Bill said. 'You'd be an amateur if you hadn't. So you know that I know people. And those people will be happy, po' boy, to take a trip to New Orleans.' He hated speaking like this.

But he needed to make himself understood. 'I don't give a fuck either way about Landau using his gun skills to help with the hardware for your activities outside Colorado. I just want to find him. And you are going to do all you can to help me, Bubba.'

He slapped Dupre on the back. The slap was heavy and avuncular and very hard. Dupre's face became pale and then he nodded and rose and Bill followed him, thinking that Frank's thoughtful cheque could no longer be described as entirely blank.

He was about to leave the lodge a full hour later when he was approached by one of the skeleton crew who ran the place in the dead winter months. He was checking his equipment in the wood-and-marble lobby, securing the harness straps on the pack that carried his supplies and bivouac before lacing on his waterproof nylon boots.

'There's a telephone call for you, sir.'

He walked to the desk and the waiting phone with a sinking heart. It would be the police. They had found a body. They would very much appreciate his help with its identification. Would he mind? But it wasn't the police. It was Julia.

'He sent me her hair, Bill. He cut off her lovely hair.' Julia was wailing, undone.

'Where was it sent from?' He gripped the receiver so hard in his fist he heard the plastic crack. 'Julia? Was there a note?'

'No note. Denver,' she said.

Then he was in the right place. 'I'll find her, honey. I swear to God I will.'

He laced his boots and shouldered his pack and walked out into the storm.

He walked west, the incline varying but almost always upward, the avalanche risk appalling if he gave the prospect serious consideration. He tried not to, but it was hard when every laboured footstep reminded him of how much snow the storm had brought. It started to abate an hour out of the lodge, full night fallen by then and the landscape blue and still, under a bright moon. It was very cold. Wind chill always made the cold variable and confusing. When the wind ceased you knew what you were up against with the cold, could judge its bitter seriousness and the strength of its intent. The wind still blew powder off the surface of the freshly fallen snow in small, swirling eddies. But they were only the storm's playful afterthought.

Its legacy was avalanches.

Bill didn't want to think about that. Instead he measured the cold. While he walked, he worked hard enough to keep himself warm inside the layers of clothing under his quilted mountain parka. But the big breaths he pulled in were knife-edged, lung-piercingly cold. He would have to bivouac. Eventually he would have to stop and rest until morning. He wanted to travel on what sense he'd gained of his quarry until then. If the storm had really gone, he would curl down in his sleeping bag in the lee of a rock or on a sheltered ledge. If it returned, he would dig himself a snow hole with the entrenching tool strapped to his pack. He walked upward. He did not kid himself that he ascended the slopes on mountain legs. His mountain legs were no more than a fond memory to him now. He climbed on the strength of hundreds of hours of pushing the pedals of a stationary bike before an audience of incredulous fighters at a boxing gym in Anaheim.

He walked upward and west on what he had learned about Landau after his talk with the Creole mobster at the lodge. Ascending, he thought about the lodge. He had seen it crouched there on dozens of occasions over the years on his passages through the mountains and never felt the inclination to pay the lodge a visit. It was a curious place, but forbidding. It reminded him of various houses, sinister and grand, he had seen mostly on his travels in England. The English had a word for this character of dwelling. The word was manse. It was a medieval word derived from Latin and had originally meant the house of a minister. Bill thought manse sounded more like an affliction than an abode. And he thought it suited the lodge perfectly. Malevolence had dwelt there. He knew that now. He had a better sense altogether of who and what it was he hunted. And so he moved west, higher, where he thought Landau would go. Where he prayed Landau had not done what kidnappers almost always did, where he prayed Landau still had Natasha held safe.

Bill was not a man comfortable with the way he had lived his life. He thought his had been a life from which meaningful accomplishment was altogether absent. There was little about his past he was proud of and much that made him feel ashamed and embarrassed. In his worst and most remorseful moments he felt truly abject. And he got drunk. And afterwards he felt worse. The day of the orange grove picnic was a good example of the consequences of this behaviour. The evening prior to it, his god-daughter had called him in tears. Blind drunk, he'd slewed along the roads at the wheel of his Jeep to their house in Orange County with a wad of hundreds in his pocket and not the remotest fucking clue as to the nature of the problem. He'd tried to fake sobriety with some ludicrous courtroom burlesque inspired entirely by a bottle of Johnny Walker Black Label. Unless a packet of Planters Peanuts provided the creative spark, but that he seriously doubted. And the following day he tried to make up for it to the girl and to restore himself in her estimation by taking her for a picnic. He was damn sure that picnics featured nowhere on any twelve-step recovery programmes he had ever heard about. But that was what he did. And they were stalked by Landau. Landau had 'Tasha in the cross hairs of his sight. And if he hadn't been so debilitated by the Scotch of the night before, Bill knew he would have spotted the fucker far sooner and chased him down and broken his fucking neck.

Jesus Christ spelled sideways! He raised a foot and wasted energy trying to kick a lump of snow invitingly sculpted in his path by moonlight. Already knee deep in snow, he missed. Way to go, he thought, start an avalanche right here, put myself out of my misery. He waited for a moment for the physical world to rumble into action and exact natural justice. But no avalanche was triggered. So he punched the lump of snow instead and then started to look around for somewhere to bivouac and eat some of the field rations he'd packed. He wouldn't risk a fire. Landau, he'd discovered, was far too good a shot. And should he be fortunate enough to find the man he hunted, he wanted his arrival to be a surprise.

He looked around. The world was entirely still and wore a profound, white hush. Julia had been wrong about his motives for coming here. He understood why she would think what she did, but she was wrong. He knew he had very little of what the psychologists termed self-love. Why should he love himself? He didn't deserve to be loved. The idea was fucking ludicrous. But he loved Julia very much and he loved Natasha like a daughter. He was very grateful to have had her in his life. She had provided him with pride and joy for seventeen years and he had enjoyed nothing in his life so intensely as being able to do what he could to help take care of her. In the days when she still liked being read to at night, he would sometimes drive to San Francisco from LA just to tell her her bedtime story. What he appreciated about these occasions most was knowing how much they meant to her, how she looked forward to him coming, got excited when she heard his knock at their door with some new adventure she had not heard between the pages of the book in his hand. You could watch her bright mind illuminate in her eyes as she gathered up the sheets and blankets, scrunching down. Looking around now, still in the tree line, he could see the firs heavy and petrified under fresh snow in the freezing night. It would be the still, cursed kingdom of Narnia to a child, this place. It would. He had read her those stories, had had each shipped over from Foyles in London the moment it was printed and they had enthralled her. She would not have been reminded of Narnia in Landau's company, though.

Bill had loved his daughter, Hannah, who had been taken by spiteful God, or indifferent fate, or whatever you chose to believe in, barely having reached the age of two. And he had loved his wife, Lucy, whose sometimes febrile spirit had not possessed the strength to survive Hannah's death. Did he love Natasha now as much as he would a daughter of his own?

There had been a spate of child adoptions in Hollywood a few years back, the consequence of one of those periodic bouts of guilt the very young and unexpectedly wealthy sometimes indulged in. He had spoken at a party to a married actor in his thirties who had two young children with his wife. They loved each other and they adored their kids. But the couple were battling over the prospect of taking a toddler from an orphanage. He was against it. He told Bill why.

'I call it the *Titanic* test,' he said. 'You're aboard the *Titanic*.'

'Unfortunate.' Bill was drunk. Of course he was drunk.

'And you end up in this arctic water with your kids. Say there are two of them.'

'You're not a Catholic, obviously.'

'Come on, Bill. You asked the question.'

'Mea culpa. Continue.'

'You're holding up the kids in the water and the cold is killing them. It's killing them. One is yours by blood. The other you adopted. And a lifeboat rows by and they say they have room for one kid. Which kid would you choose?'

Bill shook his head. 'It's an impossible choice.'

'It's no choice at all,' the actor said. 'Not for me, it isn't. And if you can't pass the *Titanic* test, you don't adopt.'

Bill had never posed himself the *Titanic* question, had never given serious thought to taking the *Titanic* test in his mind. It was an ordeal by theory he'd considered gratuitous. He grieved for Hannah still, as he knew he always would grieve for her. And he loved Natasha. And he could simply not imagine how he could love a daughter more. He had done what he could to enrich her life, at least when he'd been sober and fit for the task. And the thought that this petrified time in this desolate place might mark the end of her life, when it was only about to really begin, was an outrage to him. She was only just seventeen. She was clever and beautiful and good. And he would do everything he could possibly do to save her.

That was why he had come.

Bill bedded down and ate pemmican in his sleeping bag from a tin. And he slept and he dreamed of choppy water, dead children ringed by lifebelts floating on a freezing sea. Natasha was not among them.

Chuck, the Creole John Cheever, had taken him first to where Landau had worked and then to where Landau had lived. The Remington concession at the lodge was bigger than a mere gun counter. It was a gallery, with guns and rifles lining the walls and a workbench and a lathe and a neat row of power tools. It contained a lot of firepower.

'This isn't an armoury,' Bill said. 'It's an arsenal.'

Chuck shrugged like it was nothing to do with him.

Bill examined some of the hardware on display. 'Do people really hunt these days with pump-action shotguns and automatic rifles?'

'We get a lot of real gun enthusiasts. You know how it is.'

'Yeah. I know how it is.'

There were no pictures on the walls of Landau's living quarters. He had been provided with the most basic of the guest rooms rented and had clearly lived there for a long time. There was a patina of nicotine on the ceiling and scars from cigarette stubs on his bedside table. There was an ashtray and an empty water glass. But there were no pictures on the walls of the generic type the lodge provided in all of the rooms it rented to guests. These were the predictable mix of Frederick Remington prints and pictures of corpulent men in red hunting coats and port-ruddied cheeks with dogs at their feet as they supped at some mythic English inn. There weren't even the patches on the walls to show their recent removal in Landau's room, though. The pictures had been gone a long time. He must have taken them down as soon as he arrived there. His room was the bare cell of a seedy, cantankerous hermit. Bill examined the pattern of wear on the carpet and saw with no surprise at all that Landau was a man who paced. He'd been waiting for a long time, Landau. And the waiting had made him impatient.

Going through the bureau drawers, Bill found the only thing that really surprised him. It was a cutting from a German newspaper and when he unfolded it he found himself looking at a photograph of Martin Hamer sitting on a cot in what was obviously a field hospital. He began to read.

'You can read that?'

Chuck was looking over his shoulder. Bill turned his back to shield the cutting.

'What language is that?'

'German.'

'You can read German?'

'Also French and Spanish. My Latin is rusty, but the romance languages are still the easiest to master.'

'Jeez. No kidding.'

'When first we met, Chuck, I thought you looked a little like John Cheever.'

'Wow. No kidding.' There was a pause. 'Who?'

'A writer. From New York.'

'That a compliment?'

'Not really. I'd like a few moments of privacy, please. Would you leave?'

Chuck left.

The delayed shock of coming face to face with Martin again hit him then, and because he didn't want to sit on Landau's bed he walked over to the one straight-backed chair in the room and sat on that to gather himself. The chair creaked under his weight. The wind whistled and shrieked outside the room's one small window. His hands were shaking, the yellow cutting trembling between them. He felt he was in the presence of a ghost.

Martin had been wounded. He lay on a cot and looked like much of the life had been bled out of him. An open tunic had been draped across his shoulders and a fur-lined field cap put on his head for warmth. His upper torso was wrapped in white bandages and a bloodstain obliterated the right side of his chest up to the shoulder. A senior Werhmacht officer sat on the cot and held Martin's hand in his own, which was gloved. Snow goggles were perched above the peak of this officer's cap. He was the sort of high-ranking German always played by someone like James Mason or Anton Diffring in the movies, when ruthlessness needed leavening by a little culture and a light sprinkling of aristocratic manners. But he looked much more cruel than they did. He looked far deadlier. Because this wasn't the movies, was it? This was a portrait of war.

Julia had told him long ago in Mexico that Martin had buried a medal in the snow high on the pass they tried to escape over. Now, in Landau's melancholy cell, he found out from a German newspaper cutting how the medal had been

257

earned. The story didn't read like propaganda. The prose was flat and factual, even pedantic. Either way, the hollow look on Martin's face made the wound seem real enough.

He had been involved in the counter-offensive planned by Field Marshall von Manstein after the Russians had over-extended their forces pursuing the German army on its retreat after the defeat at Stalingrad. The Germans had counter-attacked with their backs to the frozen Dnepre River and nowhere else to run to. The Russians had made the mistake of assuming they were chasing a rabble. But at the Dnepre River, and in the subsequent battle for Karkhov, they discovered they weren't. Martin had been a tank killer, the leader of an elite unit of tank infantry charged with the task on the field of battle of destroying the Russian T34s. But his unit had been ambushed by a tank, decimated, the surviving members forced to take cover in a deep, frozen ditch. It was a position they could neither defend nor escape from. Their situation was hopeless.

Martin had been hit by a machine-gun round that punched a hole through the right side of his chest. The impact had blown him into the ditch and torn his rifle from his hand. He got to his feet and used his helmet to scrape snow to pack his wound and hinder the bleeding. Then he climbed out of the ditch and crawled under persistent fire to a shell hole in which he'd seen his sergeant take cover before being hit. His sergeant had been wounded also, had lost his right leg below the knee to a canon round. Martin used his belt to tourniquet his sergeant's leg and gave him his morphine and took his grenades. He ordered the man to provide him with covering fire. Then he left the shell hole and crawled across the snow, concealed somewhat by the smoke of gun batteries and burning wagons and tanks. He got behind the tank that had ambushed his unit and, using his pistol and grenades, killed the crew and disabled it. And so he saved his men.

And his sergeant was able to give an account of the action before dying of blood loss and trauma on his way to a field hospital. He told it to the medics carrying him. I serve under a brave officer, the sergeant said. You should know of his courage. All of you should know of his courage.

Bill paused after reading this. He bent and put the cutting on the floor and sat up again and the chair creaked and he rubbed his eyes. He looked around Landau's empty walls and looked back to the cutting. It lay open, scored by its habitual folds, against Landau's thin oatmeal carpet. Martin looked out of the picture at him, wounded. Martin would never blink in the picture. He would never smile or age or cry or perish. Though he had done all of these things but the one of them Landau denied him. Bill raised his eyes to the window. The flakes of snow were white and impossibly pure outside this dismal room through the panes of glass. They seemed less frantic now, though, more sedate in their descent from the sky. The storm was abating.

All of you should know of his courage.

Bill felt thirsty. He would very much have liked a glass of water. There was a water glass in the room, but it was empty.

And there was no faucet. It seemed Landau had been obliged to use the facilities in the rest room along the corridor outside. And the water glass on Landau's bedside table was covered in a film of dirt or dust. Bill didn't like to look at it, much less think about drinking from it. Instead he turned back to the bureau and under the false bottom of a drawer found Landau's careful cache of newspaper cuttings concerning Julia Smollen and her contented, successful life. Some of the cuttings were from the trades. The rest were from the newspapers. They had been stored neatly in a folder made of stiff card. She was smiling, groomed, in all of them a poised, beautiful woman characterized by style and self-possession. He put the folder back and rose from the chair and heard his limbs creak this time as he raised his weight and straightened up. He felt very old suddenly and awfully tired. There was a knock on the door.

'Yes?'

Chuck.

'I'm leaving now,' Bill said.

'I'm leaving too. For Denver.'

'Oh? Urgent business?'

'In a manner of speaking.' He tugged at his cravat and smoothed his hair. 'When you slapped me on the back earlier? I think you displaced a vertebra.'

Dawn came sluggish and wintry and late. The sun rose on the other side of the mountains. It would be something like noon before he saw it. By his reckoning it was probably twenty degrees below zero. The snow was cold, dry, powdery stuff it was effortful to walk in. The only advantage was that in this state it lacked the weight and mass of moisture, so that despite the huge quantity that had fallen, the avalanche risk was not so great as he had feared the previous day. A freeze followed by a partial thaw was the ideal formula for an avalanche. It was much too cold for a thaw. Bill brushed snow from the fur that edged the hood of his parka. He brushed snow from his sleeping bag and rolled it tightly and tied it in a dense roll to the top of his pack. Procedures were what kept you alive in the mountains. You followed them and you never allowed your concentration to slip. Yesterday the storm had made his quarry blind to his presence but today the sky was clear. Yesterday he had blundered upward at will with no real thought of a bullet until night fell and he dismissed the idea of a cooking fire. Today was a different proposition entirely. The moon was still high in the sky but pale, like a spectre of itself. It was January. It would be afternoon before the sun hit the slopes he intended to climb and maybe two o'clock or after before it possessed its greatest strength on the westerly side of the range. He hoped to have found Natasha by then. And Landau. He hoped to have found Landau, too.

It was a bad sign, the man leaving his cuttings behind in his abandoned room. It meant he had left no longer needing them. Their being left behind was less a tantalizing clue than a morbid proof of his intent to replace them with some more tangible trophy. His intent was absolute and it was deadly. The room and its hidden contents had been evidence to Bill that there was nothing in this man's life beyond an urgent compulsion to do harm to Julia Smollen. She had been right about that. The desire for a sort of revenge possessed him. And Bill had hunches rather than the firm leads he had sought as to where the kidnapper might now be.

Landau was very adept with his hands. He made his own bullets and he carved the stocks of rifles. The Creole guy had shown him some of Landau's work and it was finely accomplished. But he was physically small. He would have to pull a sled bearing his materials to build his bolt hole. The place would have to be made of wood. Wood was heavy. Given his size and the weight of a laden sled, Bill figured on his building no more than half a mile from the lodge. There was nothing, or very little of him, in his quarters there. In the confinement of the lodge he had brooded over Julia Smollen and paced and smoked in his room when he wasn't working. In his spare time, he had disappeared. The Creole guy had confirmed that. His refuge would need to be convenient, accessible even in bad weather, or it was no refuge at all. It defeated its own purpose. So Bill reckoned half a mile. And, of course, above the lodge, where height offered him remoteness and seclusion.

Bill could think of only two places that really provided everything Landau required. One was a narrow snowfield sloping gently above a sheer cliff face and ending in an abrupt overhang of smooth granite. The route to get to it was tricky, steep, almost a traverse. And that's what made Bill favour the second site. Landau was no mountain man and this was easier to achieve. It was north by north-west of where he stood, bearing on Martin Hamer's compass, and it was half an hour's hard walking away. It was a spot above a gully, shielded by an ancient rock-fall. It was more sheltered than the first location, though not so secret a place. He had to gamble, though. And he would, he thought, snapping the compass shut and putting it into his pocket.

Then he noticed the buzzards circling above an area a few hundred yards away. And his heart lurched inside him.

'Oh, please, God, no,' Bill said.

He had taken a pump-action shotgun and two-dozen cartridges from the gunroom in the lodge. The cartridges were in a belt around his waist. He took off his pack and pulled the shotgun free of it and left his pack in the snow and started struggling through the snow to the place where the buzzards wheeled and waited. He was afraid. He was not fearful for himself, but he was dreadfully afraid of what he would find.

When he got there, a pair of bobcats were digging at a depression in the snow with their front paws. They fled when they saw him. He remembered that his entrenching tool was still attached to his pack. Shit. Shit. He put down the gun and lay on the snow and dug with his hands, deepening the hole made by the scavenging cats, his breath coming in sobs that shook his big frame and scalded his cheeks in the cold.

'Please, God,' he said, 'please, God,' over and over again, beseeching, as the hole in the snow widened and deepened under his scooping hands and he saw blood, crimson with freshness, glistening against the white.

It was a bird. It was a red-tailed hawk and it had been shot clean through. He saw something sludge-coloured a foot away from its body and realized it was the bullet that had killed the bird. The hawk had been shot right at the limit of the range of the rifle used by the shooter. The bullet had just possessed the velocity to go through its target. And that was how Bill knew it was Landau who had killed the bird. The man was an incredibly fastidious shot. He had been told so by the Creole when the Creole had been too scared of his connections to lie to him anymore.

'He makes shots you only see shooters make in the movies,' the Creole said. 'Always shoots at the limit of his range. He's a regular Sergeant York.' He laughed. 'If you can believe a Kraut Sergeant York.'

Landau had killed the bird. Just as sure as Gary Cooper had played Sergeant York. And the position where the bullet lay, in relation to where the bird had fallen, showed Bill the direction from which the shot had come. And it showed him that his hunch had been wrong. Landau hadn't been headed towards the place he'd gambled on. He'd been headed instead for the traverse that took you to the snow-field at the top of the cliff. It was there that he had built his bolt hole. It was there, alive or dead, that he now held Natasha Smollen.

The change in location called for a change of strategy. There was no way Bill could surprise Landau if he had built his shelter where he now supposed it was. He was a skilled and experienced hunter. But it simply couldn't be done. If you approached from the front you were horribly exposed. Even if you got behind and above the place, abseiled down from the lip of the overhang, you'd be heard by anyone half alert to the possibility of approach and picked off still clinging to the rope. A shot might be possible. It might if Landau left the shelter on his own and walked far enough out in the snowfield to give you an angle. But why would he do that? The snowfield ended in a thousand-foot drop. The route down, to the left of the field and along the traverse, gave you no shot at all. And Bill only had a shotgun, not a rifle.

And he didn't have much time. The weather was clear and stable. Soon the helicopter would be up and Landau would hear the thrum of its rotor blades and he would kill her and flee. Soon the dogs would be up, unleashed, after his scent, and he would hear their barking and panic and kill her.

No.

Bill would have to go there unarmed, with his hands held high in the air, and appeal to the kidnapper's greed. Landau possessed a rare talent for killing. But the business with the eagle nests suggested the man had the soul of a thief. Some weird grudge against Julia Smollen had been the motive for the kidnapping. He was using the daughter to hurt the mother. But Bill believed he would listen to offers of money if he heard the kind of offer Bill was prepared to make. He'd say anything, after all. He'd say anything just to get close enough to snatch Landau's rifle and break it over his knee and then break Landau, break his back or his neck, crush him like something that squirms under your foot until it was unrecognizable, obliterated, gone.

All of you should know of his courage.

Bill knew he wasn't brave. He was mad as hell and desperate. He loved his god-daughter. And the man who held her captive offended him. He was an affliction. He was a stain on the world.

Bill was there. He had taken the traverse without thinking about it. So much for procedure. Well, fuck procedure. It had all gotten a little late in the day suddenly for that. He faced a squat hut and behind it, a looming rampart of grey granite. The overhang cast the hut into shadow and Bill stood now on the edge of that shadow and could feel its sunless chill. There was a door dead centre of the hut. There was a window to the left of the door and in the shadow of the rock its panes looked like they were made from black glass. Smoke rose from a round zinc chimney on the roof. The top three or four inches of chimney were all you could see above the drift snow lying thick up there. To the left of the hut from where Bill stood, he could see a snow-covered shape that he guessed from its length was a sled. Lying on the snow, sticking out from the rear of the sled, was a pair of boots. He thought it was odd the boots had been left there. But everything was odd. The silence and the stillness were odd in the shadow of the overhang and the building itself seemed bizarre, anomalous in such a remote and desolate place. It was solidly, even neatly constructed. But even from this distance he could smell a sour mingling of odours from within. It was a mix of burnt paraffin and decaying animal flesh and old tobacco and human dirt. The dogs would have no trouble finding it when they were unleashed, that was for sure. But Bill very much hoped the dogs would be too late for Landau.

He raised his hands above his head and called out the man's name. His voice echoed and magnified in the space between the crags and buttresses, across the high valleys, before fading on the thinness of the air. He watched the door. But nothing happened. Smoke rose from the zinc chimney. Snow trickled on a steep slope high to the left of the overhang in a manner that reminded him of the way sand moves sometimes in an hourglass when the opening between its chambers looms.

'Landau?'

Nothing. An echo. Stillness. His arms were starting to ache over his head. They were big arms to hold that high and his mountain parka wasn't cut to accommodate the pose. Plus it was undignified, standing there in the posture of surrender. He thought it odd that he had no sense of being watched. He reminded himself that everything in this place was odd.

'There's a million dollars in used bills in your room back at the lodge.'

Nothing.

'No police. I swear it, Landau. The door to your room is locked and I've got the key. It's a good deal. No strings. A million straight for the girl.'

Nothing.

His arms ached in the silence and the shadow slowly crept and stole, retreating from where he stood as the sun ascended.

'Landau?'

Nothing.

Fuck this. He started to walk through the snow towards the door. If he started running now, silly old fool that he was, he'd probably have a heart attack before he got there. So he walked through the snow. And he lowered his arms. Ah, much better. He swung his arms as he walked. It was thirty-seven years since he'd played nose tackle for Yale. But he still held the record for tackles completed. His pace increased. He'd set that record and he'd kept it. And he doubted any of the opponents who helped him compile it had ever forgotten the contribution they made. He tilted forward and started to trot. What was a lock, anyway? It was a few cheap screws and a tin hasp. Bill felt an old and familiar roar rising in his chest. Twenty feet from his target, he began to run. He was bellowing when he bulled into the door and it broke and splintered under his shoulder and huge momentum and he was in Landau's hovel, Natasha shivering under a shorn scalp, feet drawn up on a cot, a blanket at her throat, alone. Alive.

'Where is he, honey?' Bill was breathing hard, relief and foreboding fighting in him. The smell of the place was an intimate, feral assault. Her head was pale and shaven, cut. Dried blood ran down her temple in a zigzag trickle. I'll break him, Bill thought. So help me, I'll rip him apart. He looked around. He saw the trapdoor in the floor, the iron ring that would open it.

'He's outside. I think I killed him, Bill.'

Bill remembered the boots behind the sled. He nodded to Natasha and held his finger to his lips and because he had to, went straight back out. She seemed okay. His priority now was the man who had taken her.

Landau lay with one hand reaching for his rifle and the other trying to push his spilled guts back inside his body. His entrails were blue and purple and frozen in the deep shadow of the overhang and his face wore the rictus of fear. Bill was no expert on violent death. But this looked like a man who had died having learned in increments everything there was to know about the subject. The hand reaching for the rifle was a claw, contracted with cold and blackening, two or three inches from the weapon's trigger guard. Landau had died desolate in a desolate place. But that was also how he had chosen to live.

Bill looked for a long moment at the man who had killed the friend he had, above all men, loved. He felt no anger or vindication, no triumph or satisfaction at the sight of Landau's corpse. He just felt profoundly grateful for the life of Natasha, saved. He'd been a man much visited by grief over the course of his life and it was a burden he had faced and necessarily borne. But he did not think that on this occasion his heart would have allowed him to survive the pain and bitter familiarity of a loved one lost. Not this time. Not again. Not his god-daughter. Not his daughter in his heart and soul, Natasha.

That wasn't the reason, though, for his gratitude. For better and often for worse, his span of years had largely been lived. What remained to him was twilight, now, ashes glowing in the hearth on remembered heat. She was a girl on the cusp of adulthood. At seventeen she was only about to embark on her great and impossible adventure. He could think of nobody he'd ever met who better deserved their chance at living. To him Natasha *was* life, joyful and abundant in her qualities and gifts. She would need to get over this, though. She would need to recover from what it was Landau had said and done to her before she could ever begin.

He looked again at the corpse. He was curious to see what manner of man had willingly inflicted such turmoil, so much anguish. But Landau gave away as little about himself in death as he had apparently when living. He'd been one of those with an instinct for unobtrusiveness, someone who found it practical to live on the margins of life, where he plotted and schemed to revenge himself on others endowed with the gift for living he had been denied. He had clearly clung to what remained of his life very tenaciously at its conclusion. Beyond that, there was nothing to distinguish him, though. He was smallish and slight and pale and dead. This last characteristic, Bill thought, was the finest he'd been capable of possessing. In a man like the one whose corpse he pondered, death was an attribute for the rest of the world to be grateful for. He plucked Landau's rifle out of its sticky grave in the snow and broke it over his knee and flung the sundered stock and barrel at the granite wall facing him, where the parts clattered with a dull impact and fell to rest.

'Did he hurt you, 'Tasha?'

'He didn't rape me, if that's what you mean.'

'Did he hurt you?'

'He told me about my father.'

'And how did that make you feel?'

'Proud of my mother. Prouder of her, I mean.'

There was a silence then that, to Bill, seemed absolute.

'He must have been very brave, my father, after his own fashion. Landau told me he was given a medal.'

'The thing for which he was given the medal was not the bravest thing your father did, Natasha.'

'I know that,' she said. 'I'd like you to tell me about him.'

'I will. One day I will. I expect my opinion of him differs from the one you've heard.'

She shivered on the cot. Her eyes swivelled. 'Is Landau dead?'

'Oh yes. Comprehensively.'

She dropped the blanket and held out her arms to him and he saw the knife, huge and bloody in her lap.

'Pick me up and show me, Bill. I want to see him. I want to see him dead.'

Bill sat on the cot. He shifted the knife away from her. 'He's not a pretty corpse, hon.'

'He killed my father, who was your friend. I want to see him. He stamped on my knee and I can't walk. Take me, Bill.'

And he did. He carried her outside and she looked down at Landau which was the start, he supposed, of some sort of recovery. And when they went back inside the hut she told him how the death was accomplished. She told him as he tore the parts of the cot blanket not bloodied by the bowie knife into strips to wrap her feet with. He wrapped them tenderly. She had some frostbite and Bill feared might lose her toes.

She had realized that Landau got pleasure from being served. In a curious way he seemed to think that it was his right. He must have yearned for the days of the camp, when the slave inmates scurried to the snap of his fingers. But Natasha discovered this about him even before he told her about the camp, on the first night there, when she offered to make his coffee. On the first evening in the hut she made coffee for him twice. On the second day she went through the ritual six times. Then in the evening he stamped on her knee and she thought she might have to abandon her plan.

'But then this morning I decided to risk it. I had nothing at all to lose.'

The routine was always the same. She would make the

coffee on her knees with her back to him and when it was poured into his mug would turn and slide it across the floor to where he sat with his rifle across his lap. He would wait for her to retreat to the cot and handcuff herself, then pick up the mug and drink.

'I was counting on his being a punctilious and methodical man. I was relying on his instincts.'

She was gambling, Bill thought. And the plan would not have been practical had Landau been a taller man.

'When I slid his coffee to him I had to kind of dog-leg the mug to avoid this knot in the grain on the floor. Only this morning, I didn't. Not with the second cup. I pushed it straight and the mug tripped on the knot and the coffee threatened to spill.'

And Landau leant forward instinctively to steady the mug and prevent the spill and Natasha stood putting her left hand on the rifle stock, leaning over his back with her full weight on him, to pull the bowie knife from its scabbard.

'When I pulled back again he straightened up and tried to stand and I pushed the knife into his stomach. He let go of the rifle, so I did, too. I had both hands on the hilt of the knife then and I pushed it all the way into him. He tried to use his hands to stop me but I was stronger than he was. Then I pulled the knife out and tossed it across the room. And then I opened the door and threw his rifle in the snow. When he went after it, I bolted the door behind him.'

'You make it sound easy.'

273

'No, Bill. It wasn't easy. It was a simple plan and it worked. But it wasn't easy.'

'And now you know about your father.'

'Landau called you the rich American friend. He despised you for getting my mother out of Switzerland.'

Bill smiled, remembering, wrapping her feet in careful strips of woollen cloth. 'I got you out of Switzerland, too.'

'Can you get me off this mountain?'

'I can get you off this mountain, kid. But we'd better start right away.'

'Do we have to use the sled?'

'We can't. Not going down, we can't. The snow is too deep for it to run ahead of me and if I pull it I'll trigger an avalanche for sure.'

'God isn't going to kill me today, Bill. Not today.'

She made the remark in a dreamy, singsong manner. He thought she was maybe going into shock. He fastened the final, makeshift bandage wrapping her feet and put his parka around her and plucked her off the cot.

He carried her out of Landau's hut, out into the raw and ponderous world of the western slopes of the Rockies after a deep winter snowstorm. Everything was still. The rocks and crags were snow-draped, clumsy things. They were high and the air was static with cold and altitude. Bill was strong. He had always been strong. But the sun was ascending and the snow was becoming loose and treacherous in its heavy deposits all down their descent.

'You're the best, Bill,' she said. 'I want you to take me

home. I wish you lived with us. With me and my mom. I wish you didn't live in that Meis van de Rohe mausoleum you had built in the canyon.'

He opened his mouth to say something, something witty and light after the grim enormity of what had happened to her and the sudden weight of what she had been obliged to discover. But she was asleep in his arms already, lulled by the easy rhythm of his footsteps in the snow. So he just carried her, descending in sunlight through the virgin powder, in his boots, the burden he bore light and welcome in his arms, the hair in pale tufts growing back on her head all the while she slept and breathed.

Night had fallen by the time he got her down. The jeep was where he had left it. It was buried under a snowdrift, now. But when he used his entrenching tool to dig it out, he saw that the canvas canopy had withstood the wind and the weight of snow without tearing from its frets. So he put Natasha in the back, still asleep, still wrapped in his parka, thanking God for anti-freeze as the Jeep grumbled and misfired and then lurched into reluctant life. He drove her to the hospital in Denver and from a payphone there, called the number Julia had given him to reach her on. She arrived fifteen minutes later from the police station in a patrol car. She looked pale and thin and she squeezed Bill's arm and rushed past him in her eagerness to see and touch and talk to her child.

Bill gave a statement to a polite but persistent Denver cop. He signed the statement and the cop shook his hand and left.

He drank coffee from a vending machine and dozed on a chair. His mind was dull in the aftermath of all the tribulation. He ran a hand over his crumpled face and wondered that relief could be so exhausting an emotion. Wasn't it supposed to be one of the minor league emotions? He thought it criminally underrated if it was. Relief was an emotion that could win the World Series. He yawned and caught sight of his reflection in a window. He needed a shave. To say the least, he needed a shave. And then he had a thought that caused him to laugh out loud. It was a Thursday, wasn't it? Shouldn't he be at Frank Sinatra's place, startling the assembled throng with his all-new, all-star, iced-tea and soda-water routine?

Julia came out of her daughter's hospital room. Her hair was scraped back in a ponytail. There were dark shadows under her eyes. She wore no make-up. She looked different. She looked unburdened. Bill thought he had never seen her look more beautiful.

'She's fine, Bill. No amputations. Her kneecap has a hairline fracture. She's badly bruised and hungry and dehydrated. But she's fine.'

Bill nodded.

'What would he have done with her?'

'He would have killed her. He had a radio. He had a crystal set hidden under a trapdoor in the floor of the place they were at. He'd have used it to contact an intermediary, a newspaper maybe. He'd have made threats, threatened deadlines, the usual stuff kidnappers do. He'd have taken your money. But he'd have killed her.'

Julia looked out of the window. It was dark outside and there was nothing to see but herself looking back. 'And now she's safe.'

'You're both safe.'

'I don't know what to say to you.'

'You can say goodbye.' He smiled at her. 'I'm tired. And I've never greatly cared for Denver.'

She shook her head. 'I've said goodbye too often to you. I don't want to have to say it again.' She reached for his hand, held it. 'Take us home, Bill,' Julia said to him. 'Let's all go home.'